# SPRING RAINS

Whisper Ridge, Wyoming - Book 3

---

RJ SCOTT

Love Lane Books

# Dedication

*Always for my family.*

Spring Rains - Whisper Ridge Wyoming #3



Cover design by Meredith Russell. Edited by Sue Laybourn.

Published by Love Lane Books Limited

ISBN: 9781785644788

# Spring Rains

RJ SCOTT

Love Lane Books

# Chapter One

## Noah

Sitting in the car with the engine idling, I stared through the car window at Lily's Diner, halfway down Main Street, in the small town of Whisper Ridge. The windows were covered on the inside with broken down packing boxes and a solitary rainbow cling was stuck between the cardboard and the glass. Peering through the windshield, which was being covered by a thickening layer of snowflakes, I reached for the controls and flicked on the windshield wipers. The blades moved back and forth, clearing away the snow, so I could get a better look.

"It's strange seeing it like that," I said to Fox, nodding toward the diner.

My son, with the requisite shrug of not caring about anything these days, glanced at me, then back down at his phone.

The wipers continued their rhythmic motion, swiping away the snow that was falling heavier now. We sat in silence for a moment, the gentle patter of snowflakes against the car so pretty.

"It used to be so full of life," I added. "It's a shame to see it all boarded up like that. Well not boarded. I mean, with flattened boxes, cardboard I think. What do you think?"

Fox grumbled something under his breath, but I was used to that—he hadn't forgiven me for leaving Columbus for this trip down memory lane, whatever the reason.

I stared back at the diner and couldn't help but feel a sense of nostalgia. It was something from my past, memories of happier times before everything imploded. Despite its abandoned state—Lily had been gone for over a year now—the place was part of Whisper Ridge's history, a reminder of better times.

*Thank you, Aunt Lily. I wish I'd come back sooner. I'm so sorry.*

Out front, the *Lily's Diner* sign, with its open white flower and my great-aunt's name, swung gently. For some reason, she'd left the place to me, so Aunt Lily's little piece of Whisper Ridge was mine now, and even sitting here in my car, staring up at the sign, I didn't know if I deserved it. The town was smaller than I remembered, or maybe I felt bigger, older, weighed down by everything that had happened since I was last here. Not least the divorce, which was still a fresh hurt, and one of the reasons I'd decided not to sell the property, but to reopen the diner.

Somewhere new for us.

Safe.

A fresh start for me and for my son, Fox, because there was no way my ex, Briggs Lewiston, MLB pitcher for the

Columbus River Kings, would be seen dead in the-middle-of-nowhere Wyoming.

Not to mention, it might give me a chance to get my head straight and stop jumping at shadows.

Fox, slouched in the passenger seat, was the spitting image of his dad, Briggs, with his dark brown eyes, blond hair falling in a curtain over one eye, and that stubborn tilt to his chin telling me he was pissed. He'd been tapping away on his phone, as he had been doing the entire three days and change hotels and driving it had taken to get here, and now, as he stared at the diner, his brows were knitted in a frown that seemed to be his default expression these days. Fourteen was a wonder of mood swings and surliness and boy did Fox ace every facet of being a teenager.

"Why here, Dad? I mean, look at this place." Fox's voice was flat, his gaze not leaving the screen.

At least he was back to calling me Dad. There had been a shaky few months after I'd left Briggs and gotten custody of Fox, when he'd decided I didn't have to be called Dad. Never mind that I'd brought him up since Briggs and I married when Fox was six. I'd been the one ferrying Fox to school, attending events, helping with homework, teaching him to swim… me. I loved Fox. I was his dad in every way possible.

Hell, I'll take Fox calling me Dad again as a win in a very long battle.

I sighed, my fingers wrapping around the cool metal of the diner keys. "It's a fresh start, Fox. For both of us."

He snorted, finally checking out the diner. "A fresh start in a *freaking* ghost town. Great."

"Language," I murmured without heat.

Fox rolled his eyes. "I hate Papa, but at least we had a life back there."

The implication scared the hell out of me—was Fox thinking we shouldn't have left? If Fox ever chose to go back to Briggs over me, that would be his decision. Biologically, he was Briggs's son, but I'd have run away to a country with no extradition rights before letting Fox anywhere near his dad until he was old enough to decide for himself. Thankfully, Briggs's indifference to his son, and some of the things Fox had seen his dad do to me, meant he was with me. There was so much I could've said about why his father's world had no room for us, but the words caught in my throat, tangled up in the heartache and betrayal.

Instead, I stared at Fox, really *looked* at him, and part of me hoped the things he'd seen were forgotten, because I didn't want him carrying fear and hurt around forever. But to suggest moving back with Briggs? "Fox, your papa… he's got his life, and it's not one that's good for us. Not anymore, you know that." The DUI charge, gambling, throwing games, filing *freaking* bankruptcy… the *everything* messing up Briggs's former charmed life, was a hateful place for anyone to be, let alone a fourteen-year-old kid abandoned by one of his parents.

"Whatever," Fox said, trying for sullen, but the weight of sadness in his tone was overwhelming.

"And this diner, it's a piece of family, of history, and maybe it can be a good thing for us, a fresh start somewhere new."

He shot me an incredulous stare, as if I'd said I was

happy we'd moved to the moon. "We could've stayed in Columbus, then I wouldn't have had to leave school. Seb is having a party this weekend, and I'm missing out."

I schooled my features into sympathy, but all I could think was thank fuck he was missing any party with those asshole kids he'd hung around with. To say I wasn't fond of the friends he'd had at the academy was an understatement. The school and the pupils were obsessed with materialism, constantly surrounded by the best and most expensive things—nothing in their lives had any authenticity. I didn't want Fox to be a part of that.

I pressed on, trying to connect with him by changing the subject. "You know, my Aunt Lily used to show me how to make the most awesome pies right in that kitchen. It's where I learned to love her craft, and that's why I chose to be a pastry chef."

Fox was unmoved by my statement, taking in the weathered facade of Lily's Diner. "That's *your* ancient history, Dad. It's not mine."

"It could be yours too," I murmured, more to myself than to Fox. Memories of Aunt Lily's warm laugh, the scents of her baking, and the summers I'd spent here until I was eleven… those short weeks each year were some of the happiest times of my life. Until, just like that, they were gone. My parents divorced, my dad heading off to find himself and never coming back. Then, Mom remarried and moved herself and me to France, and an entire ocean between me and this tiny town had severed any connection I had to Whisper Ridge.

I placed a hand on Fox's shoulder, feeling the tension in him.

"I know this is hard on both of us, but how about we give it a chance, Fox, see how it goes, and if in six months you want to go back…"

He turned a hopeful gaze to me. "For real?"

What did I do? We couldn't go back to Columbus, back to the media gaze, and Briggs, and the River Kings fans who didn't believe their beloved pitcher had done anything wrong at all.

"Give me six months, to the end of the summer, yeah?"

He narrowed his gaze. "August is eight months, not six."

"Eight months then."

He grimaced, frowned, then faced the diner again, his shoulders tight. That was all I was going to get—an agreement to try at least for a few months, albeit a frustrated, angry silent one. I knew that was as much as I could ask for the time being.

I could only hope this chance I'd taken would be enough for us, that we'd open the old diner, make a go of it, find our place in this town, and then stay. I felt for a moment things could get better for us both. I had to believe that for Fox and for me. This diner wasn't only a building; it was a link to my past, and maybe it was a foundation for a new beginning if I could manage it. Everything might go wrong. I might fuck everything up, and Fox might end up hating me, but I had to try.

"Okay, you want to go inside and check it out?"

He shot me his patented do-I-have-to stare, but then he nodded.

"Okay, then coats on, gloves, hat, scarf; it's cold out there."

Fox muttered something about knowing how to dress in the cold, and we bundled up to brave the bitter iciness of this mid-January day in the Wyoming mountains. As we stepped out of the car, the crisp, cold air hit me, sending a shiver down my spine, and freezing my breath. I pulled my scarf up to cover my face, and saw Fox had done the same, his eyes wide at the shock of ice. Whisper Ridge was a stunning white canvas, the peaks of the Wind River Range barely visible, shrouded by heavy, dark clouds. Snow blanketed everything, smoothing out the rough edges of the landscape and draping the trees lining Main. The streets were deserted, but then, it was three in the afternoon on a Saturday, and I thought maybe I'd seen one or two people, but I imagined the whole town had decided to huddle indoors, away from the biting cold. The buzz I remembered of everyone going about their business was absent, replaced by a hushed stillness only a heavy snowfall could bring. With each faint crunch of my shoes against the snow-packed ground, I left a crisp imprint behind.

I paused for a moment, taking in the serene beauty of it all. The way the snowflakes danced in the air before settling, the soft outline of the stores under their snowy roofs, the quiet—it was all breathtaking. The harshness of the cold was undeniable, but so was the beauty it brought.

"It's a winter wonderland," I mumbled into my scarf, but a gust of icy wind stole my words, and Fox didn't hear my fanciful nonsense. We headed for the door.

"Aunt Lily's legacy to us," I said a little louder.

"She's not *my* Aunt Lily," Fox muttered, his voice muffled by his River Kings scarf. He was right—she was my mom's aunt, no blood relation to Fox, a bit like me, but the link through me was unshakeable.

He was a step in front of me, his reluctance showing in trudging through the banked snow, scuffing his boots as he stuck in his ear buds, but at least he'd headed out.

The key turned, and as I went inside, I waited for the jingle of the bell sounding like a welcome home, but there was nothing, the metal kick plate bent back to stop the noise. The inside was a stark contrast to the warm, buttery smells that had greeted me each morning on of those summers long ago, in the original diner. The life in this new place had surely faded since Lily's passing, and it felt like a photograph from an old album—frozen in time, colors dull—and the sound of our footsteps was the only noise as we closed the door behind us. Despite shutting out the snow, it was as icy cold inside as it was out.

There were still scuff marks on the worn linoleum floor, and we followed them in. By the glow of my phone, I located and tried the lights, but there was no electricity, which was another thing on my to-do list. Instead, I eased out the loose hooks and took down the cardboard blocking the window on that side of the restaurant. The sudden appearance of the pale sun bounced off the snow filtering inside to give us enough light to find our way.

I inhaled sharply as old memories flooded my thoughts and left me feeling something between the grief of never having come back to Whisper Ridge and a manic happiness at being here now. It was the oddest sensation, and I wondered how much of it was bound up in leaving Briggs and feeling free for the first time in eight years.

"Look!" Fox exclaimed.

I followed his finger, which was pointed toward the back wall, where, in bright neon orange, there was a crudely drawn cock and balls. Vandals had been inside, and I glanced around, searching for more damage, but couldn't see any. Stools were pushed haphazardly under the counter. The red vinyl seats had small cracks and creases and were more of a sad looking thing than a reminder of the people who'd sat there. On one of them, the stuffing peeked through the cover, and I poked at it with a finger.

"This is so sad," Fox said with a sigh, pushing open the door to the kitchen. Above the counter, a menu board hung without the descriptions of daily specials, and every corner of the place sat empty of life.

"What am I doing?" I asked the empty space, given Fox had vanished. I was worried for a moment. Then, recalling the layout of the place, knew there wasn't much space for him to get lost in. There again, were there knives in the kitchen? "Don't touch anything sharp!" I called out.

"Doh," Fox replied, his voice dulled by the closed serving pass.

*Doh* was another word that Fox used a lot, specifically when I asked him to watch out for something, as if I hadn't had to take him to the emergency room when he'd climbed the tree in the yard.

The teenager handbook, page 5, *doh*. Page 6, *whatever*. I had an entire list of things I could add to the book. Talking of lists, I took off one of my gloves and pulled out my phone. Top of the to-do list was to enroll Fox into the local middle/high school in nearby Collier Springs. Next was visiting the bank, third was a lawyer. I scrolled down and added a new line, *electric to the diner*, then pushed the glove back on before my fingers froze.

Our new home.

It needed a breath of life, a new beginning, but with the apartment above, this could be what we needed. The U-Haul wouldn't be here until Thursday, so, in the meantime, we were booked into Ridge Hotel, which, if I remembered right, had barely more than eight rooms on a good day. Plenty of time to roll my sleeves up and get the apartment in shape for Fox and me. Time to get the electricity back on because this place needed to be loved again. And maybe, just maybe, Fox and I would be the ones to bring it back to life.

And fix us in the process.

# Chapter Two

## Chris

Sitting facing a counselor had been a regular thing for me over the past decade and a half. The scents, the furniture, the diplomas on the wall, the warmth and security—they evoked a sense of déjà vu, because it didn't matter what counselor I saw; everything else was the same. The sameness was supposed to make patients feel calm, but I didn't feel relaxed. Instead, I sat across from Doctor Susan Trent. I'd randomly picked her from a list of recommended therapists and she looked at me with the same understanding gaze as every other person who had seen me. Her hands rested in her lap, she wore a gentle smile, and she chose not to point out that I was tapping the armrest.

Still, today felt different because I hadn't been ordered to see a counselor after attempting to take my own life—I'd chosen this for myself.

The moment where Laurie had gotten ahead of me

and fallen into a well on my brother-in-law's property was a nightmare I couldn't shake. My fucking prosthetic, my inability to help him, and I couldn't do a damn thing to rescue him. All I'd been able to do was try to hold on, but even then, the rope had been slippery.

Sometimes in my sleep, when I couldn't stop the fears, the rope unraveled and Laurie dropped into the darkness, and it was those nightmares that had sent me here today. My choice. Not mandated. Just me and my need to get ahold of myself and call a halt to the self-sabotaging.

The sweeping views of the city from the window were nothing but a temporary distraction from the knots in my stomach as I sat facing Susan in my neatest slacks, a button-down, and tie—every inch the professional high school English teacher that I was, waiting for any words of wisdom that would make everything better.

Susan, in her more casual jeans and shirt, kept on smiling, and something about her reminded me of my mother in that caring—*I understand*—kind of way. The last thing I wanted to be thinking about was my mom, who would hug me to death and worry if she had even the tiniest idea of how much I was struggling. Not to mention there would be a family intervention, and I'd seen that firsthand and didn't want it for myself.

I knew Susan was waiting for me to get settled and, probably stop staring out of the window. I focused back on her, steadied my breathing, noted her blonde hair—slightly tousled, settled around her shoulders—and the glasses perched on her nose, adding a touch of wisdom to her gaze.

*Stay in the moment.*

*Be present in the moment.*

I shifted in my seat.

"Are you comfortable?" she asked.

I held back a snort of self-derision. Was I comfortable sitting in a room with someone who could dissect my every word and assign meaning to the most random thing? Hell no. But I needed to be here.

"Yeah, I'm good."

She leaned forward, encouraging, understanding. "So, what brings you to my office today?"

"I don't know how to explain," I replied with hesitation, taking a deep breath.

"There's no rush," she reassured me, something else I was used to hearing. *We don't need answers straight away, your life has changed, everything is different. Don't rush into thinking you'll be okay all the time.*

After a deep breath, I began. "So, you have this on the intake form, but basically, I lost my leg below the knee in a car accident when I was nineteen. 2006," I explained and lifted my pants leg to show her the prosthetic, as if she needed to see it to verify that I was telling the truth. "This is another remnant of that same accident." I touched my face, gesturing at the scar from my temple to my chin, burns that had never healed as they should and a constant reminder of a desperate moment of terror. "The scars go down my left-hand side as well, but I think it gives me an edge. Makes me look sexy." I tried to make light of the situation with a smirk, something I'd learned in a hundred counseling sessions way back when.

She smiled along with me, but then waited for more, and boy, did I have more I needed to say.

"I don't really know why I'm here, except I've had therapy after the accident, tons of it, and I know when I'm struggling. I've dealt with the physical loss as best I can. I have a job. I love teaching high school English, and I coach baseball, and sometimes football. I have a bunch of really cool student and players who respect me." I sighed. "But now, I feel I'm in a holding pattern. Frozen. I couldn't… help this kid who could have died."

"One of your pupils?"

"No, my brother-in-law's sister's kid. Micah married my brother, but it's Micah's sister's kid, Laurie…"

"A child who means something to you."

"Yeah, Laurie is a good kid, and he's like a nephew, and… it all went wrong, and now, I'm teetering on the edge of all this self-pity that I don't want or need. Only, I can *see* that I'm allowing myself to wallow in it, and that isn't good. And that is why I'm here."

She inclined her head as if she understood. "Can you explain what happened with Laurie?"

I blinked at her, the image of Laurie clinging to a wall, pleading with me to help, when all I could do was lean there, not able to do anything. *Useless.* Until his uncle, Quinn, stepped in and rescued him. *Useless.*

*Nope. I'm not thinking that.*

*I don't think that.*

*I am strong. I have purpose. I am alive.*

"Laurie was playing, and he fell into an old well on the family ranch; well, it's Micah's ranch."

"Your brother's husband."

"Yeah." I scrubbed at my eyes—this was all too

complicated. “I couldn’t help in any way. I couldn’t rescue someone who needed me, and it was on my watch, and I couldn’t keep up with him and his friend. They ran off, and, well…” I tapped my knee. “I don’t do a lot of running now.”

“So, this incident occurred, and you felt powerless, and you blame your physical limitation.”

“Exactly. I’ve spent so much time proving to myself that I’m more than capable of overcoming the loss of half my leg, that it shocked me to the core. It’s set me back, made me rethink, made me cautious, shaky, as if I’m expecting to fail, and the helplessness of that moment is just shit.”

She nodded. “You seem to have a handle on your thought processes.”

I swallowed hard. “That’s the problem, in black and white I know what I’m doing to myself, and why I’m circling the drain, but my thoughts are dark. I’ve been down that road before, where everything was so dark after the accident that I ended up overdosing.”

She paused a moment. “Do you feel suicidal now, Chris?”

“God, no, I have everything to live for. I’m happy. The thought of not seeing my family grow old.” I shuddered. “No suicidal ideation,” I said, using the term I recalled from previous counseling. “I can see what I’m doing. Rationally, I know how to stop it, but I have behavioral dysregulation.”

Susan’s gaze was unwavering, understanding. “Using terms like ideation and dysregulation sounds like you’re very self-aware, Chris, and that you clinically understand where you're at right now. Recognizing patterns in yourself is winning half the battle."

"I know." There was a knot of emotions in my chest, and words came out in a rush. "I just keep thinking I should have done more, you know? To save Laurie. And after the accident, with the prosthetic… sometimes, I feel like less of a man. Weak."

Susan leaned forward, her expression kind. "Chris," she said, "you're a survivor. You've been through so much. Your journey, the resilience you've shown, that's your real strength."

I shook my head, unconvinced. "Doesn't feel like it. I feel as if I failed."

"Your worth isn't based on what you can or cannot do in extreme situations," she continued. "You matter because of who you are, not because of what happened with a child you said you couldn't help."

I looked down, struggling to accept her words.

"So, take me back a little bit, tell me about before."

"Before the well, or before the accident?"

She considered me carefully, and I could almost see her brain working—did we *really* have to go back to the car crash, losing one of my closest friends, being caught in a burning vehicle, dragged out to survive when I wasn't sure I wanted to live at all. She seemed to decide the same as me—we didn't need to go that far back.

The conversation flowed from then on, touching upon my closer-than-close interfering, caring, annoying, loving, family and my work, which I loved. The only stumbling block was when she probed about personal relationships, and I hesitated, unsure of what I would even tell her. My last relationship, with Yan-the-asshole, had been at least two years ago, and I'd made it work for a while, until he'd decided it was better to move on. He wanted marriage and kids, and decided for himself that this was something I could never give him, or cope with.

Fuck him.

"I don't have a significant other right now," I said, and she nodded. "But I have had relationships since the accident, so there's that." I got in there before she could ask because that was what counselors did. They always wanted to know how much I'd allowed into my life, or how much I'd been capable of. "I've had a sex life and all that," I added, also to pre-empt the question. Not that this was something I'd enjoyed with another person since Yan had left; in fact, me and my right hand were very well acquainted.

"So, can you tell me a bit about the support network you have outside of family."

"My colleagues at work, and I have friends; my best friend is… well I guess that's probably Levi up at my brother-in-law's ranch. But mostly, it's my family. I'm one of five siblings, and we're close."

"Have you talked to Levi about how you're feeling right now?"

"No." That would be an X against my name. My first counselor—the one way back post-accident, the one who'd talked me through me not wanting to live at all—said I should concentrate on forming healthy relationships outside of family. Said that talking to people not related to me would give me fresh perspective. But what could I do when I had siblings who always wanted to be part of my life to the point where sometimes it was overwhelming.

Somehow this latest thing though… the self-pitying part that was so freaking stupid… wasn't what I wanted to share with Levi. When the two of us bonded over horses, we sometimes talked about personal issues, but mostly, we just enjoyed the riding. He wouldn't want me burdening him with every single shitty thought that had emerged since the well incident about me being a failure. That was why I was here talking to a professional.

She smiled at me. "Okay, Chris, let's dig deeper."

Oh joy.

I made it back to Whisper Ridge a little after four, parking on Main to head into JJ's for coffee and catching the sign for what used to be Lily's Diner, jonesing for coffee and one of Lily's cakes. The diner had been one of my safe places before and after the accident. Lily would sit and listen to me, or give me space to sit and think, plying me with home-baked goods and coffee. I'd visited every day, until the day she passed, and the diner closed. As usual, grief curled inside me that she was gone because I missed her no-nonsense attitude to life, her morning smile, and the way she somehow got me. So many hours I'd spent in the small stock room as she fed me and kept me in drinks, all the time letting me talk out my fears. There was something about Lily that had made the accident, the scars, the amputation, and the depression manageable, and I wished she was still in my life.

The inside of the diner was dark, had been for a year now, ever since she'd passed, and no one knew what was happening to the heart of the town. I'd grown up there, from kids' parties, to teenage angst, to the post-accident depression I buried in cake, to coffee that kept me going, to the regular Friday meet-up I'd once had with my siblings. Rumor said there was a new owner, some relative out in Ohio, probably looking to sell it off for profit. I knew that much, given my younger brother Scott, part-owner of our family firm Sheridan Realty, already had plans in place for conversion to two separate storefronts should the new owner want to sell.

I hated that, but I'd been outvoted, some nonsense about moving on, blah, blah.

This abandoned place with its boarded-up windows served as a painful reminder of how Whisper Ridge had changed when Lily McGuire died before her eighty-fifth birthday. Lily's Diner was a relic of the past left untouched since Lily's sudden passing. The *CLOSED* sign hanging crookedly in the window made me sad. The diner had never been closed when I needed it.

I was lost in memories of times spent at the diner with friends and family flooding back, when a flicker of movement caught my eye, and I realized one of the windows was lacking the boarding that had blocked everything from view. Freaking vandals must have gotten inside again. I should call Neil, get the sheriff out here to pull them in, but then, what if it was one of the kids in my classes who just needed Teacher-Chris to go nuclear on their ass, and therefore, avoid law enforcement being involved?

I saw a shadow. A silhouette of a person moving past one of the booths. Nope. No way. If there was someone in there vandalizing the place, trying to rip out parts of it to sell, then I was stopping it right now, kids or not. Without thinking, I twisted out of the car—my leg wobbly until I got my prosthetic steady under me—and approached the door, trying the handle only for it to open easily.

"This is private property!" I shouted as soon as I opened the door. "You shouldn't be in here."

The interior was dim, and I blinked as my eyes adjusted, taking in everything that was familiar—the old benches, the worn tables, the counter, the signs with menus that hadn't changed in a year.

And right in the middle, a man in a defensive stance, who was as startled as me. He wasn't tall, a head shorter than my six-two, but there was an undeniable presence about him. His frame was slim, hinting at an active lifestyle or perhaps just fortunate genetics, and he was bundled up like a snowman in deference to the frigid day. However, what caught my attention the most, was the fact that when he pulled down the scarf from his mouth, he was gorgeous. Very pretty, and beautifully put together. A little closer, and I could see his wide eyes were pale, maybe blue, or gray?

An attractive stranger who didn't fit in a familiar place. He didn't look like a vandal, but he was brandishing his phone like a weapon.

"Who are you?" I demanded and yanked down my scarf. "This is private property."

"Who are you?" he snapped back, casting a glance to his left as if he were searching for something, then staring back at me, and I knew the moment he clocked the scars on my face because his eyes widened again. I was used to the stares, but this time, there was also genuine fear in his expression at me storming in. Good. If he was breaking in, then you bet I was going to scare his ass.

"I asked first," I snapped. "If you think you're going to steal a single thing from here, you're wrong."

He blinked at me, staring at my face again, and I was drawn into his steady gaze, a little lost, until I yanked my attention back.

"I can't steal what I own," he said, phone still in front of him.

"What you own?" I pulled out my cell, and he stiffened. What did he think I was going to do? Have some kind of battle of the cell phones. "I'm calling 911."

"Me too!" the stranger exclaimed.

And that made no sense at all. Were we both calling the cops? Something about that didn't sit right, and apparently, we realized that at the same time because he pocketed his phone and sighed.

"I'm supposed to be here," he said, tired and confused. "I'm Noah Lew—Bennett, Lily is my great aunt." His voice hitched. "She *was* my great aunt." He dangled keys in front of him. "She left the diner to me."

I'd never seen the piss and vinegar drain from someone so fast, nor seen a man so lost and out of place, but my suspicions didn't subside. Keys meant nothing—I had keys to a lot of places in town, didn't mean I owned them. What grabbed me was the way all the fire vanished from his intriguingly colored eyes. I couldn't work out if they were blue or gray, the light too low, but they were bright and focused, until suddenly they weren't.

"Dad?" A voice echoed from the direction he'd glanced in, and the man stiffened as I half turned to check out the voice and saw a kid standing there—nobody I recognized from school. Noah made a subtle move to stand between me and the lanky teenager, who was maybe fourteen, and was so unlike this Noah guy there was no evidence they were related at all apart from the kid using the dad word.

"Fox, stay back there," Noah snapped.

"Whatever," the kid—Fox—muttered. Shit. The kid was pissed, the man was tense, stress bracketing his eyes, and his gaze darted between us, as if I was an ax murderer and I was going to kill them both.

I took a deep breath.

"Chris Sheridan," I introduced myself, and even extended my hand. Someone who got between another man and his child had to be one of the good guys. Right? "I knew Lily well enough to hear stories of her family, yet she never mentioned a Noah. So, how about we start again?"

# Chapter Three

## Noah

I POCKETED MY CELL, THEN STOOD WITH MY BACK TO THE counter, Fox behind me where I could know he was safe. Then, arms crossed over my chest, I stared down the man with the scarred face who had come barreling into my aunt's old diner like a storm ready to break. I'd faced a man more intimidating than this guy, and I wasn't backing down and letting him scare Fox.

My initial reaction to the stranger—fear, anger, and my defensiveness—subsided in an instant. As to his face, the man had been in a fire or something, corded scars ran from his temple to his chin, edging his hair line, and half hidden by his scarf. I couldn't even begin to imagine the pain he'd had to have suffered to have those marks on his skin, and compassion edged my anger.

"This is my place now," I said.

Chris's eyes narrowed, a glint of challenge in their depths. He was tall, growly, and imposing, someone I didn't need in my space. Whisper Ridge was supposed to be a friendly place to start over, and the hostility pouring off this guy was anything but happy. His accusation of breaking in hung in the air between us, and with it, a surge of defiance swelled within my chest. I didn't come here to make enemies, but I wasn't about to lie down and show my belly either. This place was my legacy, my chance to start fresh, and no amount of brooding intensity from a stranger was going to shake that from me.

"I'm a concerned citizen," he said, and leaned to the right a little, I guess to look around me at Fox. I blocked his view because my son was not there to be judged or stared at.

"This is mine." I motioned to the surrounding space—the countertops I would polish until they gleamed, the chrome stools I'd line up perfectly. "I inherited it from my aunt."

He tipped his chin at me. "Then you won't mind me getting the sheriff out here." I saw that he still had his cell out.

"Go for it," I dared him. "Call him."

Chris moved again, a fraction more to the right, placing a hand on the back of one of the booths, and yet again, I concealed Fox. But that meant little when Fox did this complicated parkour jump thing and ended up standing right in front of me, a saucepan in his hand.

"It's my dad's place," he snapped. "Just leave him alone."

I didn't want my fourteen-year-old son defending me—he'd done enough of that in this life, and all the wariness drained out of me in an instant.

"It's okay, Fox; give that to me."

Fox hesitated, then threw me a glance over his shoulder, and I nodded in reassurance. Only a few months ago, he'd been defending me from his father, from paparazzi, from lawyers, and he hadn't turned that part of himself off since. For all his teenage angst and moodiness, he would always be in my corner when I was threatened. He turned and thrust the pan at me, as if he wanted me to have a weapon, and I fumbled it as he let go.

"I want him to leave," Fox said, his eyes bright with emotion. "Make him go." There was a streak of fear running through his words.

Chris's stance shifted, and he forced himself to relax before he pocketed his cell the same as I'd done. "Didn't mean to scare you, kid," he said.

Oh, shit. He did not just use the word kid. I waited for Storm Fox to explode and beat his sexy ass.

Fox rounded on Chris. "I'm not a kid. I'm fourteen, asshole!"

I winced. "Fox!"

"It's okay," Chris said, when clearly it wasn't. We were in a standoff. Fox vibrating with anger, and I recognized the hint of panic; Chris staring at him as if he'd seen a unicorn riding a bike; and me, right at the back, losing control of the situation.

"Okay, okay," I raised a hand and stepped between my son and Chris. "I have paperwork. I'm meant to be here, and—"

The door swung open, with a rush of wind-driven ice and snow, and another man barreled in. A flashlight filling the space with light, his eyes were wild, peering past me, until they landed on Chris. "I saw your car," he panted, the words tumbling out, "and the board is missing from the window! What's wrong? Are you okay?"

I saw the man's concern, and Chris's reaction.

"For fu—" Chris stopped the curse, probably for Fox's benefit. "I'm okay." Then, he nodded meaningfully in my direction, and the man's expression changed from worry to confusion.

"Noah Bennett," I said.

The new guy's expression of confusion cleared as he spotted us in the shadows, and he straightened. "Scott Sheridan, Sheridan Realty. I wasn't expecting to see you in here." He extended a hand, which of course I took, then he glanced back at Chris. "This is Lily's great-nephew," he explained. "And this is Chris," Scott added, "my brother."

Chris and I stared at each other for a moment. *He hadn't known who I was—he didn't mean to accuse us of anything or trigger me or Fox.*

"Is there anything you need, Mr. Bennett?" Scott asked, all business.

"Electricity—"

"I can handle that," Scott interrupted, "and when I come back, we can talk valuation because I have an interested party—"

"I'm not selling the place," I said, and heard Fox's huff of dismay. "This is our new home."

Chris raised an eyebrow, but Scott was bewildered enough to comment. "What are you going to do with it? Downstairs doesn't have residential zoning in place—"

"We're living in the apartment above and reopening the diner."

Scott glanced from me, to Fox, and then to Chris. "Reopening the diner?"

"Yep."

"The diner," he repeated, as if I'd thrown a stick into his carefully laid plans.

"Yep."

Scott cast a look around him, gave a sigh of disappointment, then smiled, and I could see the smile reach his eyes. "I'm bummed you're not selling, but yeah, getting Lily's back would be so cool. How about I set up getting the electricity back on for you?"

"You don't have to."

Scott shrugged. "It's the neighborly thing. Chris, do you need a hand?" He touched his brother's arm, and Chris scowled.

"Leave. Me. Alone," Chris muttered under his breath, then without a backward glance, left the diner with a slight limp, yanking Scott with him.

I didn't relax until the door closed and I locked it after them to stop any other unneeded visits by people from town.

"This town is weird," Fox announced.

"It's protective of its own," I defended, still feeling some of the warm and fuzzies from Scott saying he'd help me. It had been a long time since someone had helped me out for no reason, instead of the customary ulterior motives involving my ex-husband.

"Well, I hate it, and nothing you can do will make me like it."

The warm and fuzzies vanished.

Reality was a bitch.

---

THE RIDGE HOTEL, at the corner of Main and Abernathy, was as much a remnant of an older time as the diner was. Marjorie and Emmet Lowe still ran the place, and I swear, if I'd mentioned the summers I'd stayed here when we visited Lily, they'd probably even remember me and my parents. Emmet, who'd been old back then, must be seventy now, but he insisted on helping us carry a bag from the car. I tried to tip him, but he waved it away, all stoic and silent, and it was Marjorie who led us up to our two rooms. They were next to each other, and despite wanting Fox in with me—*yeah right Dad*—this was the best we could do. At least, he could get to me quickly if he needed me.

I organized him in his room as much as he would let me before I was told, in no uncertain terms, that he was okay, and could I just go away and leave him to unpack.

So, I did.

My room's layout room was a mirror of his, a sofa, a small kitchenette with coffee stuff and snacks in small boxes, and the most comfortable bed—way better than the expensive monstrosity Briggs had insisted we buy that stood in the house Fox and I had left. I munched on a cookie, made myself a coffee, and now, had an hour to kill before Fox and I headed out to find food. Of course, that was way too much time not to think about the man who'd stormed in and accused me of breaking in. I'd seen the name of his brother—Scott—on papers in the Lily-file I'd been given, an offer to buy the place from the estate, but it wasn't Scott that I was focusing on.

"Chris Sheridan," I murmured, making myself comfortable on the sofa. It was time to put my Google Fu to the test.

Sheridan Realty was the first hit, a picture of a smiling Scott front and center, and listings of properties from here to the next town over and beyond.

I typed in Chris Sheridan, got a couple of hits, but the first one led me to the high school in Collier Springs. Chris was an English teacher and sports coach specializing in baseball—go figure. I got waylaid then, clicked around the school, getting a feel for it, as this was the high school that Fox would be attending. I guess maybe Chris might teach Fox. Given their standoff and the saucepan incident, I wondered how that would go.

Just because he'd come at me like a bull in a china shop didn't mean he wouldn't be a good teacher, because I'd glimpsed compassion and understanding in Chris when he'd backed off under Fox's temper. Then, a little further down, a headline: "Local Community Mourns as Tragic Car Accident Claims Young Resident's Life."

I didn't click, and I stopped scrolling then, because somehow it felt intrusive, so I went back to my to-do list, and all the while the words *tragic accident* spun in my head.

My to-do list included balancing finances and considering whether Briggs would ever get another team to take him on after the River Kings got rid of him. I bet not even the rookie leagues would be interested in him. So much for the millions he'd earned up until then. So much for the money I'd tried to put aside for Fox.

All gone because I hadn't put the money in trust.

Now the only assets I had to my name were the diner and the apartment above, and enough money in my account to at least fix the parts that people could see and get in supplies. I hoped the kitchen was still in a useful state, and I prayed that, when I took the board from the windows and light flooded the diner, there wouldn't be in too much disrepair.

That wasn't much to ask.

Right?

# Chapter Four

Chris

IT ALWAYS ANNOYED ME WHEN MY FAMILY TREATED ME LIKE I was made of glass and fussed over me, and it always would. It wasn't comforting for someone to walk alongside me with their hand out in case I fell—it was frustrating and infuriating. Add in Scott flying into the diner worrying about me, and I was about done with him today. I could sense his gaze, his protective instinct in overdrive, but I wasn't dependent on other people, and I hadn't been for a long time. Only, Scott was hovering.

Yep, no other word for it. He hovered like an insane helicopter, and when I limped, he'd touched my arm.

"Stop fucking touching me!" I snapped and shoved his hand away. Ever since the well incident, all I could see was everyone being weird around me, awkward, and I knew what they saw—an incapable invalid who needed care and comfort. Or maybe it was me who was weird and awkward around them, not quite able yet to reconcile what I hadn't been able to do.

All I knew was that it was exasperating as hell.

"No, but—"

I rounded on Scott, my right knee crunching and scraping, and I had to hold back the yelp as I slipped on the snow a little. I'd overdone it, and I bet the stump on my left would be sore, and possibly inflamed, which was just the fucking icing on the fucking cake. Cue a visit to the hospital, or to my other brother, Daniel, a doctor who could help, which was one vicious circle given that, then, he'd worry about me and…

Yeah. It was shit.

"There is no but," I snapped. "You flew in that diner like some wannabe Batman."

"I…" He paused, and his lips twitched because, yeah, it was partly funny, and yes, he had flown in, stopping in some freaked-out superhero pose.

"You're an ass," I muttered, but the flash of anger had passed, and I yanked open my car door.

"You think I'm Batman?" Scott blinked, as if butter wouldn't melt in his mouth.

"Only if Batman is an idiot realtor who is also an asshole of a little brother."

Scott pressed a hand to his chest, dramatic, his eyes wide. "Batman is so misunderstood," he finished. I caught the flick of his gaze down to my knee. "Chris?" In that single word were so many questions—why did I go into the diner, where was I driving from, or to? Shouldn't I be covering my scars more in the icy cold? But mostly—was I in pain?

"Go away," I muttered, "I need coffee." Frustrated, I grabbed my crutches from the car, only contemplating the wheelchair for an instant, then bypassed my *hovering* brother and headed to JJ's instead. The smell of coffee was a balm to my frazzled nerves, and Scott didn't follow me, which meant I got to sit and be miserable on my own. Abby, the owner, and today's server, greeted me with her usual warmth, already moving to create my favorite coffee, extra shot, lots of cream.

"Saw you parked outside the diner," she said, and I took a stool at the counter as I waited for her to expand on all the things she'd noticed. Abby always had the inside scoop on the neighborhood gossip, and there was a lot I needed to know about Noah and his son, Fox.

Like everything.

"I saw movement inside, thought someone had broken in," I admitted and waited for her to tell me I was fucking stupid putting myself in danger. She didn't;, instead, she rolled her eyes at me as she placed my coffee in front of me. I handed over the money, then took a sip—it was heaven—and it wasn't until I was done with that first taste, that she went straight in with questions.

",I saw the new owner earlier. Noah Bennett? Did you meet him?"

"Yep."

"He has a son, Fox, fourteen. Lois said that Noah is divorced, quite high profile, so she told me." Lois—Abby's best friend—was the owner of the local beauty parlor and had her finger on the pulse as much as Abby. There's a reason I get my hair cut in Collier Springs with how easily

Lois could get information out of her victims, or as she calls them, clients.

Divorced. Prickly. Defensive. And when my phone's light had rested on Noah's face, I'd seen his eyes were blue —*beautiful* blue-gray eyes. Dark hair that peeked out of his hat. I imagined carding my hands through his hair, just to feel how soft it was, and daydreaming didn't go down so well, Abby snapping her fingers in my face.

"Earth to Chris?"

"Sorry, you were saying?" I needed to ignore all the thoughts about pretty eyes, so I sipped more coffee, licked the cream from my lips, and listened while she carried on explaining.

"So, Lily's will was solid as a rock. Everything was left to her great-nephew, bypassing the Oliver family over in Collier Springs, who are Noah's semi-cousins, or something. Do you remember Craig Oliver? He's around your brother's age? Scott, I mean."

You'd better believe I recalled Craig—a bully who never quite understood that Scott had two big brothers who would always have his back.

"Yeah, I know Craig."

"Well, he and his wife contested it, so the legal stuff was delayed, but turns out it was airtight." She waited for me to be as shocked or happy as whatever expression she had going on, then, as soon as I nodded, she forged ahead. "So, I guess he's here to tidy up the place to sell."

I was surprised that the things Noah had told me and Scott about staying and reopening the diner hadn't made it over here already—I swear any and all walls have ears in this town.

"Nope. Says he's reopening the diner. He and his son are living in the apartment above," I said.

Her eyes widened at this new piece of gossip. I wondered how long it would take for it to reach the entire town. Knowing Abby and the highly effective Whisper Ridge messaging chain, it would be less than five minutes after I left. Then, I realized what I'd done—if he reopened the diner, that could affect trade in JJ's. Abby seemed torn between shock at the news, and also wanting to know more because that is what she did.

"Well shit," she muttered, then sighed and leaned over the counter. "Anything else?"

I didn't have much more to tell in the way of actual news. Yes, there was a son called Fox, and she knew that, and I didn't want to add my own feelings—that Fox was a study in contradictions, brash and brave, then fearful, all in the space of a heartbeat. He was protective of his dad, but there'd been that fear again, and then Noah had been just as protective of his son.

"Nothing more to say," I offered.

She made this little moue of dissatisfaction, but I had given her the staying-at-the-diner part, so she had enough to look important.

My thoughts on Fox and his dad would stay with me. I went back to my car, the front door of the diner was shut, and I wondered if they were in there. I couldn't believe the two of them would be staying in the cold apartment! Was it even furnished? I had a real flashlight in my trunk, and blankets I could loan them, and for a moment, I considered knocking and giving them to Noah.

Only my right knee burned, and my hip hurt. In fact,

my entire body ached, thrown off balance, too much driving, too much tension. I wanted my home, and it wasn't as if Noah would want to hear from me this soon. What had happened in the diner was nothing but a misunderstanding, but I'd overreacted, ready to confront an intruder. I should've just asked him who he was, but coming direct from the city, stressed at having to talk about my stupid feelings, I'd jumped before I thought.

It was an impulsive move on my part, I'd pissed Noah off, riled up and worried Fox, and managed to fuel Scott's overprotectiveness all at the same time.

Great.

---

I WAS NEVER SO happy to get home and shut my front door, grabbing a bowl of water and my case of supplies, then falling onto a low chair in the kitchen and taking off my prosthetic. I could feel the soreness in my stump even before I could see it, and the skin was red, a little inflamed. I wasn't a small man—six-two, one-ninety—and I carried muscle weight in my upper body from using the wheelchair most every day at work. Being a teacher is one thing, but being a teacher always standing was another. Hence the chair, and the muscles.

Still, that was a lot of weight pushing down on a single point, and it didn't matter how much engineering went into prosthetics, they were uncomfortable and rubbed in all the wrong places. Not to mention the balance issues when I leaned to alleviate some of the weight on one side.

My lower back was a mess of knots, and I made a mental note to get a massage soon—tomorrow, if I could swing it.

I cleaned the area, a ritual I'd perfected over the years, and the warm water felt soothing against the irritated skin. I patted it dry, mindful not to rub too hard, wincing even then, I was so damn sore and achy. Then came the ointment, a medicated cream I'd come to rely on, which helped with the soreness and aimed to keep the skin healthy. I applied it with practiced fingers, massaging it in, then wrapping it in a soft new bandage, a layer of protection until the next day. I shoved everything back into the box and slid it under the cabinet in the corner—no one coming into my house would see medications and supplies lying around because, stupid as people might think I was being, dealing with my prosthetic and stump was a private affair. It would always be a part of my life. Even my overprotective brothers couldn't begin to understand why I didn't talk about it all the time, but it was something I didn't want to share. I took a few pills to help with the aches, not something I did a lot, but today had been too much for my stubbornness to win out.

Then, it was time for food, but I was tired... so tired... I grabbed a candy bar and hot chocolate, and headed into my living room, sinking into my sofa and flicking channels. I settled on a documentary about bears on a reserve in British Columbia, added yet another mental note that I needed to add that destination to my vacation list, then ate the candy, drank the hot chocolate, and closed my eyes to rest.

It was three in the morning when I woke up to an infomercial about slacks, which was scary to say the least.

Particularly given how enthusiastic Mr. and Mrs. Perky-as-hell were about pushing an expandable waist design in chartreuse, a color halfway between dog barf yellow and vomit green. What was worse was I admired the design of the slacks, and that was like pouring cold water over my head.

I was thirty-four, not seventy-four.

Grabbing the crutches I left near the stairs—top or bottom depending on where I was—I heaved my tired body up, thanking anyone who listened that it was Sunday tomorrow, so no school. I didn't need to be up until ten if I wanted to sleep in, and that was for getting up to the Lennox Ranch for lunch, and they wouldn't care if I didn't make it.

Who was I kidding? My brothers would send out a search party.

Still, I *could* stay in bed and sleep.

And not think about today, about the talking with my therapist, and the ridiculous way I'd confronted Noah, and how I'd upset his son, and how…

Fuck. Now I wasn't even tired.

It took me counting to two hundred before I could relax and ignore the insistent pressure in my left leg.

And finally, I slept.

# Chapter Five

## Noah

I STOOD IN THE MIDDLE OF THE APARTMENT OVER THE diner, checking the space I had to work with. It was small, snug even. We hadn't managed to get a good look at it last night, but it was a world away from the warm and cozy hotel where Fox and I had had breakfast. Fox, sulky and disinterested, stood beside me, his teenage angst casting a shadow over my good mood. Just yesterday, facing off against that Chris guy, and then Scott, he'd been protective, almost clingy, yet this morning, he seemed to resent every moment he had to spend in my company. The teenage paradox was real.

"Hey, Fox? The bedrooms are through there." I gestured, trying to engage Fox, who glanced up from his phone for about five seconds. "You can pick whichever one you want." It was a small offering, an olive branch to bridge the gap between his moodiness and actual enthusiasm.

"Okay," he muttered, and headed down the tiny corridor, taking a left into the first bedroom.

The apartment itself was small—two bedrooms, a tiny kitchen that seemed unnecessary given the diner downstairs, and a long thin living room. The views from that main room were breathtaking—the Wind River mountains in the distance reached up toward the snow-heavy sky—and I couldn't wait until I had a sofa in here, imagining sitting with a coffee and a book, wrapped in a blanket, and staring at the view.

*I wonder if that is what Aunt Lily did.* I didn't remember her outside the diner, just that she must have lived somewhere, and I assumed it was up here.

*I'm sorry I never came back.*

*You were just a child,* the room seemed to whisper back, and I sighed at my wishful thinking.

The place was tidy, but empty and stale. It smelled of disuse, of time standing still.

On a whim, I walked over to one window and cracked it open. Despite it being January and icy enough to steal a person's breath, the fresh, cold air felt invigorating. It carried the crisp scent of snow, but it soon became too much, and I shut it immediately, shivering in my big coat. There was still no electricity, but Scott had left a message on my cell to say it would be up and running at some point today. When, I didn't know, but I hoped that when we were connected everything worked.

Like the heating system for one thing.

"I'll have that one." Fox pointed down the corridor behind him.

"Cool." I didn't care where he was as long as it made

him smile at some point. "We need to make a list of things we need." Within a budget, of course. A tight-as-hell budget due to the whole ex-fucking-us-over thing. "Can you do it on your phone?" I gave him the responsibility he pretended not to want to, but then he pressed and poked at his screen until he had a notepad up. "A bed each," I said, and he typed it in. "Bedding, a sofa, a chair, two side tables maybe." Or we could use boxes until we were more settled—the rest of any money we had would be for the diner.

"And?" Fox pushed, and I felt like shit.

"That's it for now on our budget. I'm so sorry, Fox, I wish…" What? *That things were different. That your biological father had loved me enough to not hurt me or threaten you.*

He bit his lip, and then maybe he read my expression, but his teenager act left the room, and he hugged me. "It's okay, Dad. We don't need anything else; we'll make it work."

Jesus, this kid killed me. He'd gone through his own emotions, and considered mine, all in the space of thirty seconds.

Then, he pulled back. "You get the smallest bedroom though."

I fake-punched him. "Well, you do need somewhere for your gaming machine thing to go."

He rolled his eyes at my description, but with clothes and other essentials, his gaming machine was all packed away ready to be delivered up here.

"I'll need…" He paused and was so conflicted. "A desk, for homework and stuff. Just some wood and a couple of boxes or something." My heart broke—his room back at the old house had a pod of desks, screens, his own freaking library, and what was I giving him? Nothing.

Apart from somewhere that, maybe, he could grow up and feel safe?

"We'll get you a proper desk," I decided instantly. After all, I needed nothing but a mattress and some bedding, and I'd even go without that if it meant he had somewhere to study. "Add it to the list."

A gust of wind hit the windows, and I was thankful they were airtight, but still, a shiver ran through me. "Let's check out the kitchen and the rest of the diner."

We headed downstairs, splitting in different directions, Fox off to explore the back rooms, me to the kitchen beyond the hatch. It was clean, but the lack of any recent activity had left its mark. A thin layer of dust coated the stainless-steel surfaces, but it *had* been a year at least since the last meal was cooked here so I didn't expect spotless. The air was devoid of the familiar scents of grease and cooking, replaced instead by an icy cold when I touched the grill.

We needed blinds for the main front windows—too exposed in here when the lights were on—and I tugged off one glove to make a quick note on my phone.

Then, I put it straight back on again before I moved through the space, and my first instinct was to check what still worked. I turned the knobs on the stove, and to my relief, the gas hissed to life—so clearly, the propane tank was full—the burners igniting with a familiar blue flame. It was a small victory, but it felt significant today, and for a moment, I removed my heavy gloves and waved my hands near the heat before flicking it off.

Opening cupboards, I found them stocked with boxes of cutlery and stacks of plates, untouched and waiting. It was as if the place had simply paused, ready to spring back into action at a moment's notice, and that was on me. Closing my eyes, I could almost hear the clatter of dishes, the hum of conversation from diners, and the rhythmic dance of a busy kitchen. For a brief moment, the inside was alive again in my mind, and that was what I wanted to achieve.

"No food or anything," Fox reported, "but I found this, and it has your name on it." He dumped a taped-up box on the prep area. Why would a box in a deserted diner have my name on it?

"Maybe the lawyers left it," I mused, then used my car keys to saw through the tape before opening the lid to find it filled with various flyers from blue plate special deals, right up to a music event for the annual Spring Rains Festival. That particular flyer also featured a small addition for Whisper Ridge Pride with Lily's Diner as the sponsor. Hell, I'd never heard of that—I mean, I'd heard of the Spring Rains Festival. I'd even attended once during one of my mom's escaping-from-my-dad-and-his-latest-fling-last-minute vacations, but a specific Pride part that Aunt Lily had supported? Nope. I glanced at the window and the rainbow flag decal and smiled. Another note on my phone, just the one word, *pride*, and then I pocketed my cell and almost dropped it.

"They really have a music festival?" Fox asked, his tone dripping with doubt.

"It's more of a trail thing, going from store to store, open gardens, stalls down Main with food and drink, that kind of thing. Some live music as well, I think."

"Live music in the rain?" The doubt in his voice remained.

It was obvious I wasn't selling it, but given I was a summer visitor and had only been in town once in spring, I had little to go on. I recalled Lily had taken part in the one I'd seen. Special cakes were all I recalled, a lot of flowers and music. I didn't recall a Pride theme, but then, I'd been only ten, maybe even younger.

Something compelled me to defend the town. "It doesn't rain for the *whole* of spring."

"So why the Spring Rains Festival?" He scowled at the flyer.

"I have no idea, but it doesn't rain all the time."

Fox gestured out of the window. "Well, it sure snows a lot," he said.

"It snows in Columbus."

"Yeah, like twenty-eight-point-two inches a year, not twenty-point-two in a freaking day," Fox mumbled.

"And you know that how?"

He shrugged. "Doesn't matter," he said and ignored my question.

I could tell him about the summers here—the sunshine, the horses, the freedom in green fields—but waxing lyrical would earn me another eye roll. He wandered off to the back of the diner, into the gloom, and I rummaged in the box for something else, a letter maybe, or something that meant it had been Aunt Lily who'd written my name on the box. I found nothing, so it must have been by the person who'd cleared up the leaflets.

But how would they have known my name?

Whatever—I'd go through it all later, and I shoved the leaflets back into the box. I didn't want to think about the old festival because even though my recollections of this town in summer and that once in spring, were short and blurred, they were overshadowed by the loud arguments of my parents whenever we visited. Just like Fox had witnessed me and Briggs arguing.

The guilt was real.

I shut the box and tucked it under a booth. Then, I did a slow three-sixty. I had a lot to think about, like stocking the food; what was I going to even cook? Would the town be ready for me and my take on diner food? Would they come here out of curiosity, then stay away because I fucked up? Was the town big enough to even support a diner?

I had my head in a cupboard when the door slammed open—wide open—a tall man in the doorway, glowering at me. Something about him made me straighten and go on the defensive. What the hell?

"Morning, how can I help?" I forced a smile.

"Pastor McKenna," he replied, which I assume was his way of introducing himself.

"Noah. Noah Bennett."

"Hmm, I know," he said and scanned the diner before landing on the window. "I wanted to talk to you about that." He pointed at the rainbow flag.

I nodded, my smile faltering. "What about it?"

He cleared his throat, adopting a tone that was

probably meant to sound friendly, but came off as condescending. "Well, I assumed you'd be taking that down. Lily had her… views, but she's gone now." He made the sign of the cross. "God rest her soul." He nodded as if he'd bestowed something great on her memory, and then, the sneer returned. "Anyway, young man, Whisper Ridge isn't really that kind of town."

I felt a surge of irritation at his words. The insinuation was clear—he was expecting me to conform to his narrow view of what was acceptable.

I wanted to snap at him, to tell him right then and there that I was gay, but I held back. Instead, I leaned into sarcasm. "Oh, I see. Thanks for the heads-up, *Pastor*. I'll keep the town's… preferences in mind."

He nodded, satisfied, and after a few more of what I assumed he thought were pleasantries—something about the deterioration of morals or something like that—he left, and I locked the door.

It made me laugh when he stopped and stared at the flag and sneered, then hid the sneer when a man in a bulky sheriff's coat—taller and wider, but slimmer than Pastor McKenna—sauntered past and stopped at my door. McKenna hurried away, and when the sheriff tried the handle of the diner, I let him in.

He shut the door behind him, stamping off the snow. "Neil Wyndham," he said, extending his hand, which I shook. "Sheriff."

"Noah Bennett," I replied and gestured to my side. "My son, Fox."

"Sir," Fox said with respect, and they shook hands.

"Saw Pastor McKenna was visiting; thought I'd check in."

"Thank you."

Neil glanced around, but it wasn't with a calculated gleam, or a sneer, but genuine interest. "Whisper Ridge is a friendly town," he said. "Shame about those who preach love, but don't show it." He nodded then, as if we'd had a huge debate about something important, then handed me a card. "Had some trouble in here with vandals, kids mostly, but my office is right behind you; call me if you need anything, or just visit."

"Thank you."

"Good to see the diner opening up again." Then, he nodded and left, all tall, dark, and mysterious, and it felt as if he was giving me a silent vote of support where McKenna was concerned.

Good, I needed all the help I could get.

# Chapter Six

Chris

I LASTED ABOUT AN HOUR IN MY QUIET HOUSE AFTER I WOKE up. Enough to shower, re-affix my prosthetic, and get dressed. I was still tired, waking early, and I knew I needed something to get me out of my funk.

Horses.

Ten minutes after coffee, I headed up to Lennox Ranch, parked, then headed over to the stables, the iced-over snow crunching under my wheelchair as I approached, hoping Levi was around—Micah at a push. The air was crisp, dark gray clouds hinted at snow, but there was nothing forecast until later today. I was here for a riding lesson with Levi, and nothing would deter me.

As I neared the stables, the familiar scent of hay and horses filled my nostrils, grounding me. I loved this place, not just for the riding, but for the sense of peace it offered, but that tranquility seemed off balance when I heard cursing and recognized my brother Daniel's voice.

He was shoveling hay, his movements more agitated than the task required, and the cursing was coming from a dark place.

"Hey, Daniel," I greeted, trying to read his mood.

He glanced up, forcing a smile. "Chris, what the fuck are you doing up here in this weather?"

"Thought I'd get out riding with Levi," I replied, sensing Daniel's tension and the disappointment in his expression.

I wished Levi was standing next to me—he'd become a solid friend, especially after he'd faced off against my brothers about how I was *"perfectly fucking safe riding"* and they should *"back the fuck off."*

Well, he'd been a lot more diplomatic than that in the six months I'd been back riding—but in my head he'd been my hero. Daniel, on the other hand, was winding himself up into over-worrying mode, having switched from pissed-off mode. Why couldn't my idiot brother see that riding was okay? Hell, all I needed was a modified support to accommodate my prosthetic. I had a suction socket, because any jarring could gradually work the socket loose, and a suspension belt stopped the artificial limb pinching my leg to the saddle, add in quick-release safety stirrups and I was safe. The saddle, bridle, and reins didn't need any adaptations because I was a leg amputee, and I didn't even need leather hand holds because I was stable, balanced, and riding out here was everything I needed.

My brothers could get over themselves.

"Why go riding this early, *and* in the snow?" he asked.

"Because I fucking can," I snapped.

He returned to his shoveling, his jaw set, but not before he glanced at my leg, then back up to my face, which held the visible reminder of the accident. His posture was rigid, and I was about done with whatever he was going to say next. "What if I said I didn't think it was a good idea, what with the weather turning?"

And there it was.

The protective, overbearing concern that often put me at odds with Daniel, that big brother tendency to think he knew what was best for me, and worried because he was a doctor, and he *knew things*. I understood where his fears came from. After all, it had been Daniel who'd found me in the bathroom with the pills and yanked me back from the edge. Only, understanding why he was the way he was didn't make it any less frustrating. I gave him, and Scott, a certain amount of leeway, but this fussing over me about my riding was now six months too old.

"Levi knows what he's doing. And so do I," I said, a hint of irritation creeping into my voice.

"Well, Levi hasn't…" he began, then subsided.

"Levi hasn't?"

"He hasn't almost lost you!" Daniel snapped.

"Not this again." Temper began to curl inside me. I was a different person than the man who'd thought his life was over, and that had been years ago. I was a teacher, I was happy, I had survived trying to take my own life, and now, I lived to the best of all of my abilities. "Fuck's sake, Daniel," I began.

"Don't! Okay?" Daniel bowed his head. "I found you, and I nearly lost you."

But I didn't read the room at all, pushed ahead, defending myself again from my older brother who thought he had the right to stop me from living the way I chose to. I'd worked myself up to a full head of steam in an instant. "I know you worry about me, but stop, okay? I'm not some kid who doesn't know better. I know the risks. But I also know what I'm doing. Levi's an excellent instructor, and Beans is a well-trained horse. We take all the necessary precautions, but that isn't even your business! Fuck's sake, Danny!" I was furious, bristling, defensive.

He glanced up, then, his expression weary, yet guarded. "Shit, I'm sorry." He deflated, tears bright in his eyes, and my anger morphed into concern.

"What's wrong?"

He stared at me. "There was an accident, a big one on the highway, and I lost a mom last night," he said in a soft voice. "Her brother was there, holding her hand, willing her to live, and I couldn't do a damn thing to save her. The brother cried. He sat there, and he cried, and…" He stopped.

All my defensiveness evaporated in an instant. "Do you want to talk about it?" I asked, but I already knew the answer. I was lucky to get even that much from Daniel, who kept all the bad stuff away from his family. He'd been involved in a hostage shooting in the city before he came home to work at the hospital in Collier Springs, and we barely knew anything about it.

It was what he did—internalized everything—and sometimes, his fears just spilled over into caring too much about his family.

"No. Fuck." His voice cracked, revealing the strain he was under. "No."

"Where's Micah? Do you want me to get him?"

"He's gone to town; he's..." Daniel turned over a bucket and sat down. "I just needed to calm down before I speak to him."

"And now you're shouting at me instead?" I deadpanned.

"I didn't mean to.; I just worry you'll fall and..." he said and scrubbed his face.

Okay. I needed to be patient and not flare up. Daniel was stressed, and I could handle this.

"I can't live in fear of what might happen if I can't balance, or I fall," I said. "I appreciate your concern, I really do. But I also need you to trust me. Trust that I'm being as safe as I can be."

He was quiet for a moment, then nodded. "I do trust you, Chris. It's just hard sometimes, you know? When I saw the brother crying, then you turn up here, and it's going to snow... I can't separate the doctor part of me from the big brother part."

"Okay."

Just like that, we were done with the confrontation, but a small, selfish part of me wished it had never happened. Life constantly reminded me of the things I shouldn't be doing, and I was desperate to prove I could do anything I wanted.

We stood in silence for a moment, the only sound the occasional snort or shuffle from the horses. "Levi is out in the paddock," he said after a pause, then winced. "He's avoiding me."

I took my crutches from where they balanced on my chair, then went over to him, and bumped shoulders. "You did everything you could," I reminded him, even though I didn't know that. But I knew my brother.

"I'm gonna go find Micah," he said, then sighed. "I think I need Micah."

"Good call," I said, then left him to his thoughts and made my way to the paddock where I found Levi. He greeted me with a nod, his gaze flicking towards the stables.

"Everything okay with Daniel?" he asked.

"Yeah, just a tough night at the hospital. He's decompressing," I explained. Levi understood. He had that way about him, a quiet empathy that didn't need a lot of words. "Any chance of a ride?" I asked.

"Sure thing."

As I approached the horse—Beans, my usual mount—my prosthetic leg made a distinct, rhythmic crunch against the snow, a sound that had become part of my life. Beans turned his head to look at me, calm and trusting, and I felt peace wash over me as I scratched him between his eyes, then bent my head to touch his. With Beans, I always felt a deep connection that went past the usual bond between a horse and rider. He wasn't only any horse; he was patient and wise, seeming to understand me in a way beyond words. His calmness had been infectious, and any fears and doubts melted away. He was a companion, a friend who offered silent support and understanding. In fact, the first time I'd approached Beans after my accident, I was filled with a mix of fear and longing. I'd wondered back then if he could sense the change in me, the uncertainty that came with my prosthetic leg. But as I'd gotten closer, Beans had turned his head towards me, his eyes gentle and welcoming. It was as if he was saying, "I've been waiting for you."

He was *my* horse, and I was *his* person.

We saddled up, and as soon as Levi assisted me up in the saddle, the scent of the leather and the sturdy feel of Beans beneath me meant, in that moment, I was Chris, the rider, not Chris with a prosthetic. As Beans started to move, a familiar surge of confidence washed over me—I'd always found a sense of control and freedom in riding, and it was way past empowering to experience this, whatever Daniel thought. Where he saw danger, I saw possibility, and with the rhythm of the horse's gait, the gentle sway of our movement, it was liberating.

The ride became more of a lesson, and it went smoothly, Levi guiding me through familiar exercises designed to improve my control and confidence on horseback. I pulled my scarf up to cover my face, my woolen cap down, when fluttering snow and the icy January chill was sharp against my scars, and even though the snow held off, the sky remained a heavy gray, a blanket of clouds keeping the world muted and hushed.

As we rode, my mind occasionally drifted to Daniel. His concern, though sometimes overbearing, came from a place of love. Life had thrown a lot at him, at us, and his way of coping often involved projecting his fears onto me.

But here, on Beans, with Levi's calm presence guiding me, I felt capable and at peace. Riding was more than a hobby; it was therapy, a way to connect with a part of myself that remained steady and unshaken by the world around me.

After the lesson, Levi and I took care of Beans, no sign of Daniel, but he'd left immaculate stalls in his wake. I brushed Beans down and made sure he was comfortable.

"I've been thinking of showing you a new trail next time," Levi said.

I immediately felt intrigued. "Oh?"

"Only, it's a bit off the beaten path, winds through the hills. The views are something else—maybe even some wildlife if we're lucky, pronghorn antelope, coyotes maybe."

"That sounds amazing. I'd love to check it out."

"Great!" Levi's enthusiasm matched mine, and I loved he wasn't questioning my ability to do a new trail that might take us further from the ranch. "It's longer than our usual routes, but I think you'll really enjoy it."

Daniel's car wasn't in the parking lot, and I assumed he'd headed back to the hospital, because that was who he was. I sent him a quick text.

***Chris:*** *Here if you want to talk.*

The reply was delayed, but it took me a while to get settled in the car and warm up enough to drive.

***Daniel:*** *I know. Sorry C.*

***Chris:*** *It's all good*

I left Lennox Ranch feeling rejuvenated, and the drive home was quiet, the landscape a blur of winter browns and grays. I found myself already looking forward to my next visit, to the next lesson, to that feeling of freedom and strength that came with each ride.

I just didn't want to hang around and wait for lunch, because I had things I needed to do.

Then, I hit town, but drove straight past my house and stopped instead in the parking space outside the diner without even realizing what I was doing. There were no lights inside yet, but I could see his truck parked, and I wanted to go in and speak to Noah.

Something had passed between us—although I wasn't sure what.

Somehow, he hadn't stared at my scars, or made a comment about them, or been stupid with pity.

He'd stared of course, but then, he'd caught my gaze and held it steady.

I watched as Scott left the diner. He spotted me and headed over, and I steeled myself for whatever he was going to say. No doubt Daniel had called and told him I was out riding in a potential snowstorm, and I was prickly and defensive even as he tapped on my passenger window, then clambered inside, huffing, and puffing to squeeze in with his bulky coat.

"Saw Daniel this morning," he began without introduction. "Think something happened."

"He had a bad night at the hospital."

Scott sighed, then nodded. "And I'm betting he doesn't want to talk about it?"

"He was going to find Micah to talk."

"Okay then."

Scott's focus moved from Daniel to me. "What are you doing parked here?"

Busted. "I owe the owner an apology for accusing him of breaking in."

He smirked. "An apology? Right."

"Fuck off," was all I could say because that was all his almost-laughing deserved.

He poked at my arm, then let himself out. "Have fun!" he said and sauntered away, turning briefly to raise an eyebrow at my middle finger, then offering one of his own.

Freaking brothers. I was done with both of them today.

# Chapter Seven

## Noah

Scott had just left. Telling us it was going to be eleven before the electric company attempted to connect us. He'd also left a proposal he'd created way back when Lily's Diner was assumed to be for sale and gave us a number over in Collier Springs for a company who helped when he needed to stage a house. He'd seemed hopeful we'd be able to get furniture on a short timeline and cheaper than retail. I was all for cheap and speedy. I flicked through the folder, checking out the plans to turn the upstairs into something way better than a dingy apartment, and to split downstairs into two storefronts, then sighed. I guess I had options if my grand ideas for a brand-new Lily's Diner failed.

My cell buzzed, and I pulled it out to check, my chest tightening at the familiar Google notification.

Turned out, my ex had a girlfriend, some influencer who was number three on some list or something that made her famous. I swiped away because news about what Briggs was doing was going to ruin my day.

"I'm hungry," Fox announced.

I side-hugged him, and for once, he didn't protest. "You're always hungry."

But he was in full-on teenage hangry mode. "It's been *hours* since breakfast."

"Two, but who's counting?"

"And it's sooooo cold in here," he wheedled.

"I know. Let's head over to Collier Springs, get some furniture, and find a place to eat."

"McDonalds?" he asked with hope.

I hated to break his bubble, but did Collier Springs even have a McDonalds? "Maybe, but if not, we'll find something."

There was yet another knock on the door—it was as if the world and his wife wanted to visit. Only this time, it was Chris.

In a wheelchair.

Kind of awkwardly stuck and frowning at the doorjamb, which made getting in awkward. I grabbed the door and held it open for him, closing it when he was through, making a mental note to think about improving disabled access. He stared up at me as if he was waiting for me to ask why he was in the wheelchair, but instead, my head went to stupid jokes.

"You just missed Scott," I said.

"I know."

There was so much tension between us, and I wanted to break it. "Is this a thing? Where Scott is, you are, and vice versa?" I deadpanned.

He blinked at me, then sighed with a ton of added drama as he waved at his feet. "All too often. Protective. In my face. I go anywhere, and Scott is watching out for me, or Daniel, or hell, even Mark now that he's at home more. They're my other brothers. The only one who isn't all over me is Michelle, and that's because she has her hands full with..." He let out another sigh. "Sorry, that was probably a rhetorical question." He wheeled toward us, and Fox took a step closer to me.

Chris stopped and flicked on the brake. "I owe you both an apology," he began, his tone more subdued than yesterday. "I shouldn't have come in all guns blazing. But in my defense, Neil—the sheriff I mean—had to throw out some vandals just before Christmas, and this place meant something to me, or at least Lily made sure it did, so I get overprotective."

I nodded, with a flicker of understanding for his initial reaction. "Is that who did our resident work of art?" I asked, gesturing toward the back wall. There, in bright neon orange, was the cock and ball graffiti—a jarring sight on the otherwise unblemished surface.

"Yeah, that was them," Chris confirmed with a sigh. "I wanted to paint it over, but it's been the third break-in since the diner closed, and then, the will was settled. Suddenly, the place wasn't the town's problem and I wasn't allowed back in. Anyway, Neil—Sheriff Windham, that is—put all the cardboard up and got better locks on the doors because the place was just a magnet for bored kids looking for trouble." He paused, then added: "Of course, there are the stories about Lily haunting the place.

Doesn't help in keeping away kids who dare each other to get inside."

I looked around the empty diner, at the graffiti, and it was hard to imagine Aunt Lily's spirit lingering here. I would have sensed it, I was sure.

Unless she'd given up on me ever making it back here.

"Yay ghosts," Fox muttered, but I couldn't tell if he was excited and interested, or sarcastic and dismissive.

Chris chuckled, and the sound was like warmth and happiness, and as he sat there in his winter gear, I caught him staring at me, tracking his gaze from my rainbow beanie to my sturdy boots, I couldn't help but feel an unexpected tug of attraction.

"What's with the chair?" Fox asked, and I nearly died. Teenagers had no filter.

Chris didn't seem fazed, pulled at his pants leg to reveal a prosthetic, and all the breath left me in a rush. That was why he'd been unsteady toward the end of the conversation, yesterday when he'd leaned against the booth.

"Wow, what happened?" Fox pushed.

"Fox, that's enough—"

"Car accident," Chris interrupted, and kept his gaze locked with Fox's. It hit me then—the car accident where a teenager died must be part of the same story.

"Sheee—"

"Fox!" I warned. Then, I wondered if maybe I should say something—offer condolences? I mean, who the hell did that? Chris appeared unfazed by it all, so why in God's name would condolences be my first thought.

He glanced up at me. "I thought I could take you both for coffee?" he asked, and levered himself up and out of his chair, a little unsteady, then took a step closer, leaning on the booth the same as he had done yesterday. "Both of you, I mean, get you out of the cold in here and... I know JJ's has some good pie." He seemed embarrassed to ask, and I was torn. So torn.

He was as bundled up against the cold as I was, a thick all-weather coat, a purple scarf wrapped snugly around his neck, and a beanie pulled down over his blond hair, just a few inches of the longer layers evident on his forehead. His cheeks were flushed from the cold, and his blue eyes sparkled, and I found myself caught up in their depth for a moment. Something curled inside me that felt a lot like desire.

What the fuck?

"Coffee," I repeated.

"And pie?" Fox asked. "I could eat pie."

He pulled his scarf up around his mouth, muffling his voice, and fuck, it was freezing in here.

"What about the McDonalds you wanted?" I asked.

Fox stared at me. "I could do pie, *then* McDonalds," he said, then a smile lit his eyes. "I'm a growing boy."

"Sounds good," Chris offered, and then he smiled. "I could tell you about the school as well, if you're interested?"

Fox was less enthusiastic about the school thing, but Chris had gotten him at the word pie. We *could* go to JJ's, have pie, get out of our coats, maybe talk, and I might even flirt, just to see if Chris was flirting with me?

*No.*

This attraction to Chris took me by surprise. He was a

whole different package to my ex, and he had so much sexy going on that I was drawn to him. His gorgeous eyes didn't hold anger, or hate, or confidence that no one would stand up to him. They held something like compassion, and interest.

But, as quickly as the attraction surfaced, so did a wave of conflicting emotions. The ink on my divorce papers was barely dry, and yet, I was feeling drawn to another man who might mess with my life, and take me away from what I should focus on—Fox, and the diner, and our new beginning. It felt too soon, too raw, given I was still untangling the complicated web of my failed marriage, still trying to navigate my new reality as a single parent with no money and with nothing but an old diner to my name. And then, there was Fox to consider. He was my priority, and the last thing I wanted was to introduce more upheaval into his life, especially when he was still adjusting to the massive changes we were both facing.

But the realization that I was even capable of feeling attraction to someone else was disconcerting, and I wasn't entirely ready for it with how much guilt I still felt. I shouldn't even be thinking about Chris, however fleeting the thought might be. I didn't even know if he was straight or gay or bi or…

As I stood there, trying to reconcile all the conflicting feelings, I knew it was okay to find Chris attractive, but it didn't mean I had to act on it by flirting back.

That started with keeping my distance.

"We really need to head over to Collier Springs," I said. "Maybe another time?"

Chris didn't seem upset by that, nor did he push.

Instead, he spoke to Fox. "Guess I'll see you at school? Tomorrow?"

Fox grumbled under his scarf. "Sure," he said as politely as he could manage, which sounded okay to my ear. Chris sent me a knowing smile, as if he was confiding that he knew all about teenagers.

Then, he left the diner, bumping over the raised jamb. It could only have been a few seconds later when the lights in the kitchen turned on, and a hum from the refrigerator was loud in the silence. I didn't dare think about what the poor refrigerator would be like after all this time, and I focused instead on putting on the heating and turning out the kitchen light before flicking on the light in the main seating area. I needed to invest in timers, but the thought of the place lit up was good in that it might act as a deterrent to vandals.

"Should be warmer by tomorrow," I reassured Fox, who was back on his phone. "Let's go."

I locked up, and we headed out.

But I couldn't shake the image of Chris asking us out for pie from my thoughts.

And that was dangerous.

# Chapter Eight

## Chris

MONDAY MORNINGS AT COLLIER SPRINGS HIGH SCHOOL usually began with the hustle of students and the ringing of the first bell; however, this particular Monday was different because, as soon as I entered and wheeled myself toward the staff room coffee machine, Evie Turner—principal extraordinaire—tracked me down and summoned me to her office.

As I followed her down the familiar corridors, the tires of my wheelchair squeaking on the linoleum, I went through all the possibilities of what I might have done now. Last semester, I'd gotten into hot water for chairing a lively debate about queer novels in the AP English class, although the *concern* wasn't coming from Evie, but an anxious parent—Ainsley McKenna's dad—who didn't want any teacher turning their kid gay. It wouldn't have been significant if Pastor McKenna didn't have positions on the school board and at a local church. Ainsley, thankfully, was nothing like his dad, which was a good thing given he was best friends with another student in my homeroom, Clarke, who sported pink streaks in his hair and didn't care who knew he was gay. I suspected Ainsley wasn't straight, and I tried to make my classroom an open and safe environment. If anything, it was in the hope that, one day, I could help him the same I had help at school and outside with all kinds of things. Or indeed, any other kid who needed a sounding board.

Like about being queer. Or losing part of my leg and seizing my life back after I'd decided it wasn't worth living.

*Let's focus on today, yeah? Come on Chris, up and at 'em ... or rather, up and wheel at 'em.*

I chuckled at my own stupid joke, but stopped when the principal shot me one of her quirked eyebrow looks of concern.

Uh oh. Busted.

I couldn't recall having messed up anything since the great gay lit debate, but seeing Jerry Hensley—a fellow teacher, the PE coordinator, and my friend—hovering at the principal's door hinted that this was about the sports department, in particular baseball, which would be my territory, and probably soccer, which was Jerry's.

"Hi." I offered a fist to Jerry, which he bumped as he sat on the visitor's chair, and then, we followed Principal Turner into the room. He waited until I'd maneuvered myself in before closing the door.

"Good morning, Chris, Jerry," Principal Turner greeted us, her tone serious. "Please sit, Jerry. Now, I wish I didn't have to say this to you, but both our baseball and soccer teams are facing a funding shortfall in this year's budget. We need to significantly boost our fundraising efforts or resort to asking parents for more funds."

When she said *we*, what she really meant was Jerry and me. I noticed Bryan—our football coach—wasn't in here. I didn't have to guess that football wasn't short of funding—the football team *never* faced these kinds of problems. They always had ample money and volunteers. It was a stark reminder of the challenges lesser-followed sports like baseball and soccer often faced in schools.

None of this surprised me.

I exchanged a knowing glance with Jerry. Budget issues weren't a new thing, but it was always a challenging situation, and the lack of volunteers for our sports compounded the problem.

Principal Turner waited with something like expectation. "Please tell me you have some ideas on how we can tackle this?"

"How about Bryan gives us some of his budget?" I deadpanned, and she threw me a frosty glance. "Kidding." I lied.

"I'm asking for serious thought on this," Evie said with exaggerated patience.

Jerry and I brainstormed on the spot, which was all we could do given this was an early Monday morning shock —typically, we got told bad news last thing on a Friday. "We could write to the parents of the kids on the teams," he suggested. "Explain the situation, and maybe, set up a support roster for various fundraising activities."

I nodded, adding: "Sheridan Realty will sponsor the

Rockets as usual." For what it was worth, my family's company at least bought the jerseys.

"And the Treetops garden center is still sponsoring us," Jerry added. The soccer season went from fall and overlapped us in spring, and I'd already heard Jerry bemoan how much fuel costs were to get to away games.

"We need more than small companies and their limited sponsorships, gentlemen."

I bristled at the implication that Sheridan Realty was small, although, to be fair, she wasn't wrong. Scott ran the company. His siblings, me included, were silent partners, and we'd invested in land, buildings, and construction, but it was a minor concern in the grand scheme of things.

Jerry clicked his fingers, to pull me back into the room. "We could also organize community events, like a charity soccer match or a sponsored run, to involve more people. Get the whole of Collier Springs behind us." It was very rah-rah of him to suggest, but there was an issue with that. Collier Springs was a football town, and the Collier Cougars school team fundraising stole the thunder in every way, which I didn't need to remind him of, only when I glanced at him, he was staring at me with wide, hopeful eyes.

*Wait. He's looking at* me *for ideas.*

Fuck. Okay… what could I suggest? Events turned into auctions, which turned into getting new sponsors, and I had one small idea that I'd been thinking over, that might work.

"How about, this year, we outreach to the smaller towns our kids live in. I know Whisper Ridge, where I live, has the Spring Rains event coming up in April, we could piggyback off of that. I mean, we have a fundraising baseball game every year, and we could see what other small towns do as well?"

Jerry nodded, and even looked surprised at the idea, which was new and probably radical, to take fundraising out of the town of Collier Springs and into the far reaches of the high school's catchment area. Even Principal Turner seemed impressed with the idea.

"That's what I like to see—a proactive approach—but remember, we'll be asking the parents for more money and support if we can't fill the funding gap." Yep, way to remind us of the urgency of the matter.

Leaving the office, even despite my bright idea, I couldn't help but feel dispirited, and Jerry was the same.

"Every year…" he murmured and shook his head as we separated and headed for our respective homerooms.

*Yeah. Every freaking year.*

And given it was time for homeroom, I hadn't even gotten my coffee.

It sucked to be me on a Monday morning.

Guiding my chair at an angle into my homeroom classroom, the usual buzz of energy immediately greeted me from my ninth graders. They were always full of life in the mornings, a mix of teenage exuberance and the excitement of new things that had happened during their weekends. As I entered, they quietened, and I took my place at the front of the room, ready to start the day.

"Morning, everyone," I called.

Everyone sing-songed it back, and I smiled at them. Roll call was a smooth process; I knew all my kids well. We had about twenty-five students in this homeroom, a manageable number that allowed me to connect with each of them. After checking off names and making sure everyone was present, the conversation inevitably turned to the quality of food in the cafeteria—a crucial topic for high schoolers. We were almost through with our discussion on fries, and I was about to send them off to their first class, when there was a knock at the door.

Sally, one of our school administrators, ushered in a new face—Fox Bennett. Noah's son. My heart skipped a beat at the realization that he was joining *my* homeroom.

Fox stood there, awkward, but with his chin tilted in a brave front, his nervousness only betrayed by the way he fiddled with the stitching on his worn backpack. It was always tough for a kid to switch schools, especially in the middle of a semester, and Fox might be walking into what I thought was a cool group of teenagers, but they were teenagers, nonetheless. His gaze briefly met mine for the first time, and I saw the tell-tale flicker of fear.

"Everyone, this is Fox Bennett," I announced, trying to make the introduction as smooth as possible. "Do you want to take a seat, Fox?"

The single available seat was at the back of the room, and he weaved his way through, accepting a couple of fist bumps from the cool kids, and a Vulcan salute from Clarke, which the class laughed at, but which Fox had no trouble returning. I wished Principal Evie Turner had been more focused on classroom dynamics, than on funding issues, like giving me a heads-up about a new student, because I could have met him and brought him in myself.

As Fox settled into his seat, a couple of the girls nearby

giggled. It was typical high school behavior—a new kid, especially a good-looking one like Fox, always drew attention. I felt a twinge of sympathy for him. Starting over in a different school might be hard, but being the center of attention on the first day could be overwhelming. I needed to pair him up with someone. I took the copy of his schedule from a smiling Sally and glanced at it.

"Who has honors Math, room 201, first period?" I asked. Clarke's hand shot up, then Ainsley's, and I was quite pleased it was just them, so I didn't have to choose. They were both good kids, best friends, and connecting them up with Fox seemed like a good thing.

"Clarke, can you see to it that Fox gets to first period?"

Clarke shimmied at his desk. "Brainiacs for the win." He smiled, high-fived a less exuberant Ainsley, then gave me a thumbs up before he turned to Fox and did the same to him. I'd have a word with Clarke later, but checking Fox's timetable, I saw he was honors Math, honors English, and yeah, his science grades were good as well, all at the same level as Clarke and Ainsley.

I redirected the class's focus to today's schedule, ensuring Fox didn't feel too much on the spot. But in the back of my mind, I knew he'd be having a hard day, and I wished I could make it easier for him.

Then, maybe he'd go home and tell his dad that I was the cool teacher.

*And we're stopping those thoughts, right there.*

I caught up with Fox again in the last period of the day, honors English, for those kids who were so bright they made me work hard. He walked in with an animated

Clarke on one side, and a quieter Ainsley on the other, and I think I even saw a hesitant smile at whatever Clarke was talking about. I caught the tail end of it, something about Picard being a better captain than Janeway, which with my limited knowledge of not much at all, I assumed was one of Clarke's science fiction shows.

"Okay, guys, settle down."

I waited until all the muttering and notebook opening and pencil case shutting had stopped.

"Today, we're starting our final week with John Steinbeck's *Of Mice and Men*. Fox, I'm not expecting the essay due at the end of the week from you, but bullet notes on impressions would be good." Fox nodded as I clasped my copy of the book, its worn edges showed how many times I'd read it, and also, how often I'd taught it. I knew virtually every word by heart, every lesson that could be pulled from it—the background of the Great Depression, delving into the heart of the American Dream, and into the lives of George and Lennie.

Wheeling myself between the rows of desks as best I could, not wanting to be stuck at the front, I continued: "So, we've already ascertained that Steinbeck's writing isn't just about the plot. So, for Fox's benefit, what else does the story cover? Lisa?" I called on one of my quieter students, who shot me a look of horror.

"Struggling for a better life," she half-whispered.

"Absolutely. How about you, Luca, can you add anything else?"

"Friendship, or bonds that tie us together," Luca said, a little more confident than Lisa.

"Exactly. His language is simple, but powerful, and

paints a vivid picture of the Salinas Valley and the people who inhabit it."

I stopped near the back, happy to see everyone scribbling notes, and wheeled back to the front. "In your final essays, due in two days, guys, I've asked you to think about the characters, their motivations, their dreams, and their struggles, but also the larger world it's set in, so I want to see neat handwritten essays covering those main themes." The class groaned—I was one of the only teachers who wanted to see the kid's using writing skills and not relying on computers. "Okay?"

As I finished speaking, they all nodded at me, some saying "yes, Mr. Sheridan," pens poised for more, and my gaze flicked to Fox, who was still taking notes.

"Fox, I should have asked, have you covered this book at your previous school?" I hadn't had a chance to read his transcripts, but from a brief glance at the top list of bullet points, he'd attended a private academy outside of Columbus, Ohio.

An academy that probably had a fully funded baseball team.

Fox answered. "No, sir, I mean, Mr. Sheridan."

The class laughed, but it wasn't nasty, and even though Fox went red, he smiled when Clarke leaned in to whisper something to him.

"Okay then, who wants to talk about the symbolism of the rabbits?"

And goddamn it, Clarke's hand went up so quick I thought he might start flying. No one else even got near, so with a nod, Clarke began to give us his ideas, and I settled back in my chair and listened.

# Chapter Nine

## Noah

AFTER SPENDING THE LAST THREE DAYS CLEANING THE kitchen until it shone, and attempting the same for as much of the diner as I could, plus organizing all kinds of inspections from wiring to health, I was about ready for a break. On and off, I'd been adding to the balanced and considered draft menu for the opening, but I had to choose a moment to stop because getting this place fixed up seemed as if I was pushing an enormous stone up a big hill. At least, I'd gotten the first coats of paint over the graffiti, but this was the first moment I'd had to myself, the boarding coming down from the windows had been a message to the entire town to visit and meet me and reminisce about Lily.

I was the perfect professional in all things diner, and talked up my vision of the place, asked what people wanted to see on the menu, and made as many new friends as I could. I was the *new-guy-in-the-diner,* and I knew it was curiosity and the chance to gossip about me that got people through the door to visit, but also, I hoped they'd come back when I did the soft opening in a few weeks.

The menu was informed by what people said they'd loved in Aunt Lily's time, and what I'd drawn up was a blend of classic diner food and something a bit extra, a touch I hoped would set us apart. I couldn't do much about the breakfasts, they were standard fare, but with herbs and sauces, I could elevate them. On my list was to employ a line cook, or someone to work the counter, but that was way down to when the diner started making money. For now, when we opened, it would be all on me. My expertise lay in desserts and pastries, but I'd worked in enough kitchens, that I could handle most things. My gaze lingered on the section for pastries and desserts—my personal passion project for the diner's grand opening, planned for the beginning of March. I was missing good coffee, not wanting to offer the diner stuff that was so generic it was nothing, but I had plans for that.

I spent half an hour fixing the jangling bell at the door, which was a case of bending the kick plate until the door hit the strip of metal and poked at the leather on a broken bench forlornly—that wouldn't be such an easy fix. I researched making the step handicapped friendly, ordered the work from a local contractor who promised he'd be out the next day. Done.

Next up was taking my first step towards cross promotion and working with local businesses—there was nothing I could do about opening as yet, with so much to be done, but breaking for lunch was as good a time as any to network to make connections for later on.

I folded my draft menu and tucked it into my coat pocket, stepping out into the icy lunchtime air. My destination was JJ's Coffee Shop, a local favorite, with small round tables, and at the back, a collection of mismatched but comfortable sofas and low tables.

As I pushed open the door to JJ's, the rich aroma of coffee and the sound of quiet chatter welcomed me, and I spotted the owner—Abby—behind the counter, her hands busy with a steaming latte that she slid toward a man on his phone. I waited until he left, then dived straight in.

"Morning," I greeted, approaching the counter with the friendliest smile I could muster.

Abby glanced up, saw me, and her smiled dropped and her expression became guarded. "Good morning," she said. I remembered my first day in town, when Fox and I had popped in for coffee, and she'd been a lot more friendly; although, she now knew who I was, and what I intended on doing.

I bet there wasn't a single person in town who didn't know I planned to re-open the diner.

I got straight to the point. "Noah Bennett, from the diner, Lily's great-nephew." I held out a hand, and she shook it before sliding a finished coffee to a young woman on her phone waiting at the end.

"I know who you are," she said with a neutral expression. I waited for her to offer her name, but it was on her tag anyway. *Abby. Manager.* And I knew she owned the place as well.

"Hi, Abby, it's nice to finally talk to you properly. You

have a lovely range of pastries and pies." I was being overenthusiastic about the anemic-looking fruit loaf and cupcakes that had barely any icing, but I liked the apple pie right next to them. I hoped it tasted as good as it looked, with crumbling pastry and packed full of apples and the colors of cinnamon. "Who does them for you?"

She paused, her eyes narrowing. "The pies are mine; we outsource the rest, of course. You don't have to ask who supplies them so you can steal the ideas, you can google for local suppliers."

I didn't launch into my list of culinary skills, or my awards, or that I'd once worked for one of the most famous restaurants in Columbus as resident pastry chef.

Instead, I took a deep breath. "I'm not here to replace what you do with what I'm doing, look… I was thinking… what if I offered to do pastries for you? For free, initially to test the market. I'm looking to supply pastries and desserts to other outlets once the diner opens."

Abby's suspicion was clear. "That sounds exactly like your diner *is* going to compete with my coffee shop."

I shook my head, eager to reassure her. "Not at all. We're focusing on breakfast, light soups and sandwiches for lunch, and a rotating dinner menu, opening at six and then, closing each night at seven. Nothing like what you offer here." I dug into my pocket and pulled out the handwritten menu. "This is what I plan."

She stared down at the note, smoothing it out and reading it line for line. When she was done, she was still hesitant, but I knew it had to reassure her.

"You blend your own coffee right?"

She considered this for a moment. "Yes, why?"

"Well, I'd like to offer your coffee in my diner, if you are agreeable, with your advice on whether the machine we have is up to the job, and the best way to prepare it, but only to go with food, not for people to take out, because it's great coffee."

She stared at me as if she couldn't quite understand. "Wait, so in exchange, you're suggesting you supply me with pastries?"

"Yes," I confirmed. "Obviously, it would end up a formal agreement with balanced costs and so on, but for now, my aim with the diner is to bring something unique, based on my experience. Fresh, homemade pastries and desserts for you, something to complement your amazing coffee, but upfront I would agree, in writing if you need me to, that the things that sell here for you, on a takeout or eat-in basis, would not be offered at the diner."

Abby's expression softened, and she glanced down at the menu. "Working together on this, not against."

"Absolutely."

She thawed a little then. "Would you like a coffee; can we talk between customers?"

"Only if the coffee comes with a slice of your pie."

She smiled then, cut me a huge piece of pie, added cream, and as I carried it to a table, she made us coffee, and at last, she joined me at a table with a view of the counter. "All right, Noah. Let's hear your ideas. But no promises."

Gratitude washed over me. "Thank you, Abby. You won't be disappointed. I plan to open early March, so we can talk some cross promotion there if you like..."

Leaving JJ's after talking ideas for an hour or more, I

felt at least some sense of purpose for what I might be offering in this small town. My first stop was the grocery store, where I was lost as to what to make Abby first. I was one hundred percent behind the concept of farm to table, always using fresh local ingredients, but this was a tiny grocery store in a small town. Local honey was displayed at the front, and my head swam with possibilities for a pastry with honey... perhaps a honey-infused croissant or a sweet honey tart. As I wound my way around the tiny store, everyone I met stopped to chat to me—about the diner, about Lily—but I was lucky it was just three people who'd braved the falling snow, so I managed to get back to the diner without too much delay.

Back there, I inspected the ovens I'd cleaned, switching the smaller of them on so I could ensure they were up for the task ahead, and then, set out all the ingredients. Washing my hands, prepping the area, weighing produce, I was in the zone, and I lost myself in working up ideas, only stopping when the bell above the door jingled and I turned to see Fox locking the door behind him, then trudging in, his school backpack slung over his shoulder.

"Hey, Fox," I called out, but he barely acknowledged me, heading straight to his room. His mood wasn't good, but somehow, today, it was darker than just the teenage thing he had going on. What had upset him? Was it Briggs? His papa had taken to messaging Fox at the weirdest of times, despite our agreement that he stay away from both of us.

I bet it was Briggs.

Concerned, I grabbed the closest plate of pastries that

were cooling, and followed, knocking on his door. "Fox, can I come in?" He mumbled a quiet assent, and as I entered, plate of pastries first, I couldn't help but see the redness around his eyes. "Is everything okay? Is it your papa?"

He winced, then shrugged, avoiding my gaze. "Not him, no. It's nothing. Just school stuff."

I sat beside him, trying to offer comfort. "I'm making some pastries for a taste test. Could use your opinion."

Fox picked one up, whatever his mood, he could always eat, and then, with a hand under the pastry, he took a bite, and the flakiness and sweetness all seemed to hit him at the same time.

"S'good," he murmured, and finished the delicate thing in about four bites. I was hesitant to bring up school, but it was something I had to do, even if it stirred up trouble and made Fox mad.

I placed a hand on his shoulder. "You know you can talk to me about school, right? Whatever it is, we'll figure it out together."

He nodded. "I just… I don't fit in, Dad. I'm trying, but it's hard."

I squeezed his shoulder. "It's only your third day, Fox, yeah? I know it's tough but give it time. You'll find your place, make friends. You're an amazing kid."

He leaned into me. "Thanks, Dad."

Since his fourteenth birthday a few months before, Fox had hit a growth spurt that took us both by surprise. He'd shot up overnight, and was fast catching up to my height, but he still tucked under my arm for now.

With this sudden change came a certain awkwardness,

and all the hormones driving his moods. Fox hadn't quite gotten used to his new, taller body. I would often catch him bumping into doorframes. He moved with a cautiousness that hadn't been there before, as if he were constantly recalibrating his spatial awareness, and he'd often frown at his reflection, probably not even recognizing the young man he was becoming. I'd seen the frustration in his eyes, the struggle to adapt to a body that seemed to change every day. He wriggled free and brushed himself down.

"Want to tell me what happened today?" I asked as if it wasn't important for him to confide in me.

He shrugged, and I thought that was all I was going to get; however, it seemed the pastry had magical properties. "Mrs. Collins, the science teacher, asked us to pair off in science and, of course, I was the odd one out, so she asked for a volunteer pair to add me, and no one offered apart from these best friends from when they were born—Clarke and Ainsley—and they're nice, but I'm just going to be the odd one out." He sighed, then straightened. "I'll be okay."

I got the feeling he was being brave for me, but I side-hugged him. "Sure, you will."

His cell vibrated, and he turned it in his hand, the name *CLARKE* appeared on the screen, and he frowned. "What does he want?" he muttered, but connected the FaceTime.

"Foxy!" this Clarke boy announced, and I smothered my smile—Fox hated being called that; only in some kind of miracle, he didn't correct Clarke; and oh my god, was Fox smiling at the other kid?

"Hey," he said to Clarke, and there was that beautiful, honest-to-god *smile*.

"So, I have Ainsley here as well, about this freaking science project. I can't believe she made you sit there wondering where you were going. Jesus H Joseph, you're in our group, I told her we're a three."

Another voice chimed in. "Hey, Foxy, and yeah, he really told her, came out with all this shit after class about new student victimization, and she went green."

"That shit was funny!" Clarke smirked.

I gestured at Fox's phone, and he turned the screen to put me front and center. "This is my dad," he announced to Ainsley and Clarke in that tone that told me he was just placating me.

The two boys—one a classic jock, the other with pink streaks in his hair, eyes smudged with kohl, and lips bright with gloss—glanced at each other with an oops-he-heard-us-cursing expression, then they chorused: "Hi, Mr. Bennett!"

"Hi, guys." I slid another pastry onto Fox's side table and winked. "I'll leave you to it."

I headed downstairs, feeling lighter. Seems like Fox may have his first friends.

---

I WAS WIPING down the counter when a knock sounded at the door of the diner. It was late, and the street outside was quiet, draped in shadows and snow. I peered through the glass, spotting a tall, dark figure standing outside. There was something about him—the way he held himself, muscles tense, eyes watchful—that sent a ripple of unease through me. I was so over feeling intimidated by big men, but self-preservation was a thing.

Despite my disquiet, I went to the door to get a closer look. After all, I'd been trying to get to know everyone in town, to make a good impression as the new owner, but this man… he was different. Without making it obvious, I fished out my phone and sent a quick message to Neil, the local sheriff, whom I'd programmed into my phone for emergencies, and then, I let the stranger in. His larger-than-life presence filled the space, and I couldn't help but feel a bit cornered, despite the fact the light from the diner spilled out onto the street and anyone passing could see us both.

"Evening," I said, trying to sound casual. "Can I help?"

He checked around the diner before his gaze settled on me. "I'm Connor Mason," he said. His voice was deep, with a hint of something unreadable lurking beneath the surface.

"Hi." I nodded, feeling nervous.

Connor continued, "I work for Quinn."

"I don't think I've met a Quinn in town yet," I said, and he nodded, almost as if he already knew that.

"Well, I just thought I'd introduce myself." His eyes were steady on me, as if he were trying to read something in my expression.

I forced a smile. "Nice to meet you, Connor. What can I do for you?"

He hesitated for a moment before speaking again. "I ran a background check on you," he said. It wasn't as if he then gave me space to react with shock, because he forged ahead. "I know about your ex, Briggs."

His words hit me like an icy wave. My hand tightened around the cloth I was holding, and now, fear began to build inside me. Was this guy media? Was he going to get his camera out and throw me on social media? "Why would you do that?" I asked, struggling to keep my voice steady.

Connor's expression softened. "I look out for Quinn, and when someone new moves into town, I like to know who I'm dealing with. And I thought it was fair to be upfront about what I'd done. Don't worry, I won't take the information any further. But part of what I do is digging a lot deeper than what the media shows."

I bristled then. "Get out," I snapped, and he held up a hand.

"If what I've found out about Briggs is right..." He paused, searching my face. "I'm here if you ever need anything."

"I said, get out!"

Before he could leave—if he was going to leave, instead of hovering there like a dark shadow—the door swung open, and Neil, the sheriff, walked in. "For fuck's sake, Connor, what are you doing?" he asked, irritation clear in his tone.

Connor turned, the picture of innocence. "Just getting to know the new owner of the diner," he replied.

It was tension overload as Neil's eyes narrowed at Connor. It was obvious there was hostility between them.

"This town is not some playground for you to bodyguard your way about," Neil snapped.

"Did you just repurpose a noun into a verb?"

Neil went quiet, gritting his teeth. "I'm warning you, Connor..."

"I was just—"

Neil stepped up into Connor's face. "Stop harassing innocent citizens."

In return, Connor reached out to brush imaginary lint from Neil's uniform. "I have a job to do," he said.

Neil shoved his hand away. "Policing this town is *not* your job."

As Neil and Connor exchanged the few terse words, I couldn't help but feel intrigued, but wary. Connor's offer of help, though unsettling, was not entirely unwelcome, because yes, if Briggs did think to come here, then maybe, someone like Connor in my corner might be good, not that I was sure who Connor was. Quinn's bodyguard? Whoever Quinn was. He finally left the shop, but not before he thrust a card at me—no name, just a number.

"Any time," he said, and then, Neil hustled him out and shut the door on him, getting a salute for his trouble as Connor walked away.

"Asshole," he muttered, then straightened. "Are you okay? Did he mess with you? Threaten you?"

"No." I blinked at Neil. "He said... never mind... it was okay. I'm sorry I bothered you."

Neil didn't seem fazed by any of this. "Sure, any time."

"Can I get you a coffee?" I thumbed at the machine, although it needed cleaning if it was to be anywhere near my standard. "Muffin."

"It's a no on the coffee, but a yes to the muffin."

I went to the kitchen and parceled up a couple of

muffins warm from the test phases and handed them over.

And when he'd left as well, I turned the sign to *back later*, then pulled the single broken blind, wishing the guys fitting the new ones would come way sooner than next Monday. With lights on inside, I was in a fishbowl, and everyone could see in, which was a good thing considering a) the Connor thing and b) they could see me working and might be intrigued.

Only with that Connor guy bringing up Briggs's name and the possibility of him visiting Whisper Ridge, I was about done with people staring in.

So, I made sure everything was locked up, switched out all the key lights, leaving the small one in the kitchen lit, then headed to bed.

And hoped to hell Briggs didn't invade my dreams and turn them into nightmares.

# Chapter Ten

## Chris

TONIGHT WAS THE FIRST SPRING RAINS FESTIVAL organizers' meeting that I'd attended, and as soon as Rachel had mentioned it in the family chat group—in her capacity as co-organizer of this year—I jumped on my brother's wife for information. If I was going to leverage the event to raise money for the school team, then I needed to volunteer my time in exchange.

Turned out, as soon as I'd started asking Rachel questions, this wasn't the first meeting—Maggie and Rachel had been working on logistics for the parade, the market, and the live music since last September, so I wasn't in at the ground level, but I hoped to get something from attending tonight.

The meeting was packed—Neil was there for the Sheriff's office, local businesses had representatives, and a huge part of me hoped Noah would be there, but there was no sign of him. Shame I had to focus on work and not on staring at pretty men who confused me, and made me happy, and worried me, and then made me smile.

"Okay, everyone, welcome our newest member to the organizational committee," Maggie began and stared at me, as did the other ten or so people in the room, Rachel included. Everyone seemed curious to see me there, but I needed to bide my time before I launched into a full-on charm offensive. I gave a hint of a wave and smiled.

"Hi," I offered.

There was a discordant mumbling of hellos, and then, we all turned back to the imposing figure that was Maggie Hamilton.

"Our other new volunteer appears to be late." She pursed her lips.

All of us turned to the door as if we expected someone to walk in just because she'd mentioned them. From my perspective, Maggie was someone who'd always been a part of my life in Whisper Ridge. She was in her sixties now, but to me, she was this ageless person—a constant from when I was little. She had this warm, inviting face, surrounded by soft curls that had kept their blonde color, and whenever I saw her, her eyes were twinkling with a kind of mischievous knowledge, as if she knew all the secrets of Whisper Ridge and could see right through anyone. She was a force of nature, and if it was possible to will someone to arrive, it would be her.

I vividly recall, as a kid, being captivated by her stories about the founders of Whisper Ridge—the local legends and the tales of our community's past—with her knack for storytelling and impressive memory. She remembered many details that most of us would forget—things like birthdays and anniversaries, and she even remembered my favorite snack from when I was little. Maggie, in her own unique way, had always been there, and I liked her, and I think she liked me. I hope that went some way to making the little speech I was going to give easier.

She was the type who was involved in just about everything in town. Whether it was organizing local events or volunteering at the library, she was always there, a constant and reassuring presence. There wasn't much that happened in Whisper Ridge Maggie didn't know about or have a hand in, including leading the organizing committee for the Spring Rains Festival.

Her number-two this year was a brand-new addition —my brother Scott's wife, Rachel, and that had to count for something, right?

The door to the small community hall slammed open, a blast of icy wind heralding a new arrival, and we all turned around to see an apologetic Noah, Fox with him looking as if he'd rather be anywhere else. Noah juggled two boxes and shut the door with his ass.

His very fine ass.

"Sorry. Sorry," he apologized, "the second oven timer broke, and I lost track of time and… I brought some lemon drizzle cake and coffees, which are just in to-go cups, but there's creamer in this bag, and sugar."

Maggie glanced over at the table with the coffee station, and Noah followed her gaze and turned red. "Oops," he said, and dropped the boxes onto the table. "I'll just arrange this quickly and…"

He was scarlet as he set out the cups and containers holding cake and even some paper plates. Fox was right behind him, but he'd slunk to the back row and sat down. I couldn't stand to see Noah all embarrassed up there, so I limped over and helped him serve up cake and coffee, passing it down the line. I was just thankful Abby from JJ's wasn't here with coffee and pastries because then we might've had a coffee war. That thought was funny, and I must have been grinning at Noah because he dipped his gaze, then peered up at me through his eyelashes.

"I messed up," he said under his breath. "I'm late. I didn't know there'd be catering."

"It's not good coffee," I said in a whisper. "So your lemon drizzle will win even the hardest of hearts." We grinned at each other over our shared joke.

Once everyone was settled again, murmuring over the cake, and eyeing Noah with new enthusiasm, it was a determined Maggie who called the meeting to order with her clipboard of notes.

"We're only fourteen weeks away from the event, everyone. Firstly, Mr. Bennett, I take it from your attendance and lemon drizzle bribe that the diner will be part of the event?"

He opened and closed his mouth, as if to defend the bribe part, but in the end, he nodded. "If that's okay."

Maggie dropped her stern expression and winked. "I'm only teasing—it will be wonderful to have the diner as part of the event this year. Rachel?"

Rachel glanced up, "Yes?" Her pen was poised over a pad.

"Can you make a note to have a meeting at Lily's Diner?"

"Sure."

As I bit into the best lemon drizzle loaf I'd ever tasted, Maggie was reviewing the agenda. Noah had taken the vacant seat to my right, sipping coffee all worried, and I knocked my knee to his in reassurance.

"We've got a lot to cover today, folks. Clock's ticking, and there's still plenty to do."

Neil, in uniform, was the first to speak up. "Regarding the road closure for the market, we've hit a bit of a snag with the permits," he began, troubled. "There are some new regulations we have to comply with, and it might take longer than expected. I'm on it, but it's going to be tight."

Murmurs of concern rippled through the room. The road closure was crucial for the market setup, one of the festival's principal attractions.

Maggie made a note. "Thanks, Neil. Keep us updated. We might need to have a contingency plan in place."

"Will do, Maggie."

Next, Ed Lewiston from the hardware store spoke up. "About the stage for the live music event on Main Street," he said, adjusting his glasses, "I could use some extra hands. It's not a big stage, but this new setup is more work than maybe I expected."

I considered his request. "I could rally some of the high school students to help. Community service hours are always a draw for their college applications."

Maggie nodded thoughtfully. "Let's put out a call for volunteers. Chris, could you coordinate with the high school? See if any students are interested in helping out?"

"Sure thing," I said, already thinking about who to contact first.

The meeting continued with discussions on various other challenges, like coordinating vendors, finalizing event schedules, and laying out logistics for the parade. Despite the hurdles, everyone was pitching in, offering solutions, resources, and support.

By the end of the meeting, there was a solid action plan, and it was time for any other business, which covered me. I put up my hand, and Maggie nodded to me.

"Chris?"

I didn't know whether or not to stand up, but in the end I did, only because this was a speech I'd been rehearsing, and I needed the stage. I wobbled just a little, and no one else would have noticed, but I leaned back on Noah's knee for balance. He placed a hand there to help, a soft touch that had me thinking all kinds of inappropriate thoughts.

I cleared my throat to catch everyone's attention and break up the heated debate over whether lemon drizzle was better than cheesecake. "I've got a short proposal I'd like to share with you all," I began, feeling a slight flutter of nerves. "It's about the high school baseball team."

Everyone quieted down, turning their attention to me. "As you know, I coach the team, and we're always looking for ways to raise funds for equipment, uniforms, and travel expenses for games. Finances are tight, and the school needs our help, and I thought we could reach out to the satellite towns that feed Collier Springs High School, to participate in events like the Spring Rains Festival."

I paused, gauging the room's interest, and no one dismissed my speech outright. Noah still had his hand on the back of my thigh. And boy, was it warm in here or what? "Besides our annual baseball game against the Merton Vale Mooners, which is always a crowd-puller, I was thinking the team could have a stall at the event."

Maggie nodded, and murmurs of interest circulated around the room. "Given that it's April in Wyoming, and we're not exactly basking in warmth," I continued with a small chuckle, "I was thinking we could set up a Speed Pitch booth where festival attendees could get the chance to test their pitching speed with a radar gun. Participants would pay a small fee to throw a few pitches, with the speed of each pitch recorded and displayed. We could offer small prizes or certificates for different age groups—like Fastest Pitch of the Day or Top Pitcher in Under-Twelve Category. It would be a fun and interactive way for people of all ages to participate, and it ties in perfectly with the baseball theme. Plus, it gives the team members a chance to interact with the community, share tips, and maybe even demonstrate their pitching skills."

I looked around the room, hoping my idea would be well-received. "The boys on the team would run the stall. It would be a great way for them to engage with the community and raise the funds they need."

Silence, and everyone turned to face Maggie, her eyes bright with enthusiasm. "That's a wonderful idea, Chris. Rachel, can you add that to the list next to Noah's stall?"

Rachel scribbled. A few others voiced their agreement, and I felt a wave of relief wash over me. "Thank you, everyone. I think the kids will be really excited about this."

I sat down then, and sent a grateful glance to Noah, to which I received a small nod.

As we wrapped up, Maggie gave us a reassuring smile. "Fourteen weeks will fly by fast, but I know we can do this. This festival is going to be fantastic, thanks to all of you."

People began to file out. I crutched after Noah, optimistic about the baseball team's participation in the festival, but more than that, happy he'd touched my leg and wondering if maybe…

Possibly…

"Okay to walk with you?" I blurted as he stepped outside, Fox scampering ahead as if running might outwit the cold, and as fast as his legs would take him on fresh snow. The community hall was at one end of Main, the diner at the other, but given that Main wasn't that long, I didn't have time to prevaricate—I'd probably freeze to death if we stood around chatting.

"Sure. Should you be… y'know…"

"I'm good," I said, although I regretted the choice of crutches in the snow, and kind of wished I'd used my chair. As we began to walk along the road in a comfortable silence, I cut to the chase. "Would you like to go out for coffee sometime?" I asked. "I know, it's a stupid idea considering you own the diner and all, but…"

Noah looked shocked, then smiled, a kind, understanding smile that made me feel at ease and yet more nervous at the same time.

I rushed on, feeling a bit fumbling but needing to get the words out. "You didn't let me fall back there, in the meeting. And I was thinking, hoping really, that maybe we could be friends, or… maybe even consider a coffee or two. See where it goes? What do you think?"

There was a pause, a moment that felt like an eternity, as we continued walking toward the diner. Noah's expression was thoughtful, but he didn't say no, so I had hope.

Finally, he spoke, his voice soft and muffled by his scarf to the point I needed to strain to hear. "I have Fox to think about, and an ex… look, it's complicated." My stomach fell as I waited for what came next. "What I need right now is friends."

Wait. What?

"Friends who don't let other friends fall ass-over-head at meetings?" I teased to cover the instant disappointment that he was saying no.

"Yeah, friends like that."

"Friends who have coffee?"

"Just knock on the door anytime; I have coffee." We reached the diner, and just as we were about to part ways, Noah turned to me. "But…" He stopped again, pulled down his scarf a little so I could see his lips. "Coffee can be an uncomplicated date, and yeah, friends can date eventually," he murmured, then with a smile, turned and let himself and a complaining Fox inside. I walked away, careful where I placed each crutch, feeling as if I could kick my heels up in excitement.

Only then, I would really fall on my ass.

# Chapter Eleven

## Noah

AS SOON AS I SHUT THE DOOR, FOX'S VOICE BROKE INTO MY train of thoughts, carrying a tone that was a mixture of confusion and slight disapproval.

"It's weird you having coffee with my teacher," he remarked, his eyebrows knitting together in a frown. Well, there you go, he heard all of that then.

*Of course, he did; he has ears like a bat.*

There was a hint of discomfort in his eyes, a natural reaction to the merging of two separate worlds—home and school. I got where he was coming from. After all, it wasn't every day a parent went out for coffee with their child's teacher, especially in a small town where everyone knew each other's business.

"Fox," I began, trying to find the right words, wondering how to explain in simple terms how lonely I sometimes felt, and how my entire world had been so wrapped up in Briggs that I'd lost sight of who I was. "He's a friend, and I could really do with some friends."

Fox looked at me, his expression showing he was trying to process this new information. I could see him working through it, trying to reconcile his view of Chris as a teacher with the idea of him being a person outside of the school environment.

"I guess it's not too weird."

"Having Chris as a friend isn't going to change anything for you at school," I reassured him. "Whatever happens."

"Do you like him?"

"Sure."

"I mean *like him* like him," Fox met my gaze—it didn't seem to faze him I might *like* Chris.

"Maybe?"

He took a moment before nodding, a sign that he was trying to understand, and then he hugged me briefly. "Okay, Dad."

He headed to his room. I ended up in the diner, right at the back in the hidden corner, nursing hot chocolate and nibbling on a test cookie, staring down at an empty page of notes. I had fourteen weeks to bring the best stall of the Spring Rains Festival, less because Maggie had pulled me aside at the end and said they'd give me a little while and then pop in for my final ideas. The concept of Maggie popping in didn't sit right—she was a master planner, and I bet I was already in her diary.

One thing I learned tonight, as I couldn't focus on the diner and spent way too long imagining kissing my new friend Chris, was that falling asleep face down in a notebook was freaking uncomfortable.

---

I THOUGHT there would be days, maybe even a week, before Chris and I had that coffee he'd asked me about. So, it was a surprise when, just after school let out the day after the festival meeting, there was a knock at the diner door. I was in the kitchen, and it was Fox who answered.

"Hello, Mr. Sheridan," I heard Fox say, his tone one of innocent curiosity. I heard the smile in his voice, and it made me feel lighter. At least he wasn't reacting with hostility at me having a friend in for coffee. "Are you here for Dad?"

"Hey, Fox. Yeah, I thought I'd take him up on that offer for coffee."

I wiped my hands on a towel and walked towards the front door, a mix of nerves and excitement building inside me. Seeing Chris in his chair, just inside the threshold, felt surreal.

"If he's still up for it, of course," Chris continued, glancing past Fox to me with a smile that seemed a bit uncertain, but genuine.

I couldn't help but smile back, feeling a little surprised, but also pleased he'd taken the initiative. "Of course, I'm still up for it. Come on back, Chris."

Fox looked at us with a knowing expression and a single arched brow. "I'll be in my room, doing homework," he announced, though I suspected his sudden dedication to schoolwork was more about giving us space than any real eagerness to hit the books. Particularly when he winked at me.

"Okay," I said, smiling at him. As Fox disappeared down the hallway, Chris and I made our way to the back table. "Coffee?"

"Sure."

"And I have umm… cookies… a ton of cookies, or brownies?"

"Brownies, always," he said, and put the brake on his chair, shifting out of it and onto the bench seat.

"I'm still figuring out the machine." I poked at the steaming wand, which I'd cleaned and then cleaned some more, running through so much hot water that if coffee machines were sentient, it would be sick of me. "Do you want me to heat the brownie?"

"Yeah, please."

His voice was in my ear, and I turned to find him standing closer than I had anticipated, and for a moment, I was caught off guard and yelped. He was right there, close enough I could see the intricate details of his sky-blue eyes—the darker ring around the pupil that I'd never noticed before.

"Sorry, didn't mean to startle you," Chris said, his voice low and tinged with amusement.

"No, it's okay. I just didn't hear you come up," I replied, my heart rate picking up.

There was a brief pause, a moment when neither of us moved. We were close, so close I could feel the warmth radiating from him. Our eyes locked, and there was an undeniable tension in the air, a current of unspoken attraction we'd both been dancing around. Or I was. After all, he'd asked me out for coffee, and it was me who'd qualified it as friends only, and he'd agreed. But as I stood there, looking into Chris's eyes, this felt like so much more when his gaze drifted to my lips, and he moistened his with the tip of his tongue.

I swallowed hard, feeling a surge of something I couldn't quite name. It was more than attraction; it was a connection I didn't think I'd ever felt before, not even when Briggs had swept me off my feet and promised me the world. Whatever *this* could be between me and Chris, was something we couldn't ignore.

The moment stretched on, and I found myself leaning in, drawn to him, and Chris mirrored my movement, his hand reaching out to steady me. Our faces were inches apart, close enough to feel each other's breath, the air charged with electricity, and there was a promise of what this could be. My heart pounded, loud in my ears, and for a moment, I thought we might close the gap, giving in to the tension that had been building between us.

The steamer on the coffee machine let out a sudden puff of hot air, jolting us back to reality. We both stepped back, a bit flustered, the spell broken, and as quickly as the moment had come, it was gone.

I cleared my throat, trying to regain my composure. "Uh, your coffee," I said, a little more breathlessly than I'd intended.

Chris ran a hand through his hair, a small smile playing on his lips. "Yeah, coffee," he echoed, his voice a mix of amusement and something else I couldn't quite pinpoint.

As I poured the coffee into a cup, I could feel his eyes

on me. There was a warmth in his gaze that sent a shiver down my spine. I was treading on new ground here, and I was both terrified and excited. Oh, and that came with a side order of thinking about Fox, and wondering if this was right.

"Are you okay to take this?" I held out a mug, which he took, our fingers brushing in the exchange. The contact sent a jolt of awareness through me, and I wondered if he felt it too. This wasn't just me, right? "I'll bring the brownie and cream. I have this new twist with cookie crumbs on top, and I hope you like it because it adds texture and a hint of extra sweetness, but you need to let me know." Great, now I was rambling, and I heard his chuckle.

"Whatever you do will be amazing," he said, and he couldn't see my face, so the grin I had going on was just for me.

We sat at the back table, the air still thick with lingering tension, and the thought of a kiss. The entire time, I was so aware of him, of the way he would occasionally glance at my lips, of the warmth of his leg when it brushed mine under the table. Even though we started to talk about the diner and the festival, the undercurrent of attraction was still there, humming just beneath the surface. At least it was for me.

*Was it just me?*

"No," Chris murmured, and reached for my hand, tracing a pattern with his thumb. "It's not just you."

Fuck, had I said that out loud? I didn't want to move my hand; I wanted him to lean over, meet me in the middle, and kiss me.

But friends didn't kiss friends. I had Fox upstairs, and I'd wrenched from his life, who'd lost everything, and I couldn't up and jump into a new relationship.

"But it needs to be slow," I blurted.

Chris nodded. "It's all good."

An hour passed in a blur, and when it was time for Chris to head out for a meeting with his brother about a new plot of land, there was a moment of hesitation, a lingering glance that spoke volumes. He was back in the wheelchair, and I walked next to him to the door, not wanting to say goodnight.

As he wheeled out, I found myself unable to move from the door, watching him go, seeing him get into his car and head off down the street with a wave, and I felt a mix of relief and disappointment. What had started as a simple coffee to make a new friend, had become something much more complicated. I thought about Chris, about the almost-kiss, about the tension that crackled between us, and wondered if maybe I should call an end to this friendship before it got out of hand.

"And?" Fox asked from behind me.

I whirled to face him, feeling guilty. I was used to his questions and his knack for catching me off guard, but I played innocent for as long as it lasted.

"And what?"

"Dad," Fox began with a sigh, then smiled, "did you kiss Mr. Sheridan, or Chris, or whatever I have to call him at home?"

He leaned against the kitchen counter, staring up at me with an expression that was half-teasing, half-serious.

I paused, as I decided how to respond. I knew that

whatever my answer, it wouldn't faze him. He was just being Fox—inquisitive, and cheeky. He didn't show the same concern as last night when he had been weirded out by me having *coffee* with one of his teachers.

"No, we didn't kiss," I said, then… because I never lied to Fox, "I wanted to, though."

He considered me for a moment, then rolled his eyes. "Dad, he likes you, and you like him, kissing comes next."

"I thought—"

"I talked to Clarke and Ainsley, and they reckon it's cool even if you're getting too old to date."

I didn't know what to address first. "You spoke to your friends about me and your teacher?"

"No, I said I was asking for a friend; they kind of guessed it was you and Mr. Sheridan."

"Fox!"

"They won't say anything. Anyway, kiss him already because I like him. Also, can I have a brownie?"

The change of subject was sudden, but something had eased in me as he spoke. I needed a friend, but maybe I needed kissing more.

In the quiet of the evening, after Fox was in bed, all brownied-up and homework done, my mind wandered as I stared out of the window at the swirling snow. There was a streetlamp a few storefronts down, and the falling flakes danced in front of my eyes, mesmerizing in the glow. All my thoughts were just as messy, Chris, with his easy smile and warm presence, could be more than just a friend.

On one hand, there was the possibility of something beautiful with Chris, a chance at happiness that was hard to ignore, and for me to show Fox what a normal relationship was like. On the other, the potential awkwardness and challenges of a small-town romance gone sour, and Fox being hurt again.

In the end, I knew I had to take my time with this decision. It wasn't just about me; it was about Chris, Fox, and the community we were all a part of. I needed to think this through, considering all the possibilities and consequences before taking any step forward. For now, there could be no kissing.

Nope.

A clatter from the window pulled me from my thoughts and the concept of the worsening storm made me shiver, until there was another clatter. I crossed to the window, peering up at the sky, looking for hailstones, or a bird, or whatever was causing the noise. *Please don't let the roof be falling in.* Another clatter-splat, and it happened right on the glass, and I stared out, spotting a figure bundled up like a Michelin man standing on the sidewalk below.

Chris?

I pushed open the window, frigid wind stealing my breath.

"What are you doing?" I kind of asked/shouted.

He gestured to the diner's front door. Wrapping my huge misshapen mustard-colored jacket around me, I hurried downstairs, going back for keys, and letting Chris in from the cold. There was no sign of his chair—he was on crutches—and with light flooding the space, I could see the warmth in his smile. He headed for the back of the diner and gestured for me to follow as I locked up. When

I reached him, a ton of questions on the tip of my tongue, he was in my space, angling himself to lean on a bench seat and tug me to him.

"You're cold!" I whimpered as all of his cold bits touched my warmth.

"Well, it *is* snowing."

"I know," I added for no reason at all.

"I forgot something," he murmured and tugged me even closer, then he took off his gloves and rubbed his hands a little before cradling my face. "Can I kiss you?"

I could see a snowflake on his lashes, watched it melt, and saw his eyes widen a fraction, and all of my careful and considered reasons I needed to go slow vanished. "Please."

And then, his lips were on mine, and I didn't hesitate to fall headlong into the kiss. I laced my fingers behind his back, which was awkward given he was as padded as a bear in his coat, then stepped into his hold, and when his tongue pressed my lips, I opened up to the best kiss of my entire freaking life. We must have stood there for ten minutes, tasting, our tongues tangling, our bodies pressed close, but it was Chris who pulled back. I hoped he hadn't seen the sudden fear in my expression when reality hit me about what I'd done.

"It's not just you," he murmured, then shifted his weight.

I was immediately concerned about him standing there for so long. "Are you okay" I hurried to ask.

He pressed a kiss to the tip of my nose, then each eye, and then my lips. "You make me forget it all." He moved away, then eased the crutch under one arm. "It's just the snow," he said. "I wouldn't need them otherwise. See you tomorrow; it's not a school day. I'll visit."

"I'll need to tell Fox about this. I don't have secrets from him," I said, waiting for him to rear back in shock.

He paused for a moment and threw me a soft smile. "Of course. Can I get your number?"

I fumbled with my phone, and he read out his number, and I sent him a message—I know Fox would laugh, given we could probably tap and connect, but what the hell did I know.

When his phone lit with my message, a simple hello, he pocketed it with a smile. Then, one last touch of his lips to mine, and he was gone. I watched him head down the street, his limp pronounced, which worried me, but then, he was hidden in the swirls of white, and I'd locked up, I sent a message.

**Noah**: *Tell me when you get in.*

And a few minutes later.

**Chris**: *Here. Thank you for the muffin (cupcake emoji)*

That made me smile.

**Noah**: *Thank you for the kissing (kiss face)*

And when he sent back the same image, with an *X*, I near floated back up to bed, bumping into Fox, who had his arms crossed over his thin chest, but was smirking.

"So, there was kissing then?" he teased.

"Yeah," I said, then grabbed my son and noogied him all the way back to his room.

Kissing was good.

But freaking scary at the same time.

# Chapter Twelve

## Chris

It had been a couple of days since I'd been to the diner for that late-night kiss, and the bell above the door jangled as I pushed it open, stepping into the warmth, the worries of the day fading.

I'm not sure why I'd stayed away—maybe it was the fear in Noah's expression when we separated after the kiss, maybe it was that I had Fox in my class, hell, maybe I was just plain scared, but I couldn't have held out much longer if I'd tried.

We messaged a lot though, but it was sharing small jokes, and nothing in the way of serious at all. I was probably messing with his head by staying away, but that glimpse of fear made me worry I'd messed everything up, so I'd gone into a dark space and worked hard to get myself out of it.

The messaged jokes helped lighten my thoughts and convinced me that he didn't hate me completely.

I'd spent all of the weekend buried in lesson plans and grading essays from the ninth-grade class, including Fox's last-minute and impressive take on *Of Mice and Men*. I'd never expected an essay from him, and it was a little scrappy given he'd only had a few days to work on it, but he was talented. It was the bright light in an otherwise miserable day where my leg ached, my back killed me, it was too cold, the kids were chatty, my head hurt, and I missed Noah. I *really* wanted to organize a dinner date of some sort. I didn't want to seem too eager, and cross that invisible line into being a stalker who would freak the poor man out, but I was eager to spend time with him.

I even managed to get through Monday at school, despite my mind occasionally drifting to the diner, to him, and it didn't help that I had Fox in my class for the final class, which just reminded me of his dad. But as soon as the final bell rang and my admin tasks were done, I found myself at the diner.

*Just to visit.*

*That's all.*

I didn't have to knock though, the door was wide open, the diner in chaos as I wheeled myself in. A huge delivery of frozen goods had arrived, a man was standing with a checklist, counting in the boxes, and Noah was in the thick of it, maneuvering said boxes through the diner to the kitchen and, I assumed, to the walk-in freezer, all with a look of mild panic. When he spotted me, his face lit up.

"Chris! Hey! Perfect timing. Help!" He handed me a copy of the order. "Can you check off what we have?"

I didn't hesitate, and we worked in sync, a dance of

sorts between boxes of vegetables and stacks of meat. I ended up moving right outside the freezer, and the close quarters meant we were right in each other's space, sending jolts of electricity through me. So many times, he was close enough to yank down for a kiss, but also...

No, I don't want to be *that guy,* who couldn't control his urges.

After we finished, Noah let out a noisy sigh. "The delivery guy was three hours late, and then Fox has gone to Ainsley's house, and he won't be back until seven, and jeez..." He slumped to one of the stools. "Thank you."

"It's all good," I said and passed him the paperwork. "Teachers are experts at filling in forms."

Noah gave them a cursory glance, then set them on the counter and placed a bowl on them to keep them safe. He glanced at me, offered me a shy smile, and I couldn't help myself—I took his hand in mine and kissed his palm before closing the fingers.

"Missed you," I said.

He colored. "Me too." Then, he checked his watch. "Have you eaten? Because I think I haven't eaten all day."

"You think? Or you know."

He snorted. "I know."

"You want to go out?" Could this be our date? Our meal out? Talking and learning, and maybe some more kissing?

He tugged his lower lip between his teeth—I wish he wouldn't do that, because, jeez, sexy—then glanced at the clock and then, back at me. "How about I make something here? Do you eat chicken?"

"Does a bear shit in the woods?" I deadpanned. "Chicken is life."

He grinned, and I moved from my chair to a stool at the hatch so I could watch Noah as he worked. He moved around the kitchen with a fluidity that was almost mesmerizing, chopping bell peppers, onions, and carrots with precision, his knife tapping against the cutting board.

"How do you not cut yourself?" I asked as he poured oil into a large skillet.

"Practice." He held out his hand. "If you look close enough you can see the scars from when I started." I took hold of it, turning it this way and that, pretending I couldn't see the tiny pale scars on two of his fingers, all so I didn't need to let go. I tugged a little, and he took a step toward the serving hatch, leaned there, and laced our fingers.

"Hi," I murmured.

He glanced past me, and then, in a quick movement, he pressed a kiss to my lips, another hello of sorts, then backed away. I missed the feel of him, but he had work to do, and the oil shimmered before he tossed in chicken strips, which sizzled upon contact. Every so often, he would glance up and smile as the aroma of cooking food filled the diner, a blend of garlic, soy sauce, and sesame oil. In less than twenty minutes, Noah was sliding two plates of steaming chicken stir-fry in front of us, and handing over sparkling cutlery and napkins, plus a glass of water each.

"You're a pastry chef, right?" I asked as I stared down at the dish. "Cakes and desserts, that kind of thing."

"Well, yeah," he said, and swung himself onto the stool next to me, our knees touching. "But I've done all kinds of stuff. I just love the sweet stuff is all." He dipped his gaze, and I reached out to tip his chin, then leaned in for one more kiss. "And you're plenty sweet," he added.

As we dug in, the door swung open and Fox entered, waving at a departing car, and then, his face lit up at the sight of the food. "Wow, that smells awesome!" he exclaimed.

"Didn't you just eat at Ainsley's?"

Fox tapped his belly. "Still room."

Noah chuckled, plating up a smaller portion for him. "Well, you're just in time, Fox. Grab a fork."

He joined us, and we ate together in the warm, cozy corner of the diner, and given he was here, the conversation soon turned to Fox's schoolwork.

"Hey, Dad, guess what?" he said, with a shy glance at me. "Guess who got an A minus on their English essay!"

"You did? Wow, that's outstanding, Fox! Well done!"

Fox dug into his school bag, then held up the essay with the big *A-* in the corner. "Well-constructed arguments. Consider the rabbits," he read out. "I knew I should have put the rabbits in." He sent me a rueful smile.

"*Of Mice and Men* is not an easy text, but you nailed it despite only a few days' study. Aside from the rabbits. So, how did you feel about the essay itself?" I asked.

Fox took a thoughtful bite, then replied: "It was cool. I liked analyzing the characters. George and Lennie are like opposites, but they fit together."

Noah listened, asking questions, or commenting, and his wide smile made it obvious how proud he was of Fox.

I realized how natural it felt to be here with them, discussing literature over a meal cooked with care.

*I'm having so many feelings here.*

As the meal wound down, I found myself not wanting the evening to end. There was something about the diner, about Noah, and Fox, that felt like peace. A place where I could be myself, share my passion for literature with a pupil who loved books, and enjoy the simple pleasure of good food and better company.

Fox nodded; thoughtful. "Do you think George did the right thing at the end of the book?"

I paused, considering. "It's a tough question. In one way, George was trying to protect Lennie from a worse fate. The hardest decisions are about protecting the ones we care about, even if it hurts us."

"Like Dad did my papa," Fox murmured, and I blinked at him.

"Not now, Fox," Noah warned with a smile, although there was an underlying tone of something that put me on edge, not to mention Fox's eyes narrowed. I got the sense that this was a familiar discussion between the two of them.

"Well, it's true. You made the choice to stay with Papa because of me, and he hurt you a lot."

"Fox, please." He shot me a worried look as if I was going to ask Fox questions, but I could read the room. Only, my chest tightened. Noah's ex had hurt him. In what way? Had he laid his hands on Noah? Is that why Noah wanted to take things slowly with me? Maybe to see if he could trust me? I saw his and Fox's silent conversation, and Fox backed down after a while, as Noah attempted to change the subject.

The conversation drifted between the book, school, and life in general. I found myself relaxing, the earlier angsty moment fading into a more comfortable evening, which wound down to Fox heading to his games room, and me helping Noah to clean up.

Or rather, staying out of his way as he cleaned up because *apparently* this was his domain, and I wasn't allowed in.

"I should go," I said, when the clock showed eight. "You probably have things to do?"

*Please ask me to stay a bit longer.*

Noah cleared his throat. "Well, I've been experimenting with buttercream variations. I need an honest opinion. You up for some taste-testing?"

*Yes! He's not saying he wants me to go.* "Absolutely."

He pulled out a tray of frosted cupcakes, each beautifully decorated, and pointed to each cupcake in turn. "First, classic vanilla with a twist of lemon zest. Second, raspberry and white chocolate. And the last one might look like *just* chocolate, but it's my wildcard—I'll tell you what's in it after you try it."

"Okay, I'm going in." I selected the vanilla-lemon cupcake first, its frosting swirled to perfection. As I took a bite, the flavors exploded in my mouth—the rich sweetness of vanilla and fresh, zesty lemon. "This is incredible, Noah." I looked up to catch his gaze. He was staring at my mouth, and when our eyes locked, there was a hint of shock, or was it something more? Desire, perhaps? I couldn't be sure, but since I'd walked in, there was a tension within me, hard to ignore, and I wondered if he felt the same way. "Next one?" I asked, trying to sound casual. He nodded.

Next was the raspberry and white chocolate, and it seemed unremarkable at first glance, the buttercream pale and piled high. I bit into it, and a fusion of sweet and tangy flavors greeted me. "Oh my god!" I muttered with a mouthful of sweetness, and his smile grew wider. I wanted to finish it all, but come on, there was a chocolate one just waiting for me.

Finally, I reached for the chocolate cupcake, expecting a simple flavor. "Chocolate is my favorite," I admitted. "Expect me to be biased." As I bit into it, the rich, smooth chocolate was spot-on, but then, there was a subtle, unexpected heat. Chili? The combination was something I'd seen done, but never tasted in a cupcake, and it was delicious. "Wow," I said, "this is something else. Chili, right?"

Noah nodded. "I was trying for something unusual, and I thought I could go for something that wasn't just vanilla."

"Can't we all," I deadpanned, and his eyes widened. "In cupcakes," I qualified.

He nodded as if that was *exactly* what he thought I meant. Which I had, but seeing him dip his head and smile —well, that made me think of him in the bedroom, and him and me kissing, and hugging, and then, getting each other off, and then, me sliding inside and…

"So, they were all at least okay?" he interrupted my heated thoughts.

I swallowed hard. "Amazing." I pulled myself back to

his creativity. "Stir fry, hot chocolate, cupcakes? You've got serious skills, Noah."

We shared a look, one of those moments where words were unnecessary. It was more than cupcakes and flavors; it was about sharing a piece of himself, and me being there to appreciate it; and we fell into another kiss that blew my mind. What would it be like to deepen those kisses, for me to trace my attraction in kisses all over his body?

He pulled back and was smiling so hard it was infectious. Then, he cleared his throat, "I rarely make cupcakes, but... yeah..." He flushed, and I leaned in for another kiss, only Fox clattering down the stairs, drawn by the siren call of cupcakes, made me stop.

"Did someone say cupcakes? Can I have one?"

"Tiny bits," Noah said, sliding a small plate with bite-sized pieces towards him. "Let's see if you agree with Chris's expert opinion."

As Fox dove into the taste test with true teenage enthusiasm, we compared notes. We laughed when he tried to guess the mystery cupcake, and all too soon, it was time for Fox to head up to bed, which he did, but not without whining.

And when I wheeled myself out of the diner, without even getting a gentle kiss goodnight, fumbling over me getting out of the door and trying to stop the flurry of snow from coming in, I felt like whining as well.

I really didn't want to go.

# Chapter Thirteen

## Noah

I didn't wake this morning thinking that everything was going to go to shit. In fact, I'd been positive and hopeful that, at last, mine and Fox's lives could be turning a corner. Fox had his friends, working hard on homework, and I'd spent two hours with estimates for materials, balancing the books to make sure I could afford any renovations and order in supplies, and so far, I was coming out on top.

Yes, there was another article in the media about Briggs and his girlfriend, an interview talking about how hard it'd been to have gone through a divorce.

Fuck that—I wasn't even going to give over any space in my head to his shit.

I was costing out the menu when the bell above the diner door chimed.

"Mr. Bennett," someone snapped, and I glanced up, the door was wide open, blustery wind and the hint of snow curling into the space. "You have yet to remove the sticky flag."

Ah, yeah, Pastor something or other, McKenna I seemed to recall. No, I hadn't removed the flag, and no, I wasn't going to remove the flag, if anything, it was on my to-do list to replace it.

"Please, shut the door, Pastor," I said, calmly. I didn't add that he should leave and shut it on the way out.

"I'm not staying," McKenna scoffed, which must have meant he was happy to let my diner heat the sidewalk. "I'm sure this is just an oversight." He peered at me, and I wondered what he saw.

I crossed my arms over my chest. "Sorry?" I pretended I didn't understand.

"The flag is offensive," McKenna repeated, glancing at each corner of the diner as if he were cataloguing any other queer representations he could comment on. "Lily never listened to me about the children who might see this and turn from the true path."

"Shut the door. Please." I added the *please* when the icy breeze hit my warm skin, but he raised a single eyebrow and moved further into the diner, the gusts of wind even more pronounced after his tall bulk no longer blocked the doorway. He was trying to intimidate me, and by extension, Fox, but I was done being intimidated. I might be a foot shorter and probably a hundred pounds lighter than the pastor, but I stepped around him and shut the door. I wanted to usher him out, but it was clear he had something to say, and he might as well get it off his barrel chest.

"You said you were removing the item," he said with a disappointed tone.

"I didn't say that at all."

He frowned, as if trying to recall the conversation in which I'd let him ramble, and he'd assumed I was listening.

"If it isn't taken down, then I'll have no option but to report you."

*Who to? The flag police?*

McKenna narrowed his gaze on me and sneered, righteous anger brewing behind his eyes, and I wondered if I'd said that out loud, or maybe it was just written in my expression.

"Also, it has come to my attention that one of the Sheridan boys is trying to cause issues for you of a serious sexual nature that goes against the scripture."

I didn't give him the satisfaction of using Chris's name. "By offering kindness and friendship?" *Take that and fuck off asshole.*

McKenna sniffed. "His brother has lost his way," he announced with great drama, "fornicating and disrespecting the sanctity of a proper marriage."

"Love is love." I kept it simple.

His eyes narrowed, and he pointed at the flag. "This symbol goes against sacred scripture!" he almost yelled, then made an obvious effort to calm his temper. "You will remove it. You have one day." Then he turned, brushed past me, and left—*without* closing the freaking door behind him.

"Come back any time," I deadpanned as I went to shut him out and lock up. He must have caught my words because he turned back to me and stared, and it was creepy as fuck, this big guy staring me down and threatening me, over what? A flag? Fuck knows what he was attempting to do, but if that stare was supposed to unsettle me, then he didn't know the kind of intimidation I'd already had to deal with in my life.

I'd been married to a manipulative asshole for eight years, and Briggs was ten times worse than a pastor with an agenda.

As soon as he was gone, my polite facade crumbled, and a mix of anger and determination flooded me. The Pride window decal Lily had put up at some point was faded, and torn in one corner, but the pastor's visit had pushed it up the priority list. Going online, I ordered not one, but two rainbow flag clings for the diner's window, and they would be with me tomorrow. If anything, McKenna's visit had only solidified my resolve to stand up for who I was and to honor Lily's legacy, regardless of what people like Pastor McKenna thought. Whisper Ridge might not be *"that kind of town"* in his eyes, but as long as I was here, this diner was going to be a place where everyone felt welcome, no matter who they loved.

I didn't recall anything in the ordinances that spoke of the wrong kind of window decal or supporting queer anything. Maybe I'd mention it to the sheriff—he seemed to have no time at all for our pastor foe.

Whatever.

Fuck Pastor McKenna and the horse he rode in on.

"Look at me using ranch talk," I muttered to no one, and relaxed back into my costings. The blinds had been put up today, they gave the diner space some privacy, and I'd even started to relax a little.

But then, Fox arrived home from school.

Dark and dramatic as a storm, he ran past me, thumped up the stairs, and slammed the bedroom door. It was still ingrained in me that Briggs hated the chaos of Fox getting upset, and I had to work hard to shake my instinct to ask Fox to calm down. *My son* was entitled to find the world hard, and I was going to be there for him.

I locked the front door, then piled drinks and snacks onto a tray and headed upstairs.

"Fox?" I knocked on his door. We'd been here a week now, and I thought things had been going well for him, with Clarke and Ainsley befriending him, pulling him into their circle, with study sessions at the library, shared in jokes, and a love of movies. Both of them were good kids, and I liked to see Fox smiling when he was with them. Not to mention, he'd worked doubly hard to get an essay in to Chris about that mice book he'd been reading.

"Go away!" he yelled so loud I winced. Fox aced sulky teenager, but this was different, this was temper, and tears.

I knocked again as worry consumed me. "I'm coming in!"

"Don't you dare!"

"I'm coming in," I repeated.

"I hate this! It's my room! I hate you!" he shouted, but shoulders back in self-defense, I pushed the handle, stepped inside, and encountered chaos. The contents of his school bag were scattered around the floor, a water bottle lying on its side, the contents splashed up the wall and now soaking into the carpet, and the poster of his papa in uniform holding his Cy Young award had been torn from its pride of place and was in tiny pieces on the floor.

Fuck.

Was this about Briggs? What the fuck had he done now?

I had an alert on my phone for any news about my ex, and nothing had come up, but this had to be something *he'd* done, or said, to cause Fox to lose control like this. I faced him head on. He was in the middle of the turmoil, hands in fists at his sides, red-faced with temper, and snarling.

"Get out!" he screamed in my face, and even though with this temper he'd probably be able to hurt me if he lashed out, I knew he wouldn't do that.

"Fox, you need to take a breath."

He searched around himself, found a baseball trophy he'd won when he was at Grovewood Prep, and hurled it at the wall where it dug into wood and plaster, then fell to join the remains of the poster. I moved so that I was in front of him, not touching him, but letting him see me.

"Leave me alone! I hate you!" he yelled right in my face.

"Fox—"

"You're not even my real dad!" he roared, his eyes wide, tears streaking down his flushed cheeks.

The knife dug deep, even though I knew he didn't mean it. This was not just another adolescent outburst; this was Fox losing control, his emotions cascading one at a time, and that was where he'd ended, hating the adult who was responsible for him.

His hands were curled into fists and his chest heaved with rapid, shallow breaths, but through the pain, he was so vulnerable—still a kid—and his brown eyes, normally bright and curious, were dark with a storm of anger, frustration, and hurt.

"Fox!" I shouted over him, startling him. "Stop!" I kept my voice steady despite the worry churning inside me, trying to rein in the confusion.

"Why does everything have to be so messed up?!" Fox yelled, his voice cracking under the strain of his emotions. "Why can't anything just be normal? Why didn't Papa want me to stay?"?" He sobbed. "Why didn't he want *me*?"

I swallowed my pain at his words, then took a cautious step toward him and touched his arm, and I called it a win that he didn't move away, or flinch. "Fox, talk to me."

He glared. "I didn't even want to come to this shitty town!"

"Fox? Talk to me."

"I hate you for bringing me here!"

"Fox—"

"I hate you!" Then he pressed his fingers to his mouth. "Dad…" He stared, unblinking, then dashed tears from his eyes, and I could almost see every emotion passing over his face. "You don't understand," he whispered. "No one does!" With that, he slumped onto his bed, burying his face in his hands. His shoulders shaking with sobs.

I sat beside him, leaving enough distance to give him the space he needed while still being close. "I may not understand everything, but I'm here to listen." I kept my tone gentle, a little worried that I might scare him off, when actually this could be a pivotal moment for the two of us. If only he would talk to me about what was going on in his head.

Fox was silent for a long while before his voice emerged, muffled and small. "They took me out of the group chat."

"Who did? Clarke? Ainsley?" My heart ached—so much for friends—I thought they were the good guys.

"No," he sounded shocked. "Brad, and Lewis, and Seb, they just took me out like I don't matter anymore."

Brad, Lewis, Seb... well shit. Social media was a horrific thing for kids, taken out of chat groups, bullied. I couldn't even imagine the weight of it, but those three—entitled assholes all—had been Fox's closest friends back at Grovewood. I never asked if he was still in contact with the old group—just assumed he'd moved on, all kinds of healthy—when he joined the new school.

"I'm sorry, Fox. Maybe it was a mistake."

His shoulders shook again. "They told me. They said Papa... they said..." He sobbed some more, and I couldn't even begin to imagine what those little shits had sent Fox about Briggs. "They didn't want my name anywhere near theirs. That I wasn't worth the crap they had to deal with because of *him*."

I doubted that was what it said, for all that private education and money, I bet there were a lot more hateful things that were said than not wanting Fox's name near them.

"Well, fuck *them*," I announced, and the curse was enough for Fox to glance up at me, his eyes swollen.

He stared at me as I cursed, and I wondered if maybe I'd shocked him out of the pain, but then he crumpled again. "I don't hate you," he said, and threw his arms around my shoulders. "I'm sorry. You *are* my dad. My *only* dad. I love you."

I hugged him tight. "I know, sweetheart."

"I hate how *that man* ruined everything."

*That man. His dad. His biological dad. My ex.*

Leaving Columbus had been nothing but sacrifice for Fox—leaving behind his private academy, his close-knit circle of friends, and the only life he'd known, not to mention his papa. Briggs's actions had not only destroyed his own world, but had broken our life in Columbus beyond repair, especially Fox's. Anyone would find it too heavy of a burden to bear, especially a teenager whose entire existence was formed from chaos and emotion, not to mention the fact that his father was disgraced.

"Fox," I began, choosing my words with care, "what your dad did, it's not your fault. You're not responsible for his mistakes. And it's okay to be angry that those kids shut you out because of him."

He looked up, his eyes searching mine for answers I wasn't sure I had. "I know, Dad." He sniffed, and I reached for the ever-present bedroom tissue box, awkward given that Fox was hanging off me. I passed him the box, and he released me to blow his nose, tears still falling.

Tears that had been a long time coming.

"How do I make it stop hurting?"

I reached out, placing my hand over his. "You can talk to me, any time, and it's good to let things out, and you know what?"

"What?"

"It's okay to cry."

Fox leaned into me, his body trembling with suppressed sobs. I held him close, offering whatever comfort I could until after a while he stopped crying, but didn't move away from me.

"What if Clarke and Ainsley do the same thing? What if they decide I'm not worth it to be friends with me?"

I wanted to reassure him that they would never hurt him, but I didn't know that, so I gave him the best that I could. "Then they're not your friends in the first place."

We hugged a while longer, his face buried against my chest.

"Dad," he mumbled, "can I ask you something?"

"Anything."

Fox's voice was small, hesitant. "Is it okay if sometimes I hate Papa?"

Was it okay to hate the man who'd hurt his son, lied to us, and destroyed everything? I wanted to say hell yes, but the one thing I'd always promised was that I would never badmouth Briggs in front of Fox, in case, one day, Briggs realized what he'd lost in Fox, redeemed himself, and wanted a place back in Fox's life. So, I modified my answer.

"It's okay to feel whatever you're feeling, Fox," I said, with gentle care. "Anger, sadness, or whatever."

Fox nodded and leaned against me, seeking comfort. "It hurts so much, Dad."

"I know." And I did.

"What if Clarke and Ainsley find out about who he is

and what he did, and all that stuff in the papers? They'll hate me."

"Do you want my advice?"

"Yeah?"

"Why not tell them?"

Fox was quiet for a moment, then looked up at me. "Maybe." He sighed, and we hugged for a while, and I almost didn't hear his whispered words. "Do you think things will ever be normal?"

I ruffled his hair. "Normal is overrated." Let's tidy up a bit, yeah?"

"Okay." He sounded so small, and I wanted to make everything right.

"Then afterward, I don't know if you want to pick up where you'd gotten to back in Columbus, but how about we go up to the ranch and talk about getting you riding lessons? I mean, you used to enjoy those, right?"

His eyes widened comically. "For real?"

Was I rewarding bad behavior, or offering a gift to someone who needed something good to happen?

I didn't care why I was doing it. Fox was far from spoiled, despite all the money he used to have, and I'd find a way to pay for lessons, and I'd sure as hell find a way to make our time work in Whisper Ridge.

We both went to the floor, and he pulled over the garbage can and began to scoop up bits of torn poster.

"We can get you another poster if you want one," I said.

He sat back on his heels and considered the bits of poster in the garbage.

"Nah. I have better people than *him* that I want on my

wall." Then, he picked up the trophy and placed it in there as well. "Cy Young award," he muttered, "yeah right, shitty award if he wins it."

I didn't even call him on his cursing.

He found his phone, caressing it as if he was apologizing for throwing it, and I was relieved it seemed okay, although it was dead. He plugged it in, and we put the room in order, and when the phone reached enough charge to wake up, there was buzz after buzz from Clarke and Ainsley, and someone called Molly, which caused Fox to go scarlet.

Awww.

---

I LOCKED UP THE DINER, and we headed out to the car. It was still cold at five, and the sky was growing dark, but the snow made everything pretty, and I felt as if maybe Fox had turned a corner in the last hour. He was brighter, chattering about Clarke this and Ainsley that, and about tryouts for the baseball team at the weekend, and when we headed up and out of Whisper Ridge, following rustic hand-carved signs to the Lennox Ranch, I just listened to everything he said, and all the broken bits of my heart began the slow move to coming together again.

"Will I get to ride tonight?" he asked, near-bouncing in the seat.

"I doubt it, but we'll at least get to talk to someone. Yeah?"

His belly rumbled, and I pointed at the glove box.

"Oreo snack pack in there; you'd better eat it before you die of starvation."

He fell on the cookies as if they were the last food in the world, and the empty calories at least put a smile on his face and might hold him off until dinner if he believed they'd filled him up. Horses first, then dinner.

The drive up to the ranch took us past narrow, straight fences on either side, poking out above snowbanks, and the snowfall gave everything a Christmassy feel. I made a mental note to visit here when it was actually coming up to Christmas because I got the feeling it would be breathtaking. Lamps lit the way into the parking area, and I stopped the car next to a blue pickup, and then, wasn't sure what to do at all. Maybe I should have called the office? This was impetuous and stupid, although the opening times on the board at the bottom of the hill went up to six, and it was only—I checked my watch—shit, five-forty.

"Bundle up, and let's go find some horses," I said, and Fox beat me to it by a country mile, excitement in every inch of him. He was out of the car and hopping up and down to keep warm before I even had my arms in my coat sleeves.

"Come on, Dad!" he pestered.

As soon as my boots hit the new snow, he was off and following the path with the sign that said *office*, which seemed to be part of the main ranch house, and he thrust open the door and hustled inside, leaving it to shut in front of me.

Well, at least, he wasn't letting the cold in.

I let myself in, and stomped my snowy boots on a mat that welcomed us here.

"Sorry about this, I know it's late, but—" I glanced up as I spoke, and there he was. The man who'd taken up residence in my head, sitting behind the desk and staring at me and Fox as if we'd threatened to rob him. Chris shuffled a pile of papers on the desk before shoving them into a folder.

"Look, Dad! Mr. Sheridan is here!" Fox exclaimed and pointed at Chris.

"So, I see."

"I'm covering for Micah; he's taken Daniel out for…" He stared at me, then winked. "… anyway, I was grading papers."

"Wow." Fox shuffled closer, as if he was examining something in a zoo—there again, this was his teacher, the one he raved about, out of his natural habitat. "The Shakespeare sonnet one? Did I do okay?"

"I can't—"

"You can't ask that," I spoke over Chris. Then, nodded at the man. "Come on, Fox, we'll come back another day."

"But Daaaad," Fox whined, which I guess was better than the breakdown earlier—normal service resumed.

"It's late," I reminded him.

"It's okay, are you here for um…" Chris looked around him. "Well not for me obviously, given you didn't know I was here."

"Lessons," I blurted.

He regarded me with an amused smile. "That was going to be my next guess." He slid the folder of papers into a messenger bag, then flung it over his shoulder.

"Come with me," he said, then wheeled out from behind the desk.

"Do you need help?" I asked, gesturing at the snow and ice. Then, I wished I hadn't said a thing because he stared up at me, his expression unreadable. Shit. I've probably offended the man I was lusting after.

He winked and chuckled instead. "Well, you can get the door, and listen to me bitch about Micah not putting in a disabled access."

"Sure, sure." I opened to the gusting wind and falling snow, and he wheeled past, with Fox almost tripping over himself to keep up. Yep, Chris was in line to win all the teacher of the year awards in the entire world if Fox had anything to do with it. I pulled the office door closed.

"Do we need to lock it?" I asked, but Chris was tearing down an incline, Fox hurrying with him, then laughing when Chris did the wheelchair equivalent of a handbrake turn towards the front door to the main house. "Shit. Fox! don't go in! We don't need to worry people…" I hustled as fast as I could to reach them, by which time the front door was open and both Chris and Fox went in. "I'm sorry, so sorry, we'll come back—"

"Two more for dinner, Scott!" Chris announced.

There was a muffled curse and then, an apology—I assumed from Scott, as I stepped inside and pulled the door shut behind me.

I'd stepped into heaven. A warm, cozy kitchen, the aroma of tomatoes and garlic, and five men all staring up at me. This wasn't how I wanted to meet Chris's family, but I recognized Micah and Daniel, they'd been into the diner—Micah had wanted to make sure I had pancakes with real maple syrup on my menu, Daniel wanted granola—and of course, I knew Scott, Chris's brother. The other two I didn't know—a cowboy leaning back in his chair and a shorter man sitting on his knee, who was rocking pink hair and smiling up at me.

"Hi." I waved weakly and shook hands with Micah and Daniel, then Scott, who was in charge of dinner by the looks of it, given he was stirring a pot on the stove. Then, it was just pink-haired dude and the cowboy.

"Hi," pink hair said. "I'm Quinn, and this is Levi."

"You're Quinn?" I blurted, and then, probably went bright red as he regarded me with confusion at the outburst. "I met Connor."

Quinn rolled his eyes. "What did he do? Examine the number of times you missed deadlines for turning in papers when you were a kid."

"He uhm… no?"

Quinn rescued me. "I'm not sure how to explain Connor, but he's security on Team!Quinn." He added air quotes, and I wondered who Quinn was to warrant security. He was so sweet and unassuming, and I didn't recognize him from anything in my life—not movies, or music, or anything like that. He reached up to touch my arm. "I apologize for whatever he did. He's super intense, and watches people's backs all the time, and mostly, he looks out for me, but if you need him for anything—he's always there."

"Okay."

"Rachel's night off, so I'm cooking," Scott interrupted the intense discussion. "Sit, sit."

I didn't know who Rachel was, but if she had to cook

for all these men in her kitchen, I wasn't surprised she was having a night off.

"Rachel's my wife," Scott explained. "She's had enough of Maggie and the Spring Rains work, so it's her big night off—bath and a book—we get to keep the kids entertained, cook dinner, and we must *all* keep the noise down," Scott added the warning, and Chris saluted, getting a middle finger in return. Ah, so that Rachel was the same Rachel who was married to Scott.

Okay, I'd get this all straight at some point.

"We shouldn't impose," I said, but Fox had already chosen his seat and sent a shy glance to Quinn.

"My friend Clarke has pink in his hair," he blurted.

"It's a cool look," Quinn said with a broad smile, and frowned when the guy in whose lap he was sitting—Levi—ruffled his hair.

Chris levered himself out of the chair and put his arm over my shoulder, tucking me into his side. "I'm dating Noah," he said, and everyone nodded as if him hugging me and making that announcement wasn't a surprise at all.

"Noah, you poor bastard," Scott deadpanned, "run while you can."

"Whatever," Chris snarked. "He's all mine right now."

There was laughter and lots of banging echoed from another room, which interrupted the warm and fuzzy feelings I had going on.

"The kids are in there; Laurie, Archie, and Oliver," Scott said and pretended to wipe his brow. "At least they don't need feeding. Thank god for takeout pizza! Levi, Quinn, it's your turn to check on the boys."

Quinn scrambled from Levi's lap, and they headed out of the door, and all I could hear, then, was laughter.

"Please sit, Noah; we have a ton of food."

Overwhelmed, I did as I was told. Then, bounced back up again. "Can I do anything to help?"

Scott glanced over at me. "It's cool, take the weight off and sit down."

Chris cleared his throat and gave me a hesitant glance, leaning in to give me the gentlest of kisses. "Well, we don't have dessert, so if you want to check the refrigerator and cupboard for stuff to make something?" He winked at me as well, and when Scott turned to tell Chris something in the lines of *he's a guest*, I was already over by the cupboards, searching for inspiration.

Now, this I could do.

# Chapter Fourteen

Chris

Noah seemed to relax an inch at a time as he mixed and stirred and hummed with happiness. Given that he sometimes looked as if he carried the weight of the world on his shoulders, that was a good thing.

"Is it okay to watch you?" I asked Noah, and he glanced at me and nodded, so I eased myself out of my wheelchair again and leaned against the kitchen counter, taking the weight off my spine, watching Noah immersed in his baking. I'd left Fox engrossed in a conversation about horses with Micah and Levi, the latter having made it out alive from the kid's playroom and was intrigued to see what Noah was up to. I'd seen how awkward he'd felt, in the way he was tense, and I'd thrown him into a den of misbehaving lions and expected him not to be angry at me.

I don't know why I'd suggested they stayed for dinner —or rather guilted them—but seeing Noah appear in the office had made my crappy day a million times better, and there was no way I was letting him go yet. He made everything in my world brighter.

Noah had ingredients laid out before him: flour, sugar, and butter, and he wasn't weighing or measuring anything. He stirred the batter with practiced ease and lifted the spoon, letting it slide, then making a happy noise that implied it was mixed to his idea of perfection.

"What are you making?" I asked. I was curious, but also, the thought of another dessert of any type from him was making me anxious to get the pasta main course out of the way.

Noah glanced up, a gentle smile playing on his lips as he replied: "A cake dessert with toffee sauce." Then he frowned and glanced over at my brother. "Do you think people will like that?"

The very thought of it made my mouth water. A cake with toffee sauce sounded amazing, a perfect end to our dinner, and I nodded.

"Wow. I'm sure everyone will love it. So, what are you doing right now?"

He took down two baking tins from the shelf above the counter. "Greasing the tin. I need to get it slippery so that it slides out at the end of baking."

"'Slippery,' uh huh."

He side-eyed me. "Very slippery."

From my vantage point leaning against the counter, I watched the muscles bunching in Noah's forearms as he tilted the batter and filled two pans.

"So, you can create sweet things with random ingredients at the drop of a hat because, sometimes, I have these cravings in the middle of the night." He sent me a glance that said he knew what I was doing, then chuckled, and I leaned in a bit closer. "Are you ever available to cater for these... cravings?"

He smiled, not missing a beat. "Only when I'm sure the result will be thoroughly enjoyed," he quipped, his gaze flicking to mine in a way that sent a warm shiver down my spine.

I watched as he poured the batter into the pans, the smooth consistency reminding me of silk. "Looks like you've got quite the technique there."

Noah laughed lightly, his attention still on his task. "It's all in the wrist action," he said and smirked.

The air between us was charged with need.

"Can't wait to taste it," I said, my voice low and suggestive.

"No doubt it'll leave you wanting more," Noah replied with a grin, sliding the cake tins into the oven, and checking his watch. Then, he pulled over a saucepan, flipping it and catching it before placing it on the stove.

God, there was something so damn sexy about competence, and the way he flipped that saucepan was all... jeez, is it hot in here?

He pointed at it. "For the sauce, but I'll do that when we eat."

"Can you do that again?" I can't believe I asked that.

"Do what?"

"The saucepan thing?"

He lowered his voice. "What if I drop it and everyone laughs at me?"

I swallowed. "What if you don't drop it, and I get even more turned on?"

He leaned into me. He was so close and—

"It's done!" Scott announced, and I slumped back down into my chair, so damn hard I could probably chop wood.

Clearly, I had a saucepan-spinning kink. Or a baking one. Or maybe it was a Noah kink.

Yep, definitely Noah.

Fox fell asleep leaning against Noah a little after nine, despite declaring he was going to stay up all night because he was having fun. It was just him and me at the kitchen table as of five minutes ago. The kids were in bed, the adults had gone home, or in the case of Scott, gone upstairs to find his reading wife to see if she was okay.

Well, that was Scott's story, and he was sticking to it.

"Fox looked tired," I murmured, fixing the final lid on three small containers of the toffee cake Noah had made and placing them in the refrigerator. The dessert had been the highlight of the meal, or maybe it was sitting facing Noah that was the highlight.

"He's had a bad day," Noah murmured.

"At school?" That worried me. As his teacher, I wanted to know if he was struggling.

"No, not this school; his old life. From before."

"As his teacher, and with us… y'know… but if you need to talk…"

Noah smiled and seemed grateful for the offer, but I got the feeling he'd be happier dealing with everything himself. "I should get him home."

“Yeah, I need to go too,” I murmured and reached for our coats, grabbing all three of them.

“Fox? You need to get your coat on,” Noah said and succeeded in waking a grumpy, exhausted Fox long enough to get him wrapped up and to their car. I locked the front door of the ranch house—all the Sheridan siblings had keys—then headed to my own car. It was a lot harder to get my chair up the hill than it was to come down, but I reached the parking lot as Noah closed the door on Fox. His breath gusted white in the cold air.

“They need to install a chair lift,” I grumped.

“I could have helped…” Noah began, then stopped. I saw this all the time—people thinking they’d overstepped. I was as independent as he was, but somehow, worry from him didn’t grate—it felt like affection.

“I’ll take all the help I need, but I’m a stubborn ass, so I will probably curse you out for daring to think I can’t do things,” I said, and we exchanged smiles.

“Okay then, thank you for welcoming us in for dinner, it was…” He searched for the right words. “The best kind of night with family and friends, and it’s been a long time since Fox and I have had that. Most of the friends I had were Briggs’s people, and Fox… today… it hit home for him what he’d had to leave behind.”

He pressed a gloved hand to his temple, and I didn’t want to be sitting when he needed something from someone. Aka me. I pushed myself to stand, feeling a sense of determination as I stepped toward Noah.

“We loved having you,” I said.

“We loved being there. Sometimes, I wonder if I’m a good dad, whether we should have stayed as just friends because I need more of them, but then when we kiss, I forget…"

"What?"

"Fox deserves a better version of me, and I wonder if, maybe, I'm doing things wrong."

"You're a great dad. I don't know what went down with his dad, but Fox is a credit to you—polite, happy, focused, and determined. You did good."

"I think I needed to hear that."

"Also, your dessert was fantastic." I caught Noah's eye, and his face lit up with a smile—a genuine expression of gratitude—and some of the introspection and sadness I'd seen there vanished.

"Thanks," he replied. He didn't move, even as I stepped closer, an unspoken understanding hanging in the air between us. I reached out and pulled him, not into a kiss, but into a hug. I thought he needed it. Noah relaxed into the embrace, and after a moment, we separated—it might not have lasted long, but it felt right. Then we kissed, but it held so much emotion my heart ached with need.

"Good night," he said, then watched patiently as I collapsed my wheelchair and limped towards the driver's seat of my car. There was a quiet warmth in his gaze, and I gave a hint of a wave.

"Good night."

I followed Noah's car into town, our vehicles moving in tandem through the quiet streets. As we reached a junction, I waved again, our paths diverging as I headed to my place. We'd shared a connection tonight when I'd told my brothers about Noah—enough so that, by now, I was sure the entire family knew—and the thought of seeing him again made me grin like an idiot. All the doubts and worries that burrowed into me slid away as I drove the short distance home.

I loved my house. It wasn't big; adapted with wider doorways and a ramp at the door, and it was perfect. If I was lonely sometimes, then I wouldn't admit that to anyone, because admitting it would mean I actually cared about being alone. And until meeting Noah, it had never bothered me, only now it did. Seeing him at my brother's house, watching him bake and how he was with Fox, my stupid heart was catching so many stupid feelings.

I wasn't long inside when the texts arrived in the family chat.

***Scott:*** *Tell us everything.*

***Daniel:*** *What Scott said*

At least Mark wasn't online, but Michelle was right there with a green dot.

***Michelle:*** *What happened?*

***Scott:*** *Chris brought a date to dinner*

***Michelle:*** *What? Who? Do I know her?*

***Daniel:*** *Him.*

***Michelle:*** *Oooohhhhhh. Spill the tea*

***Scott:*** *Noah, from the diner*

***Chris:*** *I'm going to bed*

***Michelle:*** *He's with you now? Ohhhhh*

***Chris:*** *I'm going to bed. ALONE*

***Michelle:*** *:(*

***Daniel:*** *I give it a week until he's not alone ;)*

***Scott:*** *I give it three days*

I shut the group, closed my phone, and put it on silent, then worried I'd miss an important middle-of-the-night call from one of them, or worse, my parents, so ended up ignoring all the buzzing, which after twenty minutes, tailed off.

I love my family, but sometimes, when all I wanted to do was go to bed, they were just a bunch of annoying assholes.

They were ruining all the soft and fuzzies I had and the excitement of something with Noah.

And heaven knows, I needed all the soft and fuzzies I could get.

# Chapter Fifteen

## Noah

I WAS SO TIRED—MY DAY HAD BEEN LONG, BUT AFTER LAST night, I'd found it hard to fall asleep.

The way Chris had hugged me, held me, and told me I was a good dad, was everything to me, and maybe it was what I needed to hear.

And feel.

By the time I'd gotten a grumpy Fox into bed, it was almost eleven, and I'd expected to fall asleep straight away but, yeah, it didn't happen. Both of us slept in, only woken at nine, startled and disorientated by my phone ringing. A guy was downstairs with a delivery of dry goods, and *did I even want the stuff because he had things to do.* I placated him with a test coffee from the newly scrubbed and flushed coffee machine, plus an apple pastry from yesterday's test batch, and he at least left with a smile. Of course, I then had hours of sorting through everything I'd ordered, but at least my pantry area was more filled out now. Then, it was painting, and fixing, and more menu thinking, and I had one more thing on my list for today—fixing the broken bench seat with the runaway stuffing.

I'd painted yet another coat over the cock and balls on the wall, and now, I could barely see the outline, and hoped that another couple of coats would erase the monstrosity altogether. I crouched down, examining the worn leather bench, a YouTube video playing on my phone that offered a tutorial about fixing broken leather on furniture. The bench had seen better days because it was right under the window that had a crack in the wooden frame, which equaled water damage. I'd fixed the window with putty, but now the seat needed to be returned to its former glory.

I pondered the need for a nail gun, weighing its efficiency in the videos against the fact I had a needle for leather that I'd purchased from the Mercantile. I'd been reassured by Jim—he of the impressive handlebar-mustache—behind the counter, that it was the right thing to fix it the old-fashioned way. Something about honoring my past, which I'd just smiled at.

"Maybe a nail gun *would* be easier," I mulled this over, but the sound of footsteps distracted me, and Fox burst into the room.

"Dad!" Fox began, a hint of excitement in his voice. "Can I go to Clarke's house for a sleepover? Ainsley will be there too, and we can work on our science project."

I slipped into Dad mode after a few seconds. "It's okay with me as long as Clarke's parents will be there."

"His mom'll be there." Fox replied. "He lives in Collier Falls, so she's offered to pick me up, then Ainsley."

"Is she sure? I can give you a ride over there."

"She's cool with it," Fox added. "I'm gonna get my stuff!" He darted out and thundered up the stairs. At least, I'd get to meet her when she picked Fox up, even so, his first night away from me, and I was feeling weird, and my chest knotted. *He'll be perfectly safe. He'll have a great time.*

I went back to the seat, and Fox ran back down with a backpack and folders I assumed contained school work, and waited by the door, unable to sit still. After the meltdown, then last night at the ranch, it was more than nice to see Fox excited again. I didn't ask him if he'd told his friends about his dad, because it was Fox's decision when to do that, but he hadn't told me he had, so I had to assume he was still keeping secrets.

Clarke's mom arrived at the diner after twenty minutes, a pleasant woman who had a young boy in tow, stomping snow from their boots. I went towards them, hand extended.

"Noah," I introduced myself.

"Beth," she replied, and we shook hands, then I did the same with Clarke, a short kid with the widest smile.

"Hey again, Mr. Bennett," he sing-songed.

"Nice to meet you in person, Clarke."

Then Clarke and Fox were chatting, and it was time for them to go, and god, I wanted to drag Fox into a hug and never let him go. If he sensed that, I didn't know, but he took the initiative and hugged me goodbye. Then, with the folders tucked under his arm, they left for great things like pizza and picking up Ainsley. I watched the SUV drive away, then with a sigh, I turned back to my nemesis, the bench, and carried on.

I had to concentrate so hard on getting the needle and thread to work. A nail gun was a better way of doing this, but for now, I was happy with the mindless work, lost in the rhythmic in and out of the stubborn needle and wondering how Fox was getting on with his first sleepover. Yes, I worried, but I knew Clarke and Ainsley were kids Fox could count on as friends.

Nothing to worry about.

The diner was quiet, the kind of silence that came when there was no Fox around, and even though I already missed him, because I was that much of sap, I was happy in my thoughts and not ready to head upstairs to my lonely apartment, yet. I wished Chris was here, and pulled out my cell to ask him over, but a knock interrupted the silence and made me pause halfway through sending Chris a message. I pasted on my game face for potential future customers, even if it was dark and getting late. Chris was outside using his crutches, bundled up against the cold and smiling. Surprised, I hurried over and unlocked the door.

"Hi?" I asked, stepping back to let him in. Just seeing him made me happy, and the scent of him, all snow and fresh air, was enough to make my heart skip and my pants get tight.

He entered, leaning on his crutches, and he looked tired. "I was passing by and saw the lights on."

I headed to the counter, tossed the cloth there, then leaned in place as Chris joined me. "Yeah, Fox is at a sleepover, so I figured I'd finish up trying to fix that bench."

"And then what, boyfriend?"

"Boyfriends? Is that what we are?"

He kissed me then, deep, and needy and perfect. "Yep." I liked the sound of that, boyfriend, and the kissing… it was everything. "So, what are you doing next?"

What did he mean? "What?"

"What are you doing for the rest of your night?

"Um, then it's just me, a good book, and a cup of hot chocolate."

Chris raised an eyebrow, leaning back on the counter, a playful glint in his eyes. "You're like thirty, right?"

"No, thirty-five. Why?"

"And a book and hot chocolate is your wild Saturday night child-free plan?"

I laughed. "I had my fun last night at the ranch, but yeah, old before my time and guilty as charged."

He motioned towards my shirt adorned with the Whisper Ridge Diner logo. "Go get a clean shirt, Noah. I was heading out for a drink with a couple of teachers. Join us?"

I hesitated, aware of the smell of the day's work clinging to me. "I need a shower first. I smell like a mix of paint thinners and sweat."

Chris took a theatrical sniff of the air. "Ah, but I love the scent of hard work," he said with a wink. "I just wish you'd been baking."

"Do you want to sit down?"

He glanced down. "Nah, I'm all good. And don't change the subject.".

Despite myself, I chuckled. "You might like the smell of cake, but it's not cake I have on me. It's sweat and grease and… look, I need to shower."

"Then go," he said, as if that were just a minor blip in his plans. "Want some help?" he teased.

My heart skipped. The thought of Chris in that tiny shower with me morphed into me and Chris in a much bigger shower, with me on my knees and...

"Just kidding," he said, then waggled his eyebrows, "or am I?"

The memory of last night's embrace—the gentle way he'd held me—was enough to have me getting hard. I wanted him in that shower with me, but...

I cleared my throat. "Give me ten minutes?"

Chris settled on a stool, and I passed him a can of soda to keep him company. And then, true to my word, ten minutes later, with my hair still damp and shoved under a beanie, we were heading to The Summit. I'd walked past the local bar several times and knew its reputation as having a laid-back atmosphere and good beer, but knew they only offered bar snacks—fries mostly—and I'd considered connecting with them about their food offering and whether they wanted me to cater anything for them.

*And where would I fit that in my day?*

I noticed Chris moving slower than usual on his crutches, careful near the piles of melting snow, and felt a pang of concern. I fought the instinct to fuss, knowing how some people hated fuss. Just because he'd called me boyfriend didn't mean it was automatic that I was in the right to nag him to be safe. Instead, I slowed my pace a little, and we walked in comfortable silence, the cool night air a welcome relief after the warmth of the diner.

At The Summit, we found the other teachers, right at

the back, in a large booth, already with a drink for Chris lined up.

"Hi, guys, this is Noah; owns the diner."

"Maddie," a woman with long, dark ringlets waved at me. "We've met."

"Keep it simple, always have ham," I deadpanned, recalling her demand for honest things to end up on my menu.

She grinned. "Yep."

Chris introduced me to the other teachers, Oscar—Math—who greeted me with a warm smile and informed me he hadn't been in the diner, but could I guess what he'd order? That wasn't happening, but I threw out a full breakfast and coffee heavy on the cream and sugar, and he seemed amazed.

According to him, I had a superpower.

Last up was Jerry—History and soccer—who explained that coffee should always be drunk black, and that Oscar was a moron, cue laughing and innocent friendly banter.

I loved it.

Almost as much as I loved last night.

The conversation flowed, filled with stories from their classrooms and the shared experiences only fellow teachers could fully understand, but with every one, they pulled me into the conversation, and as the evening wore on, I relaxed into maybe another small friendship group. Chris was next to me, our thighs together, and every time he made a point, he touched my arm, and it was *everything*. His laughter was infectious, and it was easy to forget the worries of the day when he was around.

At one point, he was getting me to talk about my plans for the diner, and something unspoken passed between us, when I blushed at the praise he heaped on me, a connection that was startling… exciting. I enjoyed his company, how his smile could light up even the most mundane of moments, and how, moment by moment, I was falling for him.

Maddie, in her animated science teacher way, was currently recounting her latest classroom experiment gone awry, laughing out loud at the unexpected fire that had cleared the entire lab. Oscar, explaining there were never any fires in his math class earned a kiss from Maddie, which was how I found out they were a couple. Jerry and Chris were debating the merits of classic literature over modern works, and I swear, I'd never heard anything as sexy as Chris going all defensive about his love of Milton.

This quiet corner, away from the boisterous energy of karaoke and the small dance floor was heaven, and with my back to the main door, I could people watch to my heart's content. Even though the bar hummed with energy, the five of us were able to talk. I liked Chris's friends, and more important I felt as if they liked me back, even if the only story I could give them was the one about an exploding mac 'n' cheese that Fox had tried to microwave, which somehow Maddie found hilarious, laughing for at least a minute, tears rolling down her face. At which point, Jerry and Oscar went up to sing a broken version of an old Queen song and we made fun of their awful singing but were the first to clap with exaggerated enthusiasm when they took a bow.

"So, karaoke?" Chris asked.

I gave an exaggerated shudder. "No way. You go. But me? I'll just sit here and judge everyone else's singing if that's okay."

He chuckled and made no move to leave for the small stage in the corner. "Thank god!" He sipped his sparkling water, fancied up with slices of fruit and an umbrella to match Maddie's piña colada. "If I was up there, you'd see why I hold a world record in the number of wrong notes in one song."

"A world record eh?"

Chris had leaned in, so I'd hear him better over raucous clapping, and he was so close, if one of us moved a little further, we'd be kissing.

Did I want to kiss Chris in public? What if people talked and caused trouble? After all, this was where Pastor McKenna had a church.

Hell yes, I did. I wanted to throw caution to the wind, mash my lips to his—but in a sexy way—taste him, drink him in. I wanted to be the one to start, I think I did, but Maddie throwing herself into the booth on the other side of me broke the connection, and instead, Chris and I fell into a comfortable silence, the kind that felt warm and familiar.

Our conversation meandered through various topics—from the challenges of his teaching to our favorite books and movies, interspersed with chatting with the others. The laughter and banter flowed, and as the night progressed, I found my need for Chris becoming something I refused to ignore. I couldn't put a pin in what it was. Maybe it was his passion for teaching, or his sense of humor, or the way his eyes lit up when he talked about something he loved—all of it made me stare at him. Could it be that he was more than just a nice guy on the surface like Briggs had seemed and actually could be a good person all the way to his core?

Briggs had fooled me, but looking back, there were signs. I was second to everything else in his life, more like a glorified nanny than a husband. Not that I regretted that part—I loved Fox, and he was the son of my heart, if not by blood. But Briggs had never listened like Chris did—as if my opinion was important, and that maybe, I could be interesting.

Chris was laughing at a joke Maddie made about protons—I didn't get it, but I was too busy thinking about Chris to follow—and he leaned on me, sharing his happiness through touch. I reached blindly for his hand on the table and drew it to me, holding it tight.

His eyes widened, but he didn't miss a beat, lacing our fingers and asking Maddie for another stupid joke, but this time, Oscar beat her to it.

"Did you know in the math department we used to have a chicken?"

"What?" Chris asked.

"She was a matha-ma-chicken!"

Silence, and I snorted a laugh, and the entire table started laughing because there is nothing as good as a stupid joke when you've had a couple of beers.

"What did one tectonic plate say when he bumped into the other?" Chris offered. "My fault!"

Yeah, stupid jokes, beer, a lot of laughter, and holding

hands with Chris on top of the table where anyone could see.

Perfect.

The Summit, with its bustling atmosphere and amazing fries (about which I made notes) was the perfect backdrop to an evening that felt like a step forward in whatever was happening between me and Chris. As we said our goodbyes to Maddie, Oscar, and Jerry, we still didn't let go of each other, and only had to when Chris picked up his crutches and we both pulled on our outdoor gear. Even then, I stepped closer to him as we walked out of the bar, the cold seeping through our coats.

"That was fun," I murmured. "Thank you for dragging me out. Again."

"I'm glad you came," he said. "Have you seen this?"

He'd stopped, leaning on his crutches, and pointing up at the night sky.

"Not properly," I admitted. "Not since I was a kid."

"Beautiful, isn't it?" Chris's voice was soft, filled with the same wonder I felt.

I nodded, unable to find words that could do justice to the view. It held a magic Columbus could never match. "It's incredible. You don't get to see this in the city. The lights there drown out the stars. I think I missed this… openness. Is that even a word?"

"I'm sure it is. Wide. Open. Vast."

After a moment, in unspoken agreement, we carried on walking to the diner, which was way too close. When we reached the door, Chris leaned against the wall, in the shadows, and I was all concerned until he reached out and tugged me close. I went willingly, ending up pressed to him, and I sighed as he shifted a crutch and cradled my face. We stood there in silence, for a long time as he stared at me, and me at him. Then, he rubbed a thumb over my cheekbone.

"I want you," he whispered.

I nodded, he leaned down, I went on my tiptoes, and we met in the middle.

At first, it was just the touch of warm lips, then the tip of his tongue pressed for me to open, and with the cold nipping at our skin, we kissed under the wide diamond-speckled Wyoming sky.

I moaned into the kiss, grabbing his coat to steady myself, then realizing I could throw him off balance, I adjusted my stance so he could use me to lean on, losing myself in the moment. When we pulled apart, I found myself entranced by his steady gaze, wishing for better lighting to decipher the emotions in his eyes.

"One day, I want to do that again somewhere warmer," he said, and I almost blurted that he should come in.

But I couldn't.

Something inside me—dark, nasty, and self-pitying—stopped me from inviting him in.

"Not tonight," I said. I was silently pleading with him not to be angry with me, and I waited for him to explain what a fucked-up cocktease I was, but he thumbed my cheekbone again.

"I promise, I wasn't asking to come in. I'd like to see you again, do this again, kiss you again."

I was so damn grateful he wasn't pushing I could have cried. "I'm sorry—"

He stopped me apologizing with another deep kiss,

but this time, when we separated, he dropped his hand and rearranged his crutch, and I stepped back and away.

"I'll watch you go in," he said, and inclined his head to the diner.

I smiled, let myself in, and locked the door, and through all of it, he watched me, and a small brave part of me wanted to drag him inside.

*Fox, first,* I reminded myself.

He sketched a wave, then headed on to wherever he lived—I hoped it wasn't far. I should have asked him if he needed help. I'd never asked where he lived.

As soon as I was upstairs, in my PJs, curled on the sofa, I took out my cell and sent him a message.

***Noah:*** *I had fun. Thank you. Hope you don't live far. I should have called you a cab or something.*

The reply from Chris was super delayed—one part of me assumed he hadn't made it home; the other, more vulnerable part, told me I'd fucked up.

And then, my cell vibrated, and it was him.

**Chris:** *You're welcome. I'd like to go out with you again. Maybe just the two of us? Dinner? Lunch? Hell, I'll take a quick snack in the car.*

**Chris:** *Also, I'm five minutes down the road, so it was all good. See you tomorrow. XX*

I stared at the *XXs* and realized I was grinning like an idiot. He wanted to do what sounded like a proper date. For real. It wouldn't be easy to fit in, with the diner opening, plus Fox, plus… yeah, it would be hard.

Still, before I could second-guess anything at all, I replied.

**Noah:** *I'd like that. But with Fox, how about I do something here?*

**Noah:** *If that's not too weird (frowning face emoji)*

**Chris:** *If it includes dessert, I'm in.*

I searched for a photo of a cake and sent the emoji.

**Noah:** *There's always dessert (ice cream emoji)*

**Chris:** *I really want to be with you.*

I nearly caved, but tonight wasn't right.

**Noah:** *I know. I'm sorry.*

**Chris:** *Night xxx*

**Noah:** *XX Night*

I was as giddy and stupid as a kid on their first date. He liked me!

And with a smile on my face, I went to bed and realized that, somehow, the boys' night out at the ranch, then drinks with Chris and his friends, were the best nights out I'd had in years.

I'd even forgotten to worry about Fox.

And the specter of Briggs never once showed until that beautiful head-spinning kiss, and while I resent that my ex was in my head at any point, I could work through that.

Yeah.

Two good nights.

And fuck... Chris's kisses were something else.

# Chapter Sixteen

## Noah

For Fox and me, dinner time had become our time—moments together where the world outside our cozy kitchen walls ceased to exist, and where, sometimes, the teenager part of Fox subsided, and he was my son again. Tonight, was lasagna, and he ate half of the lasagna, but then, he fidgeted with his fork, a sure sign he had something on his mind, and given how quiet he'd been since coming back from school, I waited for the big reveal.

"So, Dad," he began, his voice hesitant, "I did something."

"What?"

"I uhm..." He was suddenly wide-eyed, and all kinds of horrors passed through my mind. What had he done? Got into a fight? Worse? "I put my name down for tryouts for the baseball team at school. Do you think I did the right thing?"

I paused, my fork mid-air. Baseball. That single word hung heavy between us. *Be positive, encourage him.*

"That's great, Fox!" I said, masking my initial worries and shock with enthusiasm.

Fox nodded, pushing the lasagna around on his plate. "Chris said… I mean, Mr. Sheridan said I was good enough, so I thought I'd try. I love baseball. Whatever Papa did…" He took a deep breath, his next words coming out in a rush. "Only, no one at school knows about who Papa is."

Briggs Lewiston. A name that had once brought crowds to their feet was now whispered in the shadows of scandal and disgrace. People accused the famous baseball player, now a pariah in the sports world, of so many things that I had lost count.

"I never wanted anyone here to know about him," Fox continued, a determined glint in his eyes. "After all the stuff he did, the mess he made… I just want to play because I love the game, not because of *him*. But Mr. Sheridan says I could do tryouts, and he doesn't even know who I am. Right? Or did you tell him? Is it on my records? Dad?"

"No, Fox. No." I was lying—what if it was on his transcripts? Was he being asked to try out on the strength of who his dad was? Would Chris do that?

He wouldn't.

I reached across the table, placing my hand over his. "Okay?"

"What if people find out? What if they talk? And I don't mean the team. I mean, what if Clarke and Ainsley hate me for keeping secrets?" The vulnerability in his voice tugged at my heart. All the piss and vinegar that was teenage-Fox disappeared at moments like this.

"You still haven't told them?"?" I squeezed his hand gently. "Maybe it's time, Fox?"

"I didn't want to tell anyone, but..." He pulled out his phone, scrolled to something, and passed it to me. "Look."

I already had half an idea what this was about—Briggs was dating all over the place, and I'd seen his social media—but the photo Fox showed me was of Briggs, with his current partner and her children. In the article, my ex never once mentioned Fox. Even so, all it took was an internet search and Fox Lewiston was front and center. "Why did he call me Fox? Jeez, I wish my name wasn't so different that it stands out," Fox grumbled. "I don't want people here to hate me like they do at the academy."

"They won't."

"You can't say that."

Considering the assholes-in-training who went to Grovewood, comparing them to the kids that Fox was making friends with now, I was sure I was right. But then, kids could be cruel, whatever their school. My heart ached for what my son had to go through, and the things he might have thrown at him.

"Remember, you're not responsible for your father's mistakes, Fox. You're your own person, with your own talents, and I'm sure that Clarke and Ainsley won't hate you."

"They might, if they think I've lied to them." Fox looked at me, his gaze searching for reassurance. Briggs was a thousand miles away, removed from the life we were building here; yet he was still messing up Fox's life.

"You haven't lied," I said.

Fox smiled, a small, but brave, smile. "What do I do, Dad?"

"Tell them. They're good kids. If you trust them, tell them. Then enjoy your baseball."

He nodded. "I just want to play because I'm good at it, y'know. I wouldn't be playing for *him*." I watched him take another bite of his lasagna. Fox was good at baseball, so damn good. "I'll need stuff for next Monday's practice." He reached into his pocket for a list, and I scanned it briefly. "Can we afford it?"

"Of course," I lied and thanked the heavens for credit.

"Can we order it tonight?"

"Sure we can."

"And you're sure we have the money?"

"Easily," I lied.

"And I want to tell Clarke and Ainsley."

"That's good." I hated that this was even a thing for Fox. It wasn't as if I was running around telling people who my ex was, or what he'd done. All it would take was one person to mention Briggs Lewiston's name, then Fox and I would be the center of attention again.

Maybe we *should* tell all the people around us?

It wasn't as if Briggs's influence would reach us in the middle of Wyoming.

"Tomorrow? After school? Can they come back here?"

"Of course they can."

"For food?" he added with a hopeful smile.

Cooking and creating for three ravenous teenagers—yeah, that would be easy. "Sure."

---

THE NEXT DAY, Fox had Clarke and Ainsley here, and just before they arrived, he asked me to stay longer while he spoke to his friends. But in no way was I allowed to hover, only I should stay close, but not too close. In the end, I perched on a stool at the back, being there for Fox, but not obtrusively.

It was freaking complicated being a dad.

I was on my phone, playing a card matching game when my social media alert told me Briggs was in the media again.

He and his girlfriend had been spotted arguing in a restaurant, and she'd left.

Go girlfriend.

Of course, I was mentioned in the article, as was Briggs's *"terrible time since the divorce"*. Most importantly, there was no mention of where Fox and I were now. I guessed once people knew who Fox's dad was, all the stories would circulate through small-town Wyoming, but we'd cross that bridge when we came to it.

Fox was planning to open up to his friends as a start, and I'd heard him in his room, rehearsing what he was going to say, but when it came down to it, he dived straight in. "My papa was Briggs Lewiston," he blurted, with so much tension in his voice it was painful, and there was some defensiveness in there, too. Neither of his friends reacted, and I didn't know if either of them played baseball or even followed the game, but it seemed as if they had no idea who Fox was talking about. "He was a pro ball player, but… well, he wasn't the best person. Gambled all our money away, got accused of throwing games."

I watched Fox, his expression tight. This was why we were here, starting over in this small town, away from the shadows of a legacy neither of us wanted, and it hurt every time we had to explain to anyone.

Ainsley and Clarke had listened, their expressions were a mix of surprise and empathy. "Sorry, Foxy, never really followed baseball," Ainsley admitted. "But your papa sounds like an asshole."

"Yeah." Fox didn't defend Briggs; instead, he glanced my way for support, and I threw him an encouraging smile. I knew he'd hated coming here. I knew I'd dragged him away from everything he'd known and loved, but maybe, he was settling down enough to accept this new start for us. "It's why we're here. Starting new, away from all that."

The conversation shifted as Clarke chimed in, his voice low, but steady. "I get it, wanting to start over I mean. My dad's an alcoholic, spends most of his time out of the house, y'know, not around much. For real, it's just me and my mom."

Ainsley nodded, adding his own take. "My dad's all about religion. He's a bigot. I can't even tell him I'm bi because he'd probably throw me out." He exchanged glances with Clarke, who nodded, and then, with a smile, Ainsley took Clarke's hand on the table. "He doesn't know that we're boyfriends."

"No one does," Clarke added.

Fox's gaze settled on their hands, and then he stared up at them in shock. "You're what now?"

"Boyfriends," Clarke repeated.

The simplicity and courage of their admission struck me. This was their first time coming out to anyone, and they'd chosen Fox to trust. And me, given I was lurking at the back.

Fox's response was immediate and supportive. "Oh wow, that's so cool. You could double date with me and Molly, and I'd get to have my friends *and* my girlfriend with me."

"Wait, you have a girlfriend?" I interrupted the heart-to-heart.

Fox turned in his chair. "Molly," he said. I could hear the eye roll in his words.

I goldfished for a moment, then inspiration hit me. "Call Molly, get her over. I want to meet her, and she can join you for food, and you can double date right now, where I can see you. Then, you can tell your *girlfriend* what you just told your friends."

"And I can stay because Dad doesn't even know I'm here!" Ainsley announced, thrusting his fist into the air in celebration. "He's not home this week, he's off preaching, so I can do anything I want!" He spread his hands wide, and I wondered if I should be concerned. "Last night, I watched an old episode of *Queer Eye*, and he won't ever know!"

Clarke high-fived him, and the two of them sent messages, and both beamed at Fox when they got permission to stay. I wondered what Ainsley meant by his dad not knowing he was here which somehow meant it was okay to stay? Did his dad have an issue with me? Or the diner? I was not sure I'd even met the man. Unless I had—after all, I'd had many people passing through.

Then it hit me. Preaching? Was it that pastor guy who'd balked at the rainbow flag—religious, tall, wide, not skinny though. I examined Ainsley without making it obvious, and yes, there was a likeness. Jeez, if that was Ainsley's dad, then fuck, I felt sorry for the kid.

"You don't mind if I tell Molly?" Fox asked, concerned, interrupting my train of thought, and it took me a moment to catch up. Did he really think he needed my permission to tell his own story?

"It's your story to tell, Fox; your life." I smiled at him and headed into the kitchen, but not before I stopped by the table and pressed a hand to his shoulder. "And girlfriend eh? Guess we need *the* talk again, just in case."

I couldn't help smirking when Fox muttered something under his breath, probably about idiot dads. Still, I bet he wouldn't turn down food when it was handed to him.

Molly turned up about half an hour later, her big brother dropping her off, so at least I didn't have to do the whole meet my son's girlfriend's parents thing, but I did have to meet Molly, and she was so sweet.

And also, just as passionate about cake as the rest of the group.

I made the four of them burgers, added more cookies for dessert, plus milkshakes, and then, went back to organizing the pantry to give them all space.

It was eight when they all left, Fox tracking me down

as I was organizing herbs and spices into alphabetical order—again—and giving me a quick hug.

"Thanks, Dad," he murmured, "and now I'm out of here before you get mushy."

That's my boy.

## Chapter Seventeen

Chris

THE WARM, MUSTY SCENT OF HAY AND HORSES FILLED THE air as I stepped into the stables at Lennox Ranch. The low sun filtering through heavy snow clouds cast shadows through the cracks in the walls. I leaned against the rough, weathered wood of a stall, watching Levi as he brushed down his horse. Rachel had said this was where I would find Levi, and it was his words of wisdom I needed before I talked myself out of the date with Noah. I needed someone to talk to, someone who could help me get my head out of my ass, and Levi had enough distance from what had happened all those years ago to see me as something other than the injured friend who needed help.

I watched him for a moment. "Levi," I began.

He glanced up, a soft smile on his face, but it faded when he saw my expression. "Shit, what's up?" he asked, his tone shifting to one of concern as he straightened. He went white. "Is it Quinn? Fuck—"

"No, Quinn is great I'm sure." I loved that his first instinct was to worry about his fiancé, and not about me.

He relaxed but placed a hand over his heart. "Don't do that to me, shit, you come in looking like someone died, and I was…" He puffed out a breath, then pulled himself together. "Wait, if it's not Quinn… then what's wrong?

I rolled my eyes at him, shook my head, then hesitated, fiddling with the hem of my shirt. "I've got a proper date tonight, not one with other people, but just me and Noah on our own," I began, the words feeling heavy in my mouth.

Levi's eyebrows rose. "Yeah, Micah said that Daniel said that your mom said…" He blinked at just how many degrees of separation this gossip had traveled. "Yeah, over at the Italian over in Collier Springs?"

"No, I wanted to take him there, but with Fox, his son, at home, we're doing it at his place. The diner, I mean. Which is great because Noah can cook, but then, I didn't want him worried about having to cook."

"I got the feeling he loves to cook for people."

"Yeah, he does." I sighed, feeling the weight of my messed-up thoughts. "I'm just… nervous, I guess."

Levi leaned on his pitchfork, his expression turning thoughtful. "Nervous about the date or cooking or…?"

I swallowed hard. Christ on a cracker, this was embarrassing. Maybe I shouldn't have brought this to Levi because it was too personal. "Never mind, this is stupid…" I turned to leave.

He caught me, which of course he did, given I had to take it slow on the uneven floor. "I'm here, I'm listening, and we're friends, right? You can talk to me."

"It's embarrassing, okay?"

He glanced around, and his eyes lit on the bench that Rachel had placed on the slope above the house. It was a reminder that everyone needed to slow down and think about life. He led me there, then made me sit with a gentle push to my shoulders.

"Shoot," he said as he took a seat.

"It's about… after the date. You know if things go well and the kissing leads to…"

Something dawned on his expression. "Is it like a…" he lowered his voice. "A Viagra thing?"

"What? No. Jesus…" I waved at my groin, searching for the words. "Chris Junior works just fine, thank you very much."

He snorted a laugh. "You call your dick Chris Junior."

"No, I don't. I was… fuck you, Levi. It's the… other *thing*…" I waved at my leg.

Understanding dawned in his eyes. "You're worried about your leg? Wait. You're worried how he'll react… to your amputation?" He sounded so shocked, as if it had never occurred to him that anyone would have a problem with me at all. But shit, I'd been on a few Grindr hookups since losing half a leg and knew that not being whole in other people's eyes was potentially the final nail in the coffin. I owned my own home, taught kids, played ball, and that was good right? It was just a nope on the whole leg thing. Or the un-whole leg thing. I smiled to myself at the stupid joke.

"Chris?" Levi pressed. "Anyone worth your time, anyone who truly cares about you, won't care about that. And for what it's worth, Noah seems like a good guy."

"He is. He's… I think he's perfect right now." I added the last words in an almost-whisper.

Levi grinned. "About time." He placed a reassuring hand on my shoulder. "I'm so pleased."

"It's one date."

"I saw the way he looked at you at dinner that night, and the way you were all doe-eyed over him."

"I wasn't 'doe-eyed'." He gave me a patented Levi look that called me on my bullshit, and I winced. "Look, it's not just about the physical appearance, okay? The thought of someone who matters…" I didn't have the words.

"There must be all kinds of positions you can use to take the weight off your knee." He tapped his lip. "I'm thinking, if you're on the bottom then—"

I smacked his chest. "Asshole, that's not what I meant."

Levi was confused. "So, what else is bothering you?"

There was a lump in my throat. It wasn't just the leg. It was everything—exposing my vulnerabilities, the fear of rejection, the longing for a connection that I hadn't felt in so long. It was an enormous weight to be carrying into my first official date.

"Just… nothing, I guess… I just needed someone to react exactly as you did just to prove that not everyone is shit."

He chuckled. "I'm just being honest."

"Well, thank you."

We bumped fists and exchanged grins, and somehow, my doubts about the date lifted.

"You want to get in a ride while you're up here?"

I glanced at my watch. "I probably need to get back."

He cleared his throat. “Is there… I mean… would it be okay if I asked *you* something?”

“Shoot.”

“Hi!” a voice exclaimed and both of us turned to the left as Quinn strode across the yard, his skin-tight jeans and sparkling cerise sweater at odds with the practical boots he wore and the bucket he held. “What’s up?” he asked, casting a concerned glance between his fiancé and me.

“Nothing.” Levi stood immediately, as if he wanted to make it a point that he hadn’t been sitting with me chatting about whatever was on his mind.

“You looked all Secret Squirrel,” Quinn summarized. “Is this wedding stuff?”

“No,” Levi muttered, “not everything is wedding stuff.”

Quinn chuckled and pressed his free hand to Levi’s chest. “It’s okay, Grumpy; I was joking.” He went up on his tiptoes to kiss Levi, then sashayed away, the bucket swaying next to him, turning to wink at us.

Levi smirked, and we exchanged glances.

“Go.” I shooed him off. “I have grading to finish way before the big date.”

He sent me a grateful look, then sprinted after Quinn.

Hell, I wanted someone who sprinted after *me*. “Because it won’t be us sprinting, eh Stumpy?” I tapped my knee, talking to the prosthetic as I sometimes did, as if it was this sentient part of my body. “Let’s get out of here and make ourselves look pretty.”

I turned up at the diner at seven.

Well, actually, I hovered in JJ’s while Abby was trying

to close up, because I was ten minutes early for the date, but that wasn't the point.

At seven, I knocked on the diner door, on crutches, no wheelchair, standing in the snow as if I wasn't feeling wobbly, and Noah let me in, fussing over how cold it was outside. I waved him away, even though I was frozen, and thanked the heavens for the insulating layers on my prosthetic and knee.

"I'm just…" He thumbed behind him just as the scent of garlic wafted my way. "Follow me."

"Hi, Mr. Sheridan." Fox caught my attention from where he was sitting at one of the tables at the front, homework spread out around him, which for a teacher, was one hell of a gratifying sight.

"Hi, Fox. Call me Chris when…" I waved at the diner, and caught Noah throwing me a smile. That simple smile made me feel warm from the inside, and I forgot all about being cold.

"So, you're Chris when you're on a date with my dad?" he said, blinking innocently.

I huffed a laugh. "Yeah, that."

"I'm just going upstairs." He scooped everything up, stuffing it into a backpack, which he slung over his shoulder. "I'm Face-timing Clarke and Ainsley…" He frowned, then he stopped by me. "Mr. Sheridan—Chris—if I was worried about something at school, would I need to book an appointment to see you?"

"I'm open to chat any time," I reassured him. "Is everything okay?"

He seemed confused with what he was going to say. "Yeah, it's not… I'm not sure… yeah. Later." Then, he was up by the serving hatch, taking a tray laden with snacks, drinks, and a covered plate of whatever Noah was creating, from his dad's hands. By the time I got there as well, he was already on his way out.

"I'm not coming down anytime soon. I'm playing games online—just with Clarke and Ainsley." He added that for his dad's benefit when he opened his mouth to comment. "And then bed. I'll have my headphones in!" He threw all of that as he headed into the hall and the door swung shut behind him.

"Brat," Noah said with so much affection it melted even more cold. "I worry about the online thing," he said. "Drink? I have..." He peered into the refrigerator. "Wine for later, but for now, lite beer or soda, or I could make a milkshake if you like?

"Soda is fine for now, as long as I get a milkshake later." I smiled as I settled on the same stool because my competency kink demanded I stare at him while he worked. I thought he'd lean through the hatch to pass me my drink, but he came out of the kitchen and stood next to me, half leaning on the counter.

"My milkshakes are dangerous," he deadpanned. "It's been known to bring all the boys to the yard."

I couldn't stop myself if I tried. I reached out and carded a hand through his hair and tugged him toward me. I'd been staying away for far too long, and I wanted another kiss like the one in the dark.

Then it hit me, we were in a brightly lit diner.

On Main.

With anyone walking past.

I glanced at the main windows, and the blinds were

pulled down—I'd never even noticed there were new blinds, or that they'd been shut, and no one could see in.

I kissed him, and he cradled my face and kissed me right back. As our lips met, there was a small hesitance, a testing of waters, and the first was soft. But it deepened fast, becoming something more than a hello and crossing right over into passionate. He shuffled forward a little, and I widened my legs so he could slip between them, then we locked lips as if we'd never have to breathe again. My heart raced, and the world around us seemed to fade into a blur. I was at the point where I didn't care if the entire town saw this. As we parted, he pressed his forehead to mine, and we were both breathing heavily. His eyes opened, and we shared a smile, and I felt as if something significant had just happened, as if this was the kiss that changed everything, marking the beginning of something that could be beautiful.

"Are you hungry?" Noah whispered.

I scooped some of his shirt into my hand, keeping him close. "Hmmm." I kissed him again.

He chuckled.

"For food," he admonished as we separated.

I pretended to pout because what I needed was more kisses, which earned me another tongue-tangling, groaning inside, embrace. This time when we parted it was on the tip of my tongue to suggest we go somewhere and…

Anywhere and…

Yeah.

Noah tied his chef's apron around his waist and was in his element, moving around the kitchen with that sexy grace and efficiency I found so damn attractive and mesmerizing. He was completely in his zone, and that confidence and competence was undeniably hot.

"I hope you like salmon," he said.

"Love it."

"Okay, cool, with risotto and winter squash."

The salmon sizzled in the pan as Noah flipped it skillfully, and he constantly tasted and adjusted the seasoning of the risotto. Every now and then, he would look up and catch my eye, giving me a smile that sent my heart racing.

At one point, he motioned for me to lean through the hatch. "Taste this," he said, offering me a spoonful of risotto. The flavors burst in my mouth—the rich creaminess of the rice was gorgeous. "It's incredible."

Noah's face lit up with pride and satisfaction. "I'm glad you like it," he replied, turning back to his cooking.

I got the impression food was his love language, and I was here to learn every word of it, and the fact that he was doing all this for us, for this quiet evening together, made it all the more special.

"Are you okay to sit over here?" He'd come around next to me, carrying a bottle of white wine. Then, crossed to a booth at the back of the diner, in the darker part, with a candle he lit. I went straight over, easing into the booth, which was set with fancy plates and cutlery. "This is a chardonnay, if you're interested."

"I'd love some."

He opened it, and given the bottle had a cork, I'd I bet it was better than the screw tops I was used to, and then, he poured some into two wine glasses and waited.

After a pause, I realized he wanted me to try it. I took a sip. "Delicious."

"Okay then." He seemed nervous, and I wondered how stressed he'd gotten organizing all of this. "Dinner," he announced, then disappeared into the kitchen.

When he came back, it was with the side dish. "Winter squash," he announced, "just with seasoning, baked." Next, he brought over two plates, risotto in the center, piled with the salmon on top and garnished with pea shoots and a scattering of seeds. He placed one in front of me, moving it a few degrees so it faced the way he wanted it to, and then he slid into the facing bench.

"Hi," he murmured, sounding shy, and the way he looked, sitting there, all I wanted to do was kiss him again. I was so drawn to him it was ridiculous.

And fun.

So much fun.

# Chapter Eighteen

## Noah

I'd decided to make a classic crème brûlée for dessert that evening. The rich, creamy custard topped with a caramelized sugar crust always seemed to impress, and even though I'd made it hundreds of times, I was making it for Chris, and it had to be perfect. It wasn't so difficult that I could fuck it up, but as I torched the sugar on top, my anticipation grew as to what he'd say. I lived for the reaction on someone's face when they tasted my desserts, and it was even worse when I was trying to impress Chris.

I served the dessert, and as Chris took his first spoonful, I waited. My focus was on his mouth, watching as he tested the flavor, his tongue darting out to catch a stray bit of cream. What did he think? It was important that I'd gotten it right for him.

Then it hit me.

This wasn't about dessert—I didn't need to know what he thought of it because talking about food just took me away from what I really needed to do—talk to him and tell him about Briggs.

God knows why my head went there.

"I have to tell you something," I blurted out, my voice cutting through the quiet of the room.

Chris glanced up, his expression changing from a smile to a mixture of curiosity and concern. "What's up?" he asked.

"It's about Fox's dad," I began. "I know you work with baseball at school—Fox told me—but I don't know how much you know about professional baseball?"

A shadow passed over his eyes, but he blinked it away. "Some."

"Promise me this goes no further until Fox lets people know, or until we can't hide it anymore."

"You're worrying me," he murmured, placing his spoon down next to his half eaten dessert.

"Fox's biological dad, his papa, is Briggs Lewiston."

He was waiting for more, and I let him think it through, and finally, recognition flickered in Chris's eyes. "Lewiston? Do you mean Briggs *mad-as-shit* Lewiston, played for the Columbus River Kings, right?" I nodded, but as I paused, I watched Chris's expression shift from recognition of the name to the realization of what else he might know. "Wait—Briggs Lewiston? Wasn't there a story about steroids and a gambling scandal," he murmured. "And affairs? I recall lots of media coverage, it was all over the news a while back." He bit his lip, and his eyes widened after he worked through what he knew. "His husband went to court and sued for custody of … shit, that was you? And Fox?"

I nodded again; the words catching in my throat. "The divorce is final, and there's a restraining order in place so he doesn't come near me or Fox, which is hard on Fox, but..." I swallowed and absently massaged my left wrist, which still ached after I'd pushed too hard in the kitchen. "Despite... *everything*... the judge gave Fox a choice, and Fox chose to come with me." I huffed. "The media wouldn't leave us alone, and when Lily passed and left me this place, my first thought was that we could get a breather here and wait until things died down."

"Oh," he said, then frowned. "And after your breather, is that you leaving town?"

What? Did he think we were passing through? "No, god no, this is our new life. I'm going to make this work." Chris reached for my hand, gripped it tight. "But it's complicated, and it's messy, and Briggs can make anything into a drama. He somehow managed to wipe us out financially, including Fox's college fund and all my savings, yet I still feel like the bad guy."

"For wanting to be a good dad to Fox?"

"Yeah, or as he likes to say, for stealing Fox from him." I lowered my voice. "Not that he cared about Fox unless he needed a photoshoot. Fox had appendicitis when he was twelve, and Briggs was in Vegas—this wasn't ball season, this was his choice to stay away—and he only turned up at the hospital when Fox was being released. He wasn't a father; when he married me, Fox was six, and in hindsight, he just wanted a glorified nanny that he could tie down."

"Fox knows all of this."

I nodded. "He worked it out." I massaged my wrist again as Chris's expression softened.

He reached across the table, placing his hand over mine. "I can only imagine how hard that must be for you and Fox."

We sat there for a moment; the crème brûlée forgotten.

"I'm done with Briggs." I reassured him. "He's not even a shadow in my life anymore. I'm divorced, able to…"

"… date?" he offered with a smile.

"Yeah. Date."

Using his free hand, Chris spooned up some dessert and held it up to me. I took the small bite, and yeah, it was one of my best ones. Probably because of how much love I'd poured into it.

"Thank you for telling me." Then, he slid out from his seat, and I had the horrible thought he was leaving, until he stood and took my hand. I scrambled up, slipped my hand into his, and he pulled me into a hug. "Thank you for telling me," he repeated, and then, he leaned on the table, captured my face in his strong hands and held me still. "I'm here for you," he promised.

And I believed him.

When we kissed this time, me plastered against him, but cautious of allowing myself to rest on him fully, he cursed into the kiss. "Privacy," he said.

I got with the plan straight away, grabbing his hand, thinking on my feet, and finally heading into the pantry. It was cooler in here, but with the door closed, it would be only the two of us. I had a second thought.

"Stay here," I instructed, then headed back out to pick

up a stool at the counter and drag it in there, setting it down as far from any actual food as I could, then shut the door, and encouraged him back until his ass rested on the stool. I didn't know if I'd done the right thing, but it didn't matter because he wanted kisses, I needed them, and so that is what we did.

The close quarters felt intimate, a world away from everything else, and as I settled to stand between his legs again, we broke the kiss and our eyes locked. There was a silent understanding, a shared anticipation. I wanted him so much.

I placed my hands on his upper thighs, feeling the warmth of his skin through the fabric of his jeans. I leaned in, and as our lips met, a rush of emotions flooded me. This kiss differed from any I had shared with Briggs. With him, things had always felt rushed, almost transactional, but with Chris, there was a tender unhurried exploration, and it was pure sex.

Our kiss deepened, and I could feel Chris responding, tugging me close. There was a vulnerability in being this close to someone again, and it scared me and thrilled me in equal amounts. His touch slid down my back, resting on my ass, pulling me closer, holding me, and I could feel how hard he was, and god, I wanted him so bad.

"When I said somewhere private, I didn't mean the pantry." Chris chuckled against my lips, but that chuckle turned to a groan when I reached between us for the button of his jeans.

"Can I?" I asked, even as I slipped the button open.

"Please."

I unzipped him, and he let go of me just long enough to

lift his shirt out of the way, tucking it up and holding it with one hand so I could get a better look. I wished we were in bed, in a room with bright light, where I could stare at my heart's content, and catalogue every bit of him, but for now it was touch alone as we kissed, and *finally,* I had my hand on him.

He pulled back from our embrace and cursed under his breath. "Me," he whispered, and desperately shoved my shirt and reached for the button on my loose slacks, pushing his hand inside and circling my cock. "This." It seemed as if he could only utter words of one syllable.

I'd done that to him.

It was powerful.

It was new.

We pressed and touched, moved our hands in gentle movements, the erotic feeling of his fingers on me and the rush of my orgasm slowed as we kissed, exchanging nothing more than air between us. He came first, stiffening, kissing desperate and deep as I followed soon after, the slide of his cum on my hand, and all of the emotions blocked inside me rushed out in a flood.

Tears pricked my eyes as I burrowed my face into his neck, and he grasped me so hard I had nowhere to go.

"This is going to mean something," he murmured. "I could fall in love with you as easily as breathing," he added.

I burrowed deeper.

At last, we made it out, all stupid giggles and stolen kisses, to finish the crème brûlée, and the wine, talking about everything and nothing, but I felt lighter than I had in years.

"So." He sipped at his wine—he'd been drinking most of it. I never wanted to be in a situation where I couldn't drive if Fox needed me. I set the glass down, tracing the lace pattern on the base. "It's my turn."

"Your turn to do what?"

We'd never gotten to the milkshakes, but it was snowing outside and hot drinks seemed a far better idea.

"To be honest with you and tell you about the accident."

"You don't have to." We were already raw from what we'd done in the pantry, not to mention the Briggs situation and chatting about Fox.

"No, it's like part of the safe sex thing, you know, PrEP, tested, vers, also here's why I have scars and why part of my leg is missing." He was joking, but somehow it wasn't funny, although the whole versatile thing filled me with sudden thoughts of him buried inside me, and my thoughts rampaged into a whole side quest until he started talking.

"Chris—"

"Let me do this in one go?" I nodded and waited. "So, I was in Daniel's car, with my two best friends, messing about like kids do, and we hit a bridge wrong and crashed into the wall of it. Long story short, I was trapped. There was fire. Micah pulled me out, saved my life, but the surgeons couldn't save my leg, and they tried to pretty this up, but couldn't." He gestured to his face and the scars. It was weird how I'd even forgotten they were there, as if they were only a small part of the whole picture and were inconsequential. "I could go back and get more work, but pretty isn't worth all the pain and the mess in my head."

"You're plenty pretty," I murmured, and he dipped his head. "So, was Daniel hurt as well?"

He frowned. "Daniel?"

"Micah pulled you out, but you mentioned it was Daniel's car."

"Oh no, Daniel wasn't in the car." He paused. "Micah borrowed it and was the one driving; I was in the passenger seat." He stopped again, and I could see the pain in his expression. "Isaac was the third person in the car—the three of us were best friends and completely inseparable. Isaac was in the back, and we were flying… god, the times I say that, but we *were* flying, and high on life." He pinched two fingers together. "I was this close to getting a baseball call to try out in Chicago, and the game was everything to me. Micah had the ranch he was going to inherit, and Isaac, well, he was going to go places one day, president maybe. Only he didn't make it out of the car, died on impact. Forever seventeen."

"Oh, fuck." My free hand closed into a loose fist over my heart. "Chris, shit, I'm sorry."

His shoulders shifted in a small shrug, as if it didn't matter, but I could see the pain in his eyes. "It feels like yesterday, but it's been seventeen years. It chased Micah away from town, broke him and Daniel up, even though they were freaking soulmates."

"But they're together now." I tried to reconcile grown-up Micah with a teenager who'd crashed a car, and the weight of what he must have to carry. Then, my thoughts slipped to Fox, unbidden, and I imagined him dying young, and compassion welled inside me for Isaac's family.

"Micah had to come back to town, but he was broken with it all. Daniel finally came to terms with it and found it in himself to forgive and love. We reconnected as well. I never blamed Micah, not for one minute, but I wasn't thinking straight when I first woke up." He stopped, exhaled a puff of air, giving himself a moment to breathe. "I'd lost everything I was supposed to have—I had mad pitching skills, a chance at a bright future as a pro ballplayer, and suddenly, I was left with nothing but visible scars and half a leg."

"I can't imagine how you felt."

"Like I didn't want to be here," he said and stared at me.

"Chris?"

So much emotion passed between us as I made sense of what he was implying.

"It was Daniel who found me next to pills, got me to the hospital, saved me, let me live for another day so I could become the awesome teacher and man you see before you." He finished with a smile, but I was still processing. Then he squeezed my hand. "Noah? Does that change things? I understand if it does, but I wanted you to know what I did."

"It changes nothing," I said with defiance. "But you should know that my real name is Callum after my dad," I said, softly, the words coming from somewhere deep inside. "Callum Noah Lewiston-Bennett. My ex used to call me Cal, but I've always been called Noah. It's what my aunt used to call me, and it's my chosen name, and I swear

I'm not hiding my real name, but I feel better using Noah Bennett. I don't ever want to be the Cal who let Briggs hurt him again." Everything spilled out in an instant, but he leaned over to kiss me.

"You're *my* Noah," Chris whispered.

And that was the point when my universe shifted and the protective walls around me began to crumble.

It was the moment I started to fall in love.

---

I WOKE EARLY the next day—way too early—the butterflies in my stomach doing somersaults, and so tense I didn't recall having a shower even though my hair was wet. Today was the unofficial opening of my diner, a moment I had been dreaming of and dreading in equal measure, mostly because this was make or break for us in Whisper Ridge, and I wasn't sure what else we'd do if the diner didn't work. Maybe we'd live upstairs until Fox went to college, or maybe I'd give in and sell the property, but either option was shit. Over the last week, Fox and I had spent hours putting up flyers in local businesses, and Fox had done some social media work, including a video of me creating cupcakes, all sped up, with music. He told me people liked to see chefs piping things, told me I'd had a ton of hits, and even though it might not be from local people, it was a future income stream if the diner failed.

*It won't fail.*

Fox had also updated the town's small website, which he muttered over, saying it was older than me, which, hell I wasn't sure how to take, as he snorted with laughter. I think there may have been an insult in there, but who knew with Fox. I'd even placed two large posters in the diner's window, right next to the flags. The posters were as bright and colorful as the rainbow and advertised free coffee with food, and god, I hoped that worked.

"Daaaad," Fox wheedled, "how about I stay, then go in later to school, so I can help with the diner."

I turned to him, a smile tugging at my lips despite the seriousness of his request. "How about no? As much as I'd like the help, you have school, and that's way more important." I passed him his lunchbox, probably the healthiest one at school, but in my opinion, the most exciting, with a broccoli salad I'd serve the president. Not that Fox was keen on all the green stuff, or that was what he told me in no uncertain terms. We'd yet to come to a consensus on his demand for pizza and Sunny D. "You need to go to school," I repeated.

"But I can help! I can clear tables or hand out menus," he insisted, his eagerness almost contagious.

I went to ruffle his hair, feeling a pang of affection, but his ducking game was on point, and he avoided my hand. "I know you'd be a great help, but education is important, too."

He huffed, and it was obvious he wasn't impressed with the options, although I noted he'd said he'd go in late, not that he wanted the entire day off, which I called a win. He appeared happy at school, much happier than he'd been at the academy back in Columbus.

After walking Fox as near to the bus stop as I was allowed—*I'm fourteen, Dad, not four, you're so embarrassing*—I headed back to the diner. My heart raced as I unlocked the door, the silence of the empty space greeting me, and I could almost taste the potential. I switched on the lights and the coffee machine, the familiar sounds and smells bringing a sense of calm. This was it. The moment of truth.

The first person through the door was Chris, right on cue for a morning coffee. "Morning, Noah. Good luck today." He gave me a grin that could light up the room, sneaked in a kiss, then had to leave fast to pass the school bus and get to school first. Just him coming in, all smiles and snow, and kissing me, made me feel loved. A new feeling I filed away to think about later.

As Chris left, Neil arrived in his uniform. "Morning, Noah. Thought I'd come by and see the new place." He took a seat at the counter, sipping coffee as I prepared his order. The smell of bacon and pancakes filled the air, and I felt the first threads of hope weave through my nerves.

Then, Levi came in, and I greeted him with a nod, my hands busy at the grill. "Morning. I'll be right with you." I left the bacon for a second, poured coffee for Levi, juggled Neil's breakfast, took Levi's order, calculated what would be best to go first, saw the door open with more people coming in, and none of it fazed me at all. I was in my element.

As the morning wore on, more people trickled in. Each fresh face through the door was a small victory, a sign that maybe, *just maybe*, this could work, and my cautious optimism began to solidify into something real. The proper test would be the things I'd changed on the menu from the ones Lily used to offer.

For the opening, I'd gone for putting a twist on the

scrambled eggs, adding a pinch of smoked paprika and some fresh chives. It was a minor change, but I hoped it would make an impression on the people who'd once visited Lily for food.

Fred from the Mercantile was the first of the customers to order it. He eyed the dish with suspicion as I set it in front of him. "What's this?"

"Scrambled eggs."

He poked at it. "What's the green stuff?"

"Try it and let me know what you think," I encouraged, my heart in my throat.

He poked at it for a moment before taking a bite. The diner fell into a hushed anticipation. Levi, who was still enjoying his breakfast, leaned over. "Well, Fred? How is it?"

Fred didn't answer straight away. Then, with a mouthful of eggs, he said, "Leave me alone, I'm having a moment."

Relief washed over me, followed by a ripple of laughter from the other customers. Levi shot me a thumbs-up from his seat, and I couldn't help but smile.

As the morning turned into lunchtime, the menu changed a little, still offering breakfast, but adding a couple of cooked dishes, including my own mac 'n' cheese, a classic cheeseburger, and a vegetarian quinoa salad bowl—the last was a stretch I knew, and I only sold three all day. Of the three people who ordered the salad bowl, two of them wanted me to add bacon, and a side of the gooey mac 'n' cheese. All too soon, it was afternoon, and the steady flow of customers continued.

It was a start.

Each plate I served, each *"thank you"* and *"this is delicious"* I received, built up my confidence. This was only day one, but it was going well. Abby came in for the first handover of the pastries I'd baked for her, and I handed them over with confidence, but inside, I was a wreck. She took a moment to check out the pastries, *and* the customers, satisfied that I wasn't stealing all her trade, and commenting on the pastries I'd done for her—more than adequate.

Faint praise, but, at least, she was happy.

Standing behind the counter, looking at the filled tables, I had this incredible sense of pride. The diner wasn't just a business; it was a safe place for me and Fox, it was in a town where I could be myself, where most of the people welcomed me, and I couldn't help smiling.

Fox arrived home before we closed, buzzing with excitement over the opening and wanting to hear everything. He tried the eggs, poked at a quinoa salad, and wolfed down a cheeseburger. Then, he grinned at me, ketchup around his mouth.

"This is great, Dad."

Just those simple words were enough to make everything feel lighter.

Finally, it was time to close. When spring arrived and people wanted to eat out, we would extend our hours, but I would need at least one person to work the counter before I could organize that big splashy extended opening event. I added hiring someone to my mental to-do list, along with seeing if I could afford it. Maybe it was worth dipping into my meagre savings to give someone a job here?

*Don't get ahead of myself.*

As I wiped down the counter at the end of the day, the diner empty once more, I was blown away that people had at least given me a chance, and I was determined to make the most of it. This was just the beginning, and I couldn't wait to see what the future held. Particularly, when there was a knock on the window, and Chris stood there with a pretend puppy dog big-eyed pleading expression to be let in. Which I did.

And he kissed me.

"Today was awesome," I blurted, as he leaned on the back of a booth and hugged me tight.

"You're awesome," he announced.

Right here and now, I wanted Chris to know everything about today, about Fred and his chives, and about the three quinoa salads, but instead of it all spilling out in a mess of information, I cupped his face and stared into his eyes.

"I really like you," I blurted. "Really like you. I want to... it's the first time I've wanted to fall in love."

His eyes widened, and he kissed me again. "Same."

"Yeah?" I asked.

This time, he smoothed his thumbs on my cheekbones. "Oh, yeah."

"I think that just tipped me over the edge."

And that was how we declared we were falling for each other with Fox in the background, making kissy noises and hiding his eyes.

# Chapter Nineteen

## Chris

THE FALLING-FOR-YOUS STILL ECHOED IN MY HEAD RIGHT through from yesterday, and I had a constant grin on my face because I couldn't forget the kiss, or his bright smile, or the way he murmured the words.

I was falling in love.

Chris Sheridan was falling in love.

I felt like shouting the news to the world! To the post-accident Chris who didn't want to see another day, to the Chris who'd seen his friends and family fall in love, to the Chris who'd thought the diner was being broken into.

I never imagined, for one minute, I'd fall so hard, and so fast, for Noah, but he was it for me, and I could imagine things with him, a future, vacations, making love, going to Fox's graduation, asking Noah to marry me.

Hell, I wanted everything, and so the smile never left.

The morning sun was wispy over the frosty Collier Springs High School baseball field, where the team gathered for their first Saturday practice. At least, the snow had eased enough to give us a mostly clear field, but that didn't mean snow in Wyoming was over—this was February, and we were right in the middle of storms coming our way. I leaned against the fence—my go-to position—gaze fixed on Fox, who was trying out today, enjoying the weak sunshine and ignoring my icy cold extremities. I'd kept everyone in tight, getting them to keep warm, jogging on the spot, but maybe, this would have to move indoors if the promised snow fell soon. The mountain sheltered us from the worst of the snow, thank god.

"What's wrong with you?" Melanie asked. She wasn't only my assistant coach but the parent of one of the seniors.

I glanced at her, tried to drop the smile, but couldn't. "Nothing."

"You have a thing…" She waved to her own mouth. "A smiling thing."

"It's baseball practice. It's not cold enough to freeze solid, and yeah, I'm excited."

"For the season?"

"Sure."

"We weren't that good last year." She was being diplomatic. In our local league of eight teams, we'd come in sixth.

"At least, we weren't last, and anyway, this year is our year," I said, because if I could deserve the love of someone like Noah, whom I loved right back, then anything was possible.

"You think the new kid will turn it around?"

I glanced at Fox, waiting with the rest to start.

"Who knows," I said, then blew my whistle to begin.

It was soon apparent that Fox stood out among the other fourteen- and fifteen-year-olds we had playing, not because he was new, but because he seemed almost too careful with his plays, showed flashes of real skill, and then dialed it down. Why was he holding back? I watched him as a catcher, noticing how he fumbled a few catches, and a small part of me wondered if it was deliberate, a tactic to underplay his skills. I *knew* baseball, and I *knew* he was better than he was letting on.

As the practice progressed, Fox's natural talent couldn't be contained. He found his stride, his movements becoming more fluid and confident. It was clear he was an excellent player. I watched the team go through their drills, trying to focus on the practice. But my attention kept drifting to the stands where I wished Noah had been, although I knew why he wasn't in among the parents-in-watching-their-kids-seriously mode—after all he had a diner to run. Still, I couldn't help the flutter of longing in my stomach every time I glanced over to the parents.

It was complicated, feeling that way about Noah—missing him that bad. As a coach, I was there for the team, for the game. But there was this undeniable pull towards thinking about Noah, a curiosity, an attraction that I couldn't quite shake off.

Last night, I had wanted to make a good impression and be a gentleman after we'd admitted we wanted more. Only, said good intention had lasted less time than getting to dessert. The sounds Noah made, the hitch of his breath as he came, the pleading for more as he got there, was something I'd remember for the rest of my life.

I wanted to make him lose control every day, forever, and it was silly to miss him this morning, I knew, but I couldn't help it.

But then I caught myself. This morning wasn't about me or my feelings for Noah. It was about the kids, the game. I took a deep breath, refocusing on the practice, reminding myself why I was there. I couldn't let personal feelings interfere with my role as a coach. Still, in the back of my mind, Noah's absence was a constant, subtle distraction that I struggled to ignore.

"He's good, isn't he?" Melanie said.

I nodded, keeping my eyes on Fox. "Yeah, he is. We're short a catcher since Matt moved. Fox could fill that spot perfectly."

Melanie hummed in agreement, her eyes following the play. "It's always helpful to have fresh talent, and he's clearly played at this level."

His transcripts had him as assistant captain to the Grovewood Tigers—his old school's team—with an impressive record last season. It was clear he had his papa's genes, although Briggs Lewiston was a flashy pitcher—had been a flashy pitcher—and Fox was more comfortable controlling the plays as a catcher. I wondered how that made him feel. Did he resent the quieter, but equally important, role? Fox had an ease about him, a natural affinity with the game that was hard to miss. I couldn't help but agree with Melanie that maybe it was time to make it official, to bring him into the fold, so the rest of the team could get used to him. Fox's presence had already brought a new energy to the practice, some of the team eyeing him with hope—after all, we weren't a winning side, and they'd take anything that might get us out of a rut—others whispering behind their hands about him.

"All right, everyone, gather up!" I called out, motioning for the team to huddle around me. The chatter died as they formed a semi-circle, their attention on me, including Fox, who hung at the back, worrying at a lock of blond hair that had escaped his cap.

"I want to talk about Fox," I began, noticing his surprised expression. "I think we all agree he's got talent." I paused for a moment, meeting the eyes of my team. "I'm welcoming Fox to the team. He'll be a catcher, working in place of Matt. What does everyone think?"

There was a brief silence, a moment of contemplation. Then, one by one, a few of the kids spoke up.

"He's got skills." This was from Jemima, one of the best on the team, and someone everyone else respected.

"Yeah, he's great at catching," another added, nodding.

There were no dissenting voices, only nods and murmurs of approval. The team was unanimous when they recognized Fox's skill and potential contribution to our team. Maybe they even sensed a future winning season with Fox on their side.

I turned to Fox, a smile on my face. "Welcome to the team, Fox. We're glad to have you."

Fox's mix of relief and excitement said it all. He was one of us now, and together, we were going to make this season count.

The practice continued, the sound of bats hitting balls

and the shouts of encouragement filling the air. I knew adding Fox to the team was the right call. Not just for his skills, but for the new spirit he brought to the game. It was going to be an interesting season.

*I really wish Noah was here.*

Sunday was lost to family, and riding, and even though I managed a visit to the diner, it was heaving with people, and I sat for an hour at the counter to chat, but Noah and I didn't get to do much in the way of talking. He'd done this Sunday special plate with beef, roasted vegetables, and a range of tasting side dishes. He'd put a poster in the window announcing that the inaugural Sunday Roast Dinner was twenty percent off, and word spread, and when I left, he was exhausted. I'd tried to help a little, but practice yesterday, plus playing with the kids up at the ranch at Sunday brunch, had killed my remaining energy, and then, Sunday was gone.

I'd grabbed the total of two kisses all day and felt guilty that this was even a thing for me to fret over. So, this morning, I went in for coffee, stole as many kisses as I could, and Monday night found me standing outside the diner after it had closed at five. The day had been long, filled with the usual challenges of school and through all of it, I missed seeing Noah, more than I cared to admit, even to myself.

I used the softest knock, hoping not to disturb Fox, who I knew would be around doing homework. Noah opened the door, his face lighting up when he saw me, and warmth in his gorgeous eyes. It was all I needed to feel at home as he tugged me inside.

We exchanged hellos and quick kisses, but he tugged

me back and back, until we found ourselves in the pantry area, surrounded by shelves stocked with supplies for the diner. It seemed as if this was going to be our little haven.

"Maybe we need to put a mattress in here," I muttered.

Noah stared at me, a playful glint in his eyes. "I wasn't expecting you tonight," he said, his voice a soft murmur in the quiet as he pulled the door shut.

I stepped closer, closing the gap between us. "I couldn't wait until whenever," I admitted. "I wanted to see you, now."

His response was a smile, and then, he was in my arms, his lips meeting mine in an incendiary kiss. Our kisses weren't slow, we didn't savor the moment, if anything, we were desperate, and I loved every second.

The stool was still in the pantry. I sat down, pulling him closer, and our kisses deepened, fueled by the pent-up longing building up through the day.

With Noah, everything was intensified, the coolness of the room, the faint smell of spices from the shelves, the warmth of his body against mine—it all blended into me wanting him *right the fuck now.*

His hands were gentle, yet assured, sliding down my back as I pulled him closer. Time seemed to stand still as we lost ourselves in each other. There was a rush, an urgency to be close, and when my orgasm slammed into me, I buried the groan in a deep kiss, holding him as he stiffened and arched into my hand.

"I missed you," he whispered, and I could only nod, then he chuckled. "But there is no way we could fit a mattress in here. Also, I'm not sure how sanitary it would be to keep doing *this* in here." He bit back a smile, and I kissed it because his lips were *there,* and we stayed a while longer, wrapped in each other's arms.

"When is Fox's next sleepover?" I joked, and when he stiffened in my arms, I knew I'd messed up. "I didn't mean—"

"Fox isn't someone to be pushed out of the way." Noah sounded hurt at first, but his expression was frosty, and he extricated himself from my hold. Fuck.

"Wait, no, I was joking."

We stared at each other, and I could see all this emotion in him, concern, fear, then thank god, acceptance that I was telling the truth.

"Sorry," he apologized, but that didn't sit right either, as he grasped my shirt and tried to kiss me. I stopped him with a finger to his lips.

"You shouldn't be the one saying sorry, that was all on me. It was a stupid throwaway joke."

"But I—"

"Nope. Me. I'm sorry," I said, then kissed him until he relaxed back into my hold, and I was forgiven. "I'm sorry," I repeated as we kissed goodbye.

"It's good," he murmured. "We're good."

"Mom wants me to bring you for family dinner on the weekend, both of you. And I mean *all* the family. Is that too much, too soon?"

"For me? No. And if there's food, Fox will be all over it."

When I left, stepping out into the cool night air, I carried with me the warmth of Noah's last kiss, a promise of more moments like this, of a connection that was growing deeper with each stolen kiss in the diner's pantry.

And then I went back every night that week.

And we only got caught by Fox once.

Thankfully, it happened when we were drinking hot chocolate and not getting each other off in the hallway, which was the new pantry, given the hygiene concerns for the previous hookup spot.

"You *can* come upstairs," Fox muttered, eyeing us as if he knew exactly what we'd been doing. Then he pointed at his dad. "You have a boyfriend, you kiss, you probably… yeah… just stop standing in the hallway macking on each other as if you think I don't know."

He stomped around a bit, but he winked at me and smirked as he went past us and up the stairs. "Night, Mr. Sheridan; night, Dad," he sing-songed.

The little shit.

# Chapter Twenty

## Noah

WITH ME CARRYING THE DESSERT I'D MADE—TWO PIES large enough to feed at least twenty people—Fox and I walked towards the house, feeling a mix of excitement and nerves. This was a big family dinner, and I was about to meet everyone in Chris's family.

The door swung open, and Chris greeted me with a smile. "You made it! Come on in, everyone's excited to meet you."

A wide porch wrapped around the front of the two-story Sheridan house, adorned with comfortable chairs and a few potted plants—a perfect spot for enjoying summer evenings.

Beyond the garden, the land sloped away gently, providing a view of the Wyoming landscape with its rolling hills and distant mountains, and best of all, it was the kind of place that felt like home as soon as I set foot on the property. It seemed to wrap its arms around me the moment I entered, filled with warmth and family history. The walls of the hall were adorned with family photos, each capturing a moment, a memory, a piece of the story that made up Chris and his family, and I loved checking them out before his parents came to find us.

Chris's parents were the epitome of warmth and hospitality. His mom, with the blonde hair and blue eyes, which Chris had inherited, had a smile that lit up the room. She was the kind of person whose presence felt like a comforting embrace. His dad was tall, with a sturdy build speaking of a lifetime of hard work and strength. Yet, despite his height, each of his sons seemed to have outgrown him, standing just a bit taller.

"I brought dessert," I said, presenting the pies. "Apple and cinnamon, and my take on lemon chiffon, I hope they're okay. I have cream in a cooler, as well."

Chris's mom clapped her hands in delight. "Oh, Noah, those look amazing! Thank you!"

As we walked down the hall, Chris's mom began pointing out various photographs. There was one of Chris as a child, another of the whole family at a beach, and then, she paused at one where a younger Chris had his arm in a sling.

"Oh, this one's a classic." She chuckled, drawing our attention. "Chris, remember the treehouse incident?"

Chris rolled his eyes. "How could I forget? You're not going to tell that story, are you?"

His mom laughed. "Of course, I am. It's a family favorite." She turned to me. "Chris here decided he was going to build the ultimate treehouse. Mind you, he was about twelve at the time."

Chris interjected, "It would've been the ultimate treehouse if I had finished it."

"Well," his mom continued, "he was so determined, up in that tree every day after school. But one day, he slipped and fell. Broke his arm in two places."

Chris's dad joined in, a twinkle in his eye. "We found him on the ground, still holding a hammer in his other hand, insisting he was fine and could climb right back up."

Chris shook his head, but there was a smile on his face. "I was convinced I could finish it with one arm. I was a stubborn kid."

"Stubborn is an understatement," his mom said, still smiling. "But that's our Chris, always determined to finish what he started, no matter what."

It was clear that these stories were threads in the fabric of their family, told and retold with love and a hint of nostalgia, and they sucked Fox in as he asked a load of questions.

The house was filled with the sounds of laughter and conversation. Chris introduced me to his siblings: Daniel, with his husband, Micah; Scott, alongside his wife, Rachel, and their kids; Michelle, and her husband, Bob, with their child; and Mark, who was only home for the weekend from his internship up in Seattle. We gathered in the spacious dining room. The conversation flowed, and with the family so warm and welcoming, I felt at home.

We all took our seats at the large dining table laden with a variety of dishes. The food was delicious, and the company even better.

The conversation shifted to lighter topics, with everyone chiming in. I listened, contributing on occasion, feeling more and more like a part of this wonderful family.

As dinner wound down, it was time for dessert. I warmed the apple pie, then served slices of both the apple and the lemon, and everyone seemed to enjoy it. Chris leaned over to me, whispering, "You've outdone yourself. They love it."

Sitting there, surrounded by laughter and the warmth of family, I felt a deep sense of belonging, and as the evening came to a close, I helped with the cleanup, feeling content and happy. This dinner had been awesome.

I wanted so many more of them.

# Chapter Twenty-One

Chris

"How has it been going?" Dr. Trent—*please, for goodness' sake, call me Susan*—asked.

This was our fourth meeting, and I still hadn't called her Susan because she'd been riding the roller coaster of emotions about Noah right alongside me, and it just felt wrong she seemed more like a friend, than a therapist.

"Fox... Noah's son," I qualified in case I was one of a hundred clients and she'd forgotten. "He knows about us and doesn't seem to have any problem with it. He's respectful at school, he's joined the baseball team I run, and he's mostly a good kid who attempts to push boundaries when we meet up because I'm with his dad."

Everything fell out in a rush, only because I'd rehearsed how to say that on the way over.

"That's wonderful."

"I eat dinner with them sometimes, and I always go in for breakfast, and Fox sees me there, so, yeah..."

"And the physical intimacy?"

"It's good," I blurted and felt my face heat. "I mean, yes, there's been physical intimacy."

"And how is that going?" I know she meant the sex in general, and not anything about the sounds Noah made, or how we'd said we were falling for each other.

"It's going well… he um… he moves a stool so I can rest against it."

"Does that worry you?"

"Worry me how?"

"That he's fussing over you?"

"I love it. I love that he is considerate but doesn't treat me as though I'm about to break. I love that," I repeated. "I think he's dangerous because I think…"

"Yes?"

"This is it for me. I really like him. He makes me smile, and I think… I'm falling in love, and shit…"

"It scares you?" Susan finished, almost as if she was reading from a script of things I didn't want to answer. Did how I felt about Noah scare me? Did I imagine more than just the stolen moments we had? Did I imagine a forever?

"Some," I admitted. "I worry about the…" I waved at my leg. "About the long-term effects of the prosthetic, the altered gait, joint pain, bone density, the psychology of getting old with it, getting tired, not keeping up." I stopped, then, because I hadn't even been aware I was worrying about those things, but clearly, it was all there bubbling under the surface. "But Noah and me having sex? Yeah, the mechanics of it might be different, but none of it scares me when I want to be intimate with him." God,

I was even using words like intimate in full sentences—Susan's influence was messing with me. "Noah doesn't care about that," I added, "he makes me feel… sexy. Like we're having fun." I stopped then, because everything we'd done was in the semi-dark, in low-lit places, we'd not been naked yet, not managed to get to a damn bed. "But, he hasn't seen it yet. Not really."

She nodded. "What do you think his reaction will be?"

"I *know* he doesn't feel sorry for me; he accepts I am who I am, and you know what, I think he'll probably hold me, tell me he wants me, and that will be it."

Wow, that was some epiphany. I was more than the sum of my broken parts, and Noah saw that, and best of all, I knew it in my heart.

"That's all positive," Susan said. "So, to take away from today, be aware of negative thoughts about yourself and continue to actively challenge them. Replace them with positive affirmations about your strengths and qualities, particularly when you are intimate."

"I will."

"And engage in open dialogue with Noah if you feel worried."

"We talk a lot."

Susan gave me an approving smile, and it made me feel so much lighter.

# Chapter Twenty-Two

## Noah

"Do you know why the town is called Whisper Ridge, Dad?"

I glanced up from measuring out the rolled pastry. "Sure, something about standing-on-the-ridge and shouting your name and getting a name back."

"Yep, Clarke told me the story and another one about that Spring Rains thing the town does." I'd already given thought to the festival—about honoring the tradition of a Pride theme at Lily's diner, and I was so down for that.

Fox wriggled on the stool, then sneaked another bite of the cheesecake square. I didn't have it in me to disapprove of his snacking at the moment, not when my head was full of pastry and cakes.

"You mean the festival, right?" I still needed to work up some ideas of what I'd do for my feature food—something easy to eat, not too sticky, or flaky, but something that spoke about what I could do, about the diner... Croissants might be good, with different fillings, sweet and savory, as many colors of the rainbow as I could, but then, they might be too flaky. Only, if I got some napkins printed with the diner logo, not that we had a logo, it was just the word Lily in cursive, and maybe a rainbow design... I added that to my mental list and—

"Dad? Are you listening?"

I snapped back into the room. "Sorry, yes. Go for it."

"So, there was this woman, right? And she was up on the mountain in spring, and she was singing a sad song because her husband had gone away to war. I don't know which war, but one of them. Anyway, when her voice echoed in the valley, the spirit in the mountain cried, and that is the rain that falls in spring, which is why we have the Spring Rains Festival." He made jazz hands. "Ta da!"

"I didn't know that."

He rested his chin on his hands. "And there's food and drink, and we get to play a baseball game in town."

"Really?"

"It's a thing. We play the Merton Vale Mooners." He rolled his eyes. "They're shit, though."

"Fox!"

"Oops, sorry. They're uhm... not good, but we get to play them in their spring thing, which isn't half as cool as ours. They don't have the trail, all they do is have this quiz night thing, and the game, and Mr. Sheridan said that in ten games, we've beaten them eight times." He puffed up a little at that, already proud that he was part of the team, even if they hadn't played their first game. "Maybe you could be there?" He sounded wistful.

I nodded quickly. "I'll be there."

"You will?"

I made a show of taking the family calendar down from the wall and pointed at the date. It was three weeks away, which meant my Pride planning needed to kick up a notch, also it was way past time to hire in some help on that temporary contract I contemplated; otherwise, I'd have to shut the diner. "See, I wrote it down." I'd scribbled in *'Baseball game'*, and he seemed satisfied as I placed the calendar back on the hook.

"Daaddd…" Fox wheedled a little, and I waited for whatever ask he was going to make. "Can you make special Team!Rockets cupcakes for the game?"

I reached to ruffle his hair, and he went for the duck again, but I caught him in a gentle headlock and noogied him as he tried to get away. By the time the scuffle broke up, him having gotten out of my hold and hip-checked me into a wall, we were laughing so hard my sides hurt.

"Of course, I will."

"With the logo and everything?"

"Sure."

He bumped elbows with me, and grinned. "You're the best, Dad."

"I'm a cupcake enabler," I deadpanned.

"That's why you're the best!" He went back to his book and his cell vibrated, and after checking it, he let out a whoop. "Can I go to Clarke's tonight? Stay over? His mom is ordering in pizza."

I wanted to be responsible, maybe offer to make the boys and Clarke's mom some healthier, more balanced snacks, but who was I to impede a boy and his cheesy crusts?

Pizza 1, Quinoa 0

"Sure."

He sent back a hurried text. "They're picking me up at six," he said, and glanced at the clock, which was already at five-thirty, rolling off the sofa and heading for his room.

I waited until he finished packing up.

I waited until he'd gone back to his room because he'd forgotten his Switch.

I waited until Clarke's mom arrived.

I even waited five minutes after the car had disappeared around the corner.

Then, I opened the message thread with Chris.

***Noah**: Dinner? Come to my place. Get here soon.*

***Chris**: On my way. Everything okay?*

I paused for a moment, considering what I had upstairs, wondering if the supplies in my drawer were still usable.

***Noah**: Get condoms and lube.*

Silence, and I wondered if that was a sign. Then my screen lit up.

***Chris**: On my way.*

***Chris**: Fast*

---

THINGS FELT different between us as soon as I opened the door to let him in, then locked it behind us.

"Hey," he murmured, shifting his backpack from his shoulder, waiting for me to speak.

"Hey, you," I murmured, lost in his eyes, and wondering where we went next.

"I um… I have…" He waggled the bag. "As you said."

"Fox is staying at Clarke's place," I whispered, as if someone passing by might hear us. The blinds at the windows blocked people from seeing, and I drew him closer to kiss him.

Everything beyond here seemed far away, and none of it mattered now that Chris was by my side. We stayed in one place kissing, and then, I took his hand and tugged him through the diner, up the stairs, and left at the top and into my room.

"I took the smaller bedroom," I explained, as I judged the room through his eyes. Tired, faded wallpaper, flowery orange and brown drapes that needed replacing, and the king-size bed taking up most of the space. Out of habit, I closed the door behind us, and leaned there as Chris dropped the bag onto the bed and stared down at the—clean—bedcovers.

"We should talk about the leg. I mean, I need to prepare you for—"

I was probably doing this all wrong, but I cut him off with a kiss. I wanted him so much I didn't want to stop and talk or think. All that mattered was him.

"PrEP, negative, no one since Briggs." The words ran on, a repeat of conversations we'd already had. "I want you so bad."

"PrEP, negative, no one since… fuck, I don't know when—"

More kissing was needed, but I put a small amount of space between us, still joined at the lips, unbuttoning my shirt, and wishing I'd just pulled on a Lily's Diner T-shirt —a clean one of course—because that would have been so much quicker.

And now, he might have taken off his outside stuff, but he was way behind in getting naked. I growled at him—god knows if that was sexy or not-- but I needed to see him, and when Chris began to take off his shirt, he did it so slowly I wanted to growl again.

That was so not me.

I stopped when I got my first glimpse of his chest in the light—every other time had been in the dim pantry, and then, the hallway, and while I'd mapped each inch of him with my fingers, to actually get to see him… mind blown.

He was slim and toned, and I saw more burn scars running down his left arm, matching the ones on his face, which I knew were there by touch. I forgot about getting my jeans off and, instead, reached out to trace a path from his chin to his nipples and back. He wasn't the hairiest of guys, but what he had felt crinkly under my fingers, and looked perfect.

"Oh god," I muttered. "You're so beautiful."

He let out a sigh, grabbed me for a kiss, and helped me unbuckle my belt and take off my jeans, leaving me in jersey boxers and socks, which I toed off because socks are not sexy. Then, it was his turn, and he hesitated, and I hated that this was a big deal for him, that maybe he was scared.

I encouraged him to the bed, and he sat on the edge.

"Can I do it?" I asked, on my knees between his legs, my hands on the zipper of his pants. He stared at me, reached out and pressed a finger to my lips, searched my gaze for *something*, and then nodded. I was so hard, but I wanted to go slow and gentle. I wanted to show him what he meant to me, and when he shifted his ass so I could slide his pants down, I let them pool on the floor, taking the time to remove his shoes and the sock on his left foot.

I was faced with the prosthetic, something I'd never seen up this close, and it intrigued me.

"Can you tell me what to do?" I asked, wanting to understand how not to hurt him, desperate to get this right. I'd researched transtibial prosthesis, knew about the socket that would be custom-made to fit the stump, knew that in most technical descriptions it was called a residual limb. I indicated the socket, wondering what else to call it. "What is this called?"

"Stumpy," he deadpanned, and then, raised a hand. "Not my idea—it's what Daniel and Scott came up with. I fell asleep once, and they drew a face on it and called it Stumpy."

My heart hurt for him, but he didn't seem upset. "Did that make you feel bad?"

"What? No, it's gallows humor. It's okay."

"I meant the parts of the prosthetic, so I don't get it wrong."

"Oh, that, well that is the socket, and it has soft material in it, and the suspension system keeps it attached to Stumpy." He quirked a smile at that. "I have a suction cap, which is good for riding as well. Then further down foot, ankle, blah blah."

"How do I take it off?" I asked.

He went quiet. "You want to take it off?"

"Yes."

"Let me," he said, and I nodded, trying to show that it was no big deal.

He removed his prosthetic leg, setting it aside. I could tell he was watching me, maybe worried about how I'd react. But it changed nothing for me. He was still Chris, the guy I enjoyed spending time with, the man I kissed, the lover I wanted to taste.

"Okay?" I asked.

He frowned a little. "Shouldn't I be asking you that?"

I wanted him to know that I saw him, *all* of him, and that he was beautiful to me. "Chris," I said, trying to keep my voice steady. "You are beautiful. All of you."

He looked a bit surprised, maybe relieved too, and he smiled with caution.

"I'm vers," I said before he could think anymore. "Can I ride… can you… will you make love to me?" Oh god, now I was tripping over my words, and I could tell he was still a bit cautious, maybe unsure about how I felt, but then, his eyes darkened, and he shimmied up the bed. I didn't know what he could do, or what he would want to do, but I wanted him every way I could, starting with him inside me.

"Fuck yes."

I couldn't help but stare for a moment at him lying there, his cock hard, wanting me as much as I wanted him, and *god, I wanted him*. His scars and the stump where his leg used to be—they were parts of his story. I tipped up his bag, a box of condoms and two pump containers of lube tumbled out, and then, I kissed him because I'd never seen anything so sexy as all those condoms and so much lube.

He reached for the slick; his eyes hooded. "Can I get you ready?" His chest heaved with unsteady breaths as he unclipped the pump, squirting so much lube we could probably wrestle in it. I needed that—it had been so long since I'd bottomed, and fuck, he wasn't small, all hard and pretty and flushed red.

"How do you want me?" I murmured.

He made a motion for me to turn, and as soon as I did, I bent and licked his cock, and at last I had my lips on him. He made an abortive thrust into my mouth. I smiled around him, using a hand to close the space and twisting gently, smoothing the length of him as he pressed cold lubed fingers to my hole and groaned when I gasped. Chris gripped my thigh, as I sucked and tasted, the scent of him so perfect, shower gel and man and everything I wanted.

He worked in a finger, and I pushed back, the burn was too much, and then, it wasn't enough.

"More," I demanded around his cock, and he chuckled.

He fucking chuckled, then slapped my ass. "Be patient. I'm doing this slowly!"

I never thought I'd be into spanking, but fuck, the way that pushed me to the edge was way too much, and I applied more pressure to him as I bobbed my head.

"You have to… stop!" he said, between harsh breaths.

I was torn—did I want him coming down my throat or did I want him inside me? In the end, I clambered off him and around, stroking him, putting on the condom, then rubbing the tip of his cock against my hole.

"Ready?" I said with a grin, kissing him as I held his cock and lowered my weight to him, shimmying until the tip was only just in, and god, the burn was exquisite, a touch on the wrong side of pain, until my muscles eased, and he slid in one slow inch at a time.

"Noah… gah…" Chris tensed under me, his jaw tight.

"Am I hurting you?" I was worried, had I sat wrong? "Am I doing this right?"

"Any more right, and I'll come in you now," he said through gritted teeth.

Oh. That kind of *gah*.

I rocked back, my hands on my thighs, watching his face as he scrambled to get hold of the covers, shifting under me, and only when he opened his eyes again did I begin to move. I wanted to see his beautiful crystal blue eyes, and the rhythm I set was slow and steady, even if I wanted to get off.

"Touch me?" I asked.

He released his hold on the quilt and used one hand to circle my cock, the other pushing between us, finding the point where we joined, and calling my name.

I wish I could use words, but what we were doing had stolen every one of them, and I wanted to come so bad I moved faster, and he twisted his fingers and…

My orgasm barreled into me, and I painted his chest with cum, and then, he was coming too, violently, and fast, and it went on forever, until I slumped forward, and he held me close.

"Noah?" he whispered.

"Huh?" Yep, head scrambled.

"Is it too soon to say I think I'm falling in love with

you?"

I shook my head—difficult given I was sprawled over him, the sticky mess between us—and somehow he dealt with the condom, but I was boneless.

"I think I'm falling in love with you, too." Then, I lifted my head and kissed him—he deserved me to be honest. "I know I am. I've never felt anything like this before, not only making love, but everything. I think I'm in love with you." I snuggled closer.

"Same," Chris murmured.

"Every single part of you," I added and kissed him again.

He chuckled and deepened the kiss. "Same," he repeated and smiled at me.

I could do this forever.

I was awake early, crawling out from under Chris and heading downstairs to decorate today's cupcakes, focusing on getting the smooth swirl right. Each cupcake was a little canvas, and I took pride in making the appearance as good as the taste. The kitchen was quiet, except for the soft hum of the refrigerator and the occasional *clink* of my icing spatula against the bowl. I loved that Chris was upstairs; I loved that at any moment I could go back to my bed and find him there, and I placed a special cupcake to one side.

Only, the front door flew open, and Fox bounded in, his energy filling the room. "Hey, Dad, I'm back!"

"What are you doing back so early?" I asked him, a little worried that Chris was still upstairs and that this wasn't how I wanted Fox to find out I'd had a sleepover of my own.

"Molly had a dentist thing, so her mom dropped me back." He waved at a car leaving, and I sketched a wave also in case she could see inside.

"Did you have fun?"

"Yeah, big time," he said, and then hovered next to me. "Can I help?"

I smiled, pointing at the array of cupcakes still waiting to be iced. "Sure, grab an apron. There's plenty to do."

Fox tied an apron around his waist and picked up a piping bag. "So, what's the plan? Swirls, stars, something fancy?"

"Let's stick with swirls for now," I said, demonstrating the technique. "Nice and easy, just like this."

He nodded, concentrating hard as he began to work on a cupcake. His first attempt was uneven, but he soon got the hang of it.

"Dad, can I tell you something?"

"What's wrong? Is everything okay?" I caught myself when he glanced at me. I'd fucked up—why did I immediately assume things weren't okay?

"I really like Molly."

Oh, it was one of those chat. Girls. I could handle this. "So do I." That was me being supportive.

"But I don't just like girls," he added in a run-on sentence. "I like boys too, in the kissing kind of way, maybe."

Ah, the chat had changed direction. "Cool." What else was there to say? It *was* cool.

We exchanged grins and were halfway through the icing project when Chris walked in, not seeing Fox at first, and then coming to a dead stop.

"Morning Mr.—Chris," Fox murmured, and sent me a wry smile.

"Morning Fox."

Silence. Then Chris cleared his throat. "This looks like fun. Can I join in?"

"Of course," I said, passing him a piping bag. "We're doing swirls."

Chris kissed me, and he tasted of toothpaste. Then he chuckled, squeezing the bag of butter cream. "I can't promise they'll look as good as yours, but I'll give it a shot."

Together, the three of us worked on the cupcakes, falling into a simple rhythm. Fox and Chris's cupcakes weren't as neat as mine, but that didn't matter. Some had lopsided swirls, others too much icing, but each one was perfect in its own way.

As we finished the last batch, I stepped back to admire our handiwork. The cupcakes were a mix of perfection and imperfection, but staring at them lined up, I felt an overwhelming sense of happiness. It wasn't *just* about the cupcakes; it was about this moment, together in the kitchen, sharing laughs and creating memories.

"These look great," Chris said, smiling down at the colorful array.

Fox nodded, his eyes shining with pride. "We make a pretty good team, don't we?"

I wrapped an arm around each of them, feeling grateful for these moments. "We sure do. These cupcakes are perfect, just the way they are."

And they were. They were perfectly imperfect, the same as us. And I wouldn't have it any other way.

# Chapter Twenty-Three

## Chris

I WAS DONE WITH AP ENGLISH, THE LAST CLASS OF THE DAY, when Ainsley approached me with determination. He was usually inseparable from Clarke, and now Fox, so it caught me off guard when he ignored both of his friends waiting for him in the hallway and stopped in front of my desk.

"Can I talk to you, sir?"

"Sure, is this about the project?" I cast a glance over to where Fox and Clarke stood and caught Ainsley shaking his head at them. What was wrong?

"Not the project, sir, something personal."

Okay then. Worse than only a simple project question. "Sure, Ainsley," I said, and noticed Clarke hovering at the door, Fox's hand on his arm, both of them looking at me with intense expressions. Ainsley shut the door on them and leaned there.

"Clarke doesn't understand," Ainsley blurted. "Wants

to drag me away from my house and save me. But he can't save me like that."

What? Okay. This sounded serious. "Save you? Ainsley, do you need me to call someone to be in here with you?"

He frowned and tilted his chin. "No. I just need help, and Fox said I should talk to you." He took a chair in the front row, waiting as I wheeled out from behind my desk and stopped in front of him.

"Mr. Sheridan, I… I need to… talk to someone," he started, his voice barely above a whisper.

I leaned forward, my teacher instincts kicking in. "Whatever it is, Ainsley, I'm here to listen."

He took a deep breath, his eyes flickering with a mix of fear and resolve. "I'm bisexual," he blurted out, and it was as if I could see a great weight shift from his shoulders at vocalizing who he was. "And I argued with my dad because he started in on Clarke, and he said… he hates Clarke." His voice hitched and he was shaking as he held out his arm, pushed back the sweater he was wearing and exposed bruises on his wrist and up his forearm. I had to school my features to hide the spark of temper in me.

Ainsley's dad was loud and outspoken about anything he deemed immoral, and he ran his church on hate. A chill ran down my spine at what Ainsley was implying. This was a delicate situation, hell, a child protection issue.

I had to approach this with care; procedures were in place. "Ainsley, did your dad do this?"

He blinked at me for a moment. "He didn't mean to, I mean, he was just…"

"If he hurt you in anger, that's wrong," I said, in the simplest language I knew how. "What happened?"

"I was arguing about Clarke." He shot a glance at the door as if he expected Clarke to come barging in. "He hates Clarke, says he's a bad influence, that he's unnatural, and that I shouldn't see him." Ainsley's eyes swam with tears. "But Clarke is… my best friend. No!" He balled his hands into fists in his lap. "He's my boyfriend, and I want to be with Clarke, but Dad hates him, and he's going to hate who I am."

Oh. Well, that put a unique spin on things. Clarke and Ainsley together—that made absolute sense. After all, they were best friends, and tactile. Why hadn't I seen this before? I glanced at Ainsley's wrist, but he'd hidden it again.

"Dad's always talking about sin. I'm scared he'll… I don't know, kick me out. And I don't care about that—me and Clarke will be okay, we'll move to the city and get a place or something, but I'm scared right now of what Dad might do to me. Or Clarke."

I didn't point out flaws with two fourteen-year-old boys heading to the city because Ainsley was scared, and that was my priority. My heart ached for him. No kid should have to fear being themselves. Why should anyone have to hide who they are, let alone a child? We should live in a world where every young person feels safe to express themselves, where their uniqueness is not only tolerated, but celebrated. Families should be sanctuaries of unconditional love, where kids can show their true colors without fear of rejection. Not places where there was hate.

"Has your dad threatened Clarke?"

Ainsley nodded, and then tipped his chin. "Not to his

face, but to me."

"Okay, Ainsley, here's what's going to happen. Firstly, you're not alone in this. There are people who can support you, one of them being me."

He shook his head, and I caught him glancing at my chair. "My dad is tall and strong."

I understood his fear—Pastor McKenna was a big man physically, but he was also well-known in town. "Okay, let's think this through. Do you have any other family members you trust? Anyone you feel safe with?"

He thought for a moment. "Not my mom. She's just as scared of him as I am." He blanched. "I mean, I love her, but she never stands up to him. Maybe my aunt. She's always been kind to me, but she lives out of state, and I'm not leaving Clarke."

"Well, an aunt advocating for you is a start." I felt a flicker of hope. I paused for a moment to consider what next—I had a mandatory responsibility to report this. Did Ainsley know that? "You know, I need to report the incident to the appropriate authorities for your safety. I can't promise to keep it to myself."

He met my steady gaze with one of his own. "I know. I'm sorry. I didn't know who else to trust, and Fox said I can trust you." His voice broke.

I nodded. "I've got this, and I'm glad you told me," I assured him. "Your safety is my priority." God, that sounded so damn official. "I've got this." I softened my voice. "I'm on your side."

His weight settled on *my* shoulders, the reality of what he'd shared hitting me hard. I knew what my next steps had to be. My first responsibility was to ensure his safety, and that meant escalating this to the principal, at least.

*Okay. Focus on what you know. What the procedures are.*

I recalled every word of my training for situations like this, the emphasis on never promising confidentiality because I had a duty of care.

"Thank you," Ainsley murmured, tears tracking down his face, looking dejected.

My role as a mandated reporter was clear, and the urgency of the situation didn't allow for any hesitation. I made a mental note of the details of our conversation, knowing that accurate documentation was crucial.

I also thought about the immediate support Ainsley would need. I needed to talk to the principal, to set up a support system for him, and report this to law enforcement for child endangerment. This situation was bigger than him. I pulled out my cell and set it on the desk next to him. "Will you tell me again, so I have it on record?"

For a moment, he hesitated. "Can I get Clarke in here?"

I sat back in my seat. "Sure."

Ainsley opened the door, and Clarke was right there, Fox behind him. I exchanged a nod with Fox, who stared at me with frustration in every line of him, then turned on his heel and left, and Clarke came in and sat next to Ainsley, reaching for his hand, and holding it tight.

"Are you okay?" he asked Ainsley, and Ainsley nodded.

"Mr. Sheridan will help me," he said, and Clarke glanced at me with a fierce and determined expression. They were expecting me to fix everything, and the weight of that was so heavy I couldn't breathe. Then everything eased as I glanced at their joined hands. It was Ainsley finding out who he was; it was both of them falling in young love at fourteen; it was on me to fix whatever I could.

“Okay, if you’re okay…” I pressed record on my memo app, “start from the beginning.”

# Chapter Twenty-Four

## Noah

SITTING AT A TABLE IN THE QUIET OF THE DINER BEFORE opening hours, scattered notes and flyers surrounded me, I was brainstorming ideas for the Pride event at the upcoming Spring Rains Festival. I had another meeting with the organizers at ten, and caught up in Fox, and in all the feelings I was catching for Chris, I'd fallen behind and still lacked inspiration. The festival was a big deal in town, and this year, it felt significant that I do something in Lily's name.

But what?

I rummaged deeper in the box that someone had left for me—I liked to think it was Lily before she passed—and pulled out even more leaflets from festivals dating back to the seventies with Lily's notes offering me an inspiring journey through evolving tastes and trends that went from seventies Jell-O Salad, right through to the cupcakes of the first decade of the 2Ks, and on to what she'd done the two or three years before she passed. For these past years, she'd veered away from tradition, focusing on a selection of desserts that featured cupcakes in Pride colors, but she'd also included croissants.

I found one from the nineties and the design of it caught my eye. Set out to mimic a PC screen, it had the Lily's Diner wording and featured lemon cheesecake as the main offering, and it was familiar. The next one—for the first year of the new decade—was covered in notes in any white space, and on the back. The penmanship was Aunt Lily's, but was faded, only as I peered at the pale writing between customers, it soon became obvious that it was a recipe for a lemon cheesecake, and that there was a separate message at the bottom that said, *Noah, taste test, 150 percent.*

I rocked back. That was me! I'd said that.

Hell, it was a vivid memory of saying the cheesecake was a hundred and fifty percent amazing. She'd smiled down at me, and god, that *Noah* was just an innocent kid who'd visited for the festival with Dad—the last time I'd really done anything with Dad. I recalled lemon cheesecake and being so blown away I wanted to know how to make it. That was my first attempt at cooking something, even if it was mostly crushing and mixing and not much baking at all. I'd watched Lily make a hundred tiny cheesecakes, each decorated with dark chocolate shavings; and felt so much pride as they lined up on a serving dish.

*I remember.*

Lost in thought, I barely heard the bell above the door chime as Maggie and Rachel walked in chattering nineteen to the dozen about anything and everything, each weighed down with a box of something. I glanced at the clock—how was it ten already?

"Morning, Noah!" Maggie greeted me with a bright smile and Rachel, shyer, waved her hello.

I stood, shaking their hands. "Thanks for coming by. I wanted to run some ideas by you."

Maggie, ever the practical one, got straight to the point. "What are you thinking?"

I reached for a leaflet from the table, feeling a surge of pride. "I want to honor my Aunt Lily and what she did for the queer residents of Whisper Ridge." I held my breath, but all they did was nod, serious and focused on what I was saying. "I want to do a take on lemon cheesecake." They didn't seem overly impressed with something as boring as a cheesecake, but then I'd always known that would be a hard sell. "But also, croissants, both savory and sweet varieties."

Their eyes lit up. "Lily's croissants were legendary!" exclaimed Maggie.

I nodded, feeling a wave of nostalgia that was more about the lemon cheesecake than the croissants. "Yeah, I want to bring that back. Add my twist to it, oh, and the cheesecake." Because *that* was what I would focus on."

Maggie leaned in. "That sounds wonderful, Noah. It's a lovely way to remember Lily. She was a big part of this town," she added to Rachel, who smiled and nodded as she made notes.

Feeling encouraged, I offered to make them lunch. As I prepared salads for them, with added bacon of course, we chatted about the festival, exchanging ideas and stories.

They seemed interested in my plans for the diner's stall, and their excitement was infectious.

When I served lunch, both women were full of praise. "This is amazing, Noah!" Maggie said between bites.

Rachel nodded. "I can't wait to try those croissants at the festival."

The door opening interrupted our conversation, and an older man walked in, then came to the counter, exchanging hellos with Maggie and Rachel, who were just about to leave. He had a quiet, introspective air about him, and I could tell he was nervous.

"Morning," I offered, and reached back for a menu. "If you want to take a seat…"

"Actually," he said, sitting at the counter extending his hand, which I shook. "My name is Merle Lebron."

"Hi, Merle. What can I get you?"

"A job!" he exclaimed and went scarlet. "I mean, I thought you might be looking for some help around here?"

I extended my hand. "Noah. Yes, I am. Can I get you something?"

A group of moms and babies interrupted us, plus one dad pushing twins. They were regulars now—if them saying they'd like to use the back of the coffee shop every other week made them regulars.

"Please, serve customers first."

The order included a large amount of salad and mac 'n' cheese, as well as toddler versions of the same. I was in the kitchen doing my thing when I suddenly realized that Merle was behind the counter, taking care of the drink orders. He saw me glancing his way and nodded.

"Worked my way through college in a coffee shop. It's been a while, but I think I still remember a thing or two," he said to me as he steamed milk.

Surprised, but intrigued, I nodded. "Um… okay, go ahead."

He moved behind the counter with an ease that spoke of familiarity. As he worked the coffee machine, dealing with new customers alongside me, he told me about his early retirement from a city job and how his wife had passed away. "Came back to Whisper Ridge to find some peace," he said, pouring a perfect cup of coffee. "I'm fifty-nine, so I know I'm probably too old, but I'm not looking for a job because I need the money, just… something to do. And I love to be around people. Got it from working in the campus coffee shop way back when we thought having three options on the menu was fancy."

I didn't have to interview him. He was slipping seamlessly into working next to me, the moms (and dad) laughing and chilling and ordering a second round of coffee and desserts, and for the first time since I'd opened the doors, I felt more in control.

I took a sip of the coffee he'd made—it was excellent. His story touched me. Here was a man searching for a purpose, a way to heal and connect with people. After the lunch crowd thinned, it was moving into the slow rundown to closing, and I placed a couple of twenties under a slice of the lemon cheesecake I was working on. "I pay a fair wage, and we can arrange a schedule. How about you come in tomorrow, give it a try? We can see how it goes."

Merle's face lit up with a smile, a mixture of relief and gratitude. "I'd like that. Thank you, Noah."

As he left, I felt good about the decision. Merle wasn't only an employee; he could bring something special to the diner, a life experience that was invaluable. Plus, his coffee skills were a definite bonus.

And today, I felt good in my place, and it was more than serving food; it was about building a community, a place where people like Merle could find a sense of belonging and purpose.

Lily's Diner was mine, and I was making it work.

---

I WAS FINISHING up some paperwork when the last of the customers left their table—Hardware-Store-Ed, who said he could find matching leather from his suppliers if I needed it for the bench seats. He sketched a wave, and I waved back as he left, a swirl of snow the only evidence he'd been there. Well, that and the plates and mug, which were easy enough to deal with.

Although, the dishwasher was leaking, and I really needed to fix it. So many things to juggle when it was your own place, jarring when back in Columbus I'd been head pastry chef with a team supporting me. Not that I hadn't known what I was taking on, but a leaking dishwasher did not bode well.

The bell jangled, and I pasted a smile on my face, which widened when I saw it was Fox walking in from school. But he didn't smile back, and it was easy to see he was upset about something with his shoulders slumped and avoiding my gaze. He almost slunk past me to the hall, but I called his name, and he stopped and turned.

"Hey, buddy, what's wrong?" I asked, concerned when I got a closer look at him and thought he'd been crying. "Bad day?"

He hesitated, then blurted out, "I didn't know what to do, and I got scared because all I could think about was…" He slumped to a stool, burying his face in his hands.

Fuck. What scared him? Was it Briggs? Had his asshole of a papa contacted him? Or turned up in town? He mumbled something, and I went to the door, turned the board to closed so no one could interrupt whatever was going on here, and locked up, then hurried back before Fox thought I was ignoring him.

"What happened?" I asked.

"Ainsley. And I didn't know what to do, but I said Chris could help. Mr. Sheridan I mean. But Clarke went with him, and Ainsley wanted help, and then, when I was getting on the bus home, Ainsley's dad drove up, and he was so angry, and I should have stayed because Ainsley is my friend, but I couldn't!" Hot tears spilled over his hands.

"Okay, back up, start again." I sat on the stool next to him, put my arm over his shoulders and hugged him to me. "What happened? Did someone hurt you?" *Who did I need to kill?*

"Not me," Fox hiccupped, "Ainsley. His dad hurt him like…" That started off a fresh round of tears, and my heart sank.

"Hurt? How?"

Fox sniffed, and I reached for a handful of napkins

before he wiped his nose with his coat, which he'd yet to take off. "They had a fight. Ainsley's dad grabbed his wrist really hard. He showed it to me. It was all red and bruised, and it looked like… when…"

It hit me. It looked like when Briggs had done the same thing to me, grabbing my wrist, and shoving me against a wall, breaking two bones, leaving my wrist swollen and bruised.

He'd done that in front of Fox, and that had been the day we'd left with nothing but the clothes we wore, and relied on the kindness of friends who offered us a place to sleep. That had been the night before the media exposé on what he'd been doing. He was a pressure cooker waiting to explode, and he'd used his strength fueled by anger to hurt me.

"Oh, Fox, sweetheart," I whispered.

He turned into me, and I held him tight and close, and was thankful this corner of the counter was hidden from the street. He'd never wanted anyone to see how he felt back in Columbus, and he wouldn't want to start now. "That part of our lives is done now; your papa is nothing to us until you decide you want to see him again."

"I don't want to. *You're* my dad." My heart swelled. I might not be Fox's dad biologically, but it made me so happy to hear that I was the dad he trusted and wanted to be with. "But, when I saw Ainsley's dad, he was so angry, and I don't want him to hurt anyone."

"You said that Ainsley is telling the school, Chris—Mr. Sheridan."

"That's what they were doing, him and Clarke, and I

wanted to stay. I got on the bus, then I wanted to go back, but I was scared. How stupid is that?"

Oh God. I hugged my boy even tighter, as if by doing that I could make the demons vanish. So much counseling, so much pain when Briggs had demanded custody, so much pain when he'd hurt me in front of Fox, and then, with us uprooting everything, losing the old house, all of our money gone. I'd have been surprised if Fox could handle what he'd seen today.

"It's not stupid, and you know that, Fox." I pressed a kiss to the top of his head. "You're entitled to feel these things."

"I don't want to; I want to be a good friend and help."

"You couldn't have done anything," I reminded him. "If Ainsley and Clarke have taken this to a teacher, then that is the best thing."

"Ainsley's really upset," Fox continued, his voice shaky. "He wants to come out. He's scared his dad will kill him."

I didn't know if that was teenage exaggeration, or whether that was true. Before Briggs, before seeing how he'd turned on me, I would have never thought someone had so much anger and hate in them.

"The school should know what to do. They can help him, and if you're worried, we can visit the sheriff, or call Chris."

Fox looked up at me, his eyes filled with more questions than I had answers. "But what if it makes things worse?"

I sighed, knowing these situations were delicate. "Sometimes, telling someone is the only way to make things better. Ainsley's brave for wanting to speak up.

And it's not just about his wrist, right? There are other things?"

"Yeah," Fox said. He was so quiet, torn between what he wanted to say and what he could say.

"Fox, I want you to trust me and tell me anything. But if Ainsley is in danger, then I will escalate this. You understand that, right? I want to keep your secrets, I want to be the person you talk to, but if Ainsley is in danger…"

Fox nodded. "He hasn't said he's unsafe, just that his dad is always really mean to his mom, yells a lot."

"Okay. Is it like…"

"What Dad did to you? The moments when I was scared, and you got between us?" He tipped his chin and our eyes locked, and I hated what Fox had seen—hated he'd been scared for even a moment of his young life. I nodded. "Ainsley said he doesn't feel scared, but then, he hasn't told his dad about who he is."

"It's not okay for him. It's important that he tells someone who can help. You did good by getting him to go to a teacher."

"What if Mr. Sheridan messes it up?"

"He won't."

Fox nodded, relieved, but still red-eyed. "I just want him to be okay."

I pulled him into a hug. "I know, buddy." He went quiet, and I gave him one last squeeze. "Are you hungry? I have cupcakes, and I could make a hot chocolate with all your favorite toppings."

He gave me a watery smile, and then leaned his head on my chest and hugged me back.

"I love you, Dad."

"Love you too."

I entered the kitchen, and he followed me, shedding his outdoor clothes as he came, but he hadn't finished talking.

"Why do some people have to hate others?" Fox's question caught me off guard, his young voice filled with confusion and pain, and fuck, I wish I had an answer. But then Fox continued. "And why did Papa stop loving you?"

I wanted to snap that Briggs had never loved me, but that wouldn't be fair because I'd loved him for a long time before all the lies had been exposed, and I suppose it was possible he'd loved me back at some point.

"Sometimes people hurt each other because they're dealing with their own problems, their own pain. It's not right, it's not an excuse, but it happens." I paused, choosing my words carefully. "As for your papa, I don't know if it was about falling out of love. He had his struggles, his own issues that made him act the way he did."

Fox stared down, fidgeting with a napkin. "But why did he have to hurt you? Why didn't he want to fight for us?"

"That's something I've asked myself a lot," I admitted. "But we can't always understand why people do what they do." I pulled out the bag of tiny marshmallows and sprinkled some onto the hot chocolate, then placed that and the cupcake in front of Fox. It was telling that he didn't immediately fall on the sugary confections like a hyena on a fresh kill.

He poked the marshmallows under the surface of the

drink, his expression thoughtful. "Can I ask you something, Dad?"

"Of course." I sat down next to him again with a coffee, wondering what grenade I'd be thrown next.

"Did he ever say sorry to you?"

Oh shit. Way to tear into my chest and expose all the raw nerves. "No, he didn't."

"Oh."

"I'm sorry." I'm not sure what I was apologizing for.

Fox glanced up at me, his eyes clear. "Nah, it's all good, Dad. As long as we're together, it's okay."

His words filled me with a mix of pride and relief. Despite the challenges we'd faced, Fox was growing up to be resilient and understanding. In his young mind, he had accepted the situation, to look ahead, rather than dwell on the past.

I hugged him, feeling grateful for his strength and wisdom, far beyond his years. "You're an amazing kid, Fox. I'm so proud of you."

"Can you message Chris and ask him what's happening?"

"Sure."

***Noah****: Fox is here with me. Is everything okay with Ainsley?*

Sending the message was enough for Fox to calm down, and when he griped at me about not having enough marshmallows, I knew my fierce teenage Fox was back.

I just hoped to hell Ainsley was as resilient.

## Chapter Twenty-Five

### Chris

As it turned out, I didn't get to take Ainsley to the principal because she called for me to go to the office first. Ainsley came with me, but when I saw Pastor McKenna through the door, I made Ainsley sit outside, a worried Clarke hovering next to him.

"What is he doing here?" Ainsley asked, then rounded on me, his eyes wide with fear. "I'm not lying, Mr. Sheridan. I'm not lying."

I pressed my hand to his forearm. "I know you're not lying. We've got this," I reassured Ainsley, who gripped Clarke's hand and held it tight.

I knocked on the door of the principal's office, then wheeled in, passing Pastor McKenna, who stared at me without emotion. A religious man, he was not only a parent, but also one of our most influential board members, and he had made it clear, on more than one occasion, that he held me personally responsible for what he saw as the moral decay of the school. I sat there, trying to maintain my composure while McKenna voiced his disapproval. His words were laced with a disdain all too familiar to me, but he didn't know what Ainsley had just finished telling me, nor that I'd already uploaded the recorded interview through the correct channels.

"Thank you for joining us, Mr. Sheridan," Evie said.

McKenna sneered. "Mr. Sheridan, is setting a poor example." He pointed in my direction. "My son came home and began talking about subjects not suitable at a dinner table. We can't have someone like *him* influencing our children, and I'd like to know what the school intends to do about this."

I exchanged a glance with Evie, who subtly shook her head.

McKenna's conservative views and influence on the school board were undeniable. As he directed his ire towards me, I felt a mixture of frustration and disbelief, and anger that he'd laid hands on his teenage son.

I bristled at the accusation, my mind racing for a response. He wanted to know what the school was going to do about what? "I'm teaching a state-approved ninth grade syllabus, Mr. McKenna. Not providing some kind of gateway to…" I struggled to find the right word, knowing whatever I said could either escalate or diffuse the situation. "… to radical thinking," I concluded.

"Your lack of respect is abysmal!" McKenna bellowed, turning away from the principal, who lifted her phone from the desk and pressed buttons—I hoped she was getting Neil out to the school—we could do with the sheriff on the property given what this asshole had done to Ainsley. "Is this the kind of influence we're allowing in the school?" His words were laced with such vehemence that I felt a chill run down my spine. McKenna's religious fervor was well known, but to witness it being directed at me was unsettling. I couldn't even think what it must be like to be a child of his, struggling with my identity. McKenna was relentless. He leaned towards the principal, speaking in a hushed, urgent tone. "I found filth on Ainsley's phone. Men… kissing men. It's abhorrent." He was so damn smug, and I just knew what was going to happen next—he was going to pull the Bible verse defense.

Just then, the door burst open with such force it silenced everyone in the room. Ainsley stood there, his chest heaving with what seemed like a mix of anger and bravery, and I pushed myself out of my chair, ready to go to battle if needed—pain be damned.

"What are you doing here, Dad?" Ainsley demanded, his eyes flicking between his father and me, Clarke right behind him. Ainsley's eyes were wide, and there was fear there, and a hell of a lot of confusion and anger.

McKenna was taken aback by his son's sudden appearance, but then he sneered. "Ainsley, this is not the place…"

But Ainsley was undeterred. "Why are you here? Did you know I was going to tell them you hurt me?" The evidence of betrayal in Ainsley's expression killed me. "Why are you shouting at Mr. Sheridan?"

McKenna's face reddened, a mixture of embarrassment and anger.

"Ainsley, I can't believe you took this outside the family—"

"You hurt me!" Ainsley snapped and held up his wrist.

Evie's eyes widened, and we exchanged glances. I nodded, which was enough to confirm what had happened, and there was a new determination in her stance.

"Sit down, Pastor McKenna."

"Ainsley McKenna, you will not stand there and—"

They spoke over each other, but it was Ainsley who stopped them both.

"I'm bisexual, okay!" Ainsley's voice echoed in the still room. He stared straight at his father, a silent plea for understanding in his eyes, as if his dad might understand, and apologize, and somehow become a better man in an instant.

"No. You're not." McKenna was calm, but his jaw was set and his eye twitched with suppressed temper. "No son of mine is *like that.*"

Ainsley reached back and pulled Clarke, with his pink hair and his lip gloss, into the room. "And this is my boyfriend, Clarke," he added, his arm around Clarke's shoulders.

McKenna's face turned a shade paler, shock and disbelief replacing his frigid expression as Ainsley's words hung in the air. The man who had been so vocal in his criticism moments ago was now rendered speechless, his gaze darting between Ainsley and Clarke.

"Okay, I need everyone to sit down," Evie began.

But even as Evie attempted to defuse the situation, McKenna's voice rose, infused with a fervor stemming from his deep-seated convictions. "This goes against everything you believe in, Ainsley," he declared, his words sharp and unyielding. *Yep, here comes the quotes.* "The Bible clearly states that homosexuality is a sin. It's right there in the scriptures!"

"You're wrong!" Ainsley shouted.

I moved a little closer to him, given how McKenna's hands were clenched into fists. Maybe it was the one-handed air quote his son had used, but McKenna was turning purple.

"Leviticus. Romans. How can any reasonable person ignore these teachings?"

I wanted to shout that a reasonable person wouldn't be forcing his son to stand there and be told he was *wrong*.

"I've called the sheriff," Evie announced in the hateful silence.

McKenna rolled his eyes. "Now why would you do a silly thing like that?" he said, and it was so oily and repulsive I didn't know where to move, or who to protect first.

*As if you could protect anyone.*

I shoved all the negative thoughts to one side, and took another step between McKenna and Ainsley, pressing my hand to his chest.

"You need to move away from Ainsley, Mr. McKenna."

McKenna stiffened and poked at me. "People like you are drifting away from the word of God, and it's leading our children down a dangerous path. I can't stand by and watch."

"No one asked you to watch," Ainsley muttered.

McKenna lunged, but I was steady on my feet, my

prosthetic lodged under my wheelchair, which had its brakes on. No one was moving me, and McKenna wasn't getting through me to his son.

McKenna's voice softened, but only a little, his tone cajoling, but tinged with desperation. "Son, you need to understand. This lifestyle, it's not what God wants for you." As McKenna continued, citing more scripture, and lamenting the perceived moral decay of society—all down to *people like me*—the tension in the room escalated, and I wished to hell that Neil would get here quick. McKenna's tirade had started with his belief I was the corrupting influence, and he'd circled into hate.

"I'm queer, but there are plenty of churches who will love me as I am." Ainsley tipped his chin.

Fuck. McKenna's face contorted into an expression of pure fury, and I braced myself as he shoved, the pain in my knee as it twisted was enough to make me nauseous, but I kept my position, and as much as he tried, he still couldn't get past.

"This is unacceptable!" McKenna bellowed, his voice reverberating through the room. His eyes blazed with a mix of outrage and disbelief as he stared at Ainsley. "You can't be serious. This is not how I raised you!"

His words were like daggers, and I glanced back at Ainsley, who flinched, but also stood his ground, Clarke firm at his side.

"You can't be like this. You're my son!" McKenna continued, his tone laced with a mix of command and desperation. In his worldview, there was no room for this truth from his son. "I won't allow it. We'll fix this. We'll get you help."

Evie nodded at me—Neil must be on the school grounds—and I knew I just had to hold McKenna back for a little longer. His fist flew, catching me on the temple, rocking me back, but I shoved him away.

"Stop!" I yelled.

But McKenna was beyond listening. He turned his glare towards me, his anger finding a new target, spittle flying. "You're the reason my son is like this!"

I wasn't scared. If anything, I felt a surge of protectiveness toward Ainsley and Clarke. It was one thing to face discrimination myself, but seeing it directed at these kids was something else entirely.

"Sir, step away." Thank fuck. Neil was here and between us, easing his way in front of McKenna, guiding him back to the wall, looking from Evie to me, and to the kids behind. "Does someone want to explain what is going on here?"

"Dad hurt me." Ainsley's voice, though strained, was firm.

"That's a damned lie!" McKenna lunged for me again, only this time, he caught Neil square on the chin, and Neil was there, spinning McKenna to face the wall and pulling out handcuffs.

"You're not my son if you choose this... lifestyle!" McKenna yelled over his shoulder, his words dripping with poison.

Neil was reading him his rights for assaulting an officer, then he grabbed McKenna by the shirt and marched him out of the room. "My office," he ordered everyone.

Ainsley was solid, Clarke right at his side, and the

bravery he'd shown in standing up to his dad was amazing, but I couldn't help but worry about the fallout from this confrontation.

As the door swung shut behind McKenna, leaving dead silence in its wake, the principal turned to us with compassion in every inch of her. Ainsley and Clarke were shaken, still near the door, their hands clasped tightly together.

"We *will* need to take this to the sheriff's office, boys. You too, Mr. Sheridan."

Would this be the last straw? Was Ainsley going to go home? Would McKenna end up sending his son to some kind of conversion camp? Would he put Ainsley's life in danger? I slumped back into my wheelchair, all my energy gone, the agony in my knee too much to ignore, and I wiped blood from my face, then gripped the arms, my knuckles white.

The principal leaned forward, her gaze first settling on Ainsley and Clarke. "Before we go, I want you both to know that you have my full support," she began, her voice steady and sincere. She shot me a glance full of calm. "It takes a great deal of courage to speak your truth, especially in the face of such… vehement opposition. Please know that this school is a place where you should always feel safe and accepted, no matter who you love. Now, Clarke, please call your parents, and Ainsley—"

"No. I don't have anyone here."

I spoke up then. "Your aunt, the one out of state, do you have her number?"

Ainsley nodded. "I'll call her." He pulled his cell from his backpack, but then, stared at the screen."

"I'll do it," Clarke murmured, pressing buttons, then talking in low tones to whoever answered.

"Mr. Sheridan?" Evie asked, tearing my attention from Clarke and Ainsley. "Chris? Are you okay?" I nodded. "We'll need a medic to check you out, but I hope you'll be able to accompany Ainsley and Clarke to the sheriff's office. I want it on record that I'm thankful you were here."

"Okay." I nodded, feeling a mix of relief and apprehension. The principal's support was reassuring, but I knew the road ahead would be challenging if this was going to be an open battle.

I really wanted to be there for everyone, to make things right, but also…

… I needed a hug.

Only, I couldn't take this to Noah—that wasn't fair—he didn't deserve the mess that was me getting riled up and ranting at the world.

When we were done with the sheriff, answering questions, it was already six, and dark, and I was done with the evening. I wanted to head over to Noah, but my heart hurt; although, I smiled when I saw Noah had sent me a quick message about Ainsley.

***Chris:*** *It's all reported. Ainsley is safe. Tell Fox he did well.*

***Noah:*** *Thank you for letting me know. I will tell him. Are you coming here?*

I wanted to, so badly, but I couldn't. I was too raw, and the pain was too much.

***Chris:*** *Bad day, early night.*

***Noah:*** *Do you want to talk?*

No. I didn't. Or rather, I couldn't.

***Chris:*** *It's okay x*

***Noah:*** *Do you need anything? I have so many desserts, I need to feed someone.*

I almost caved.

*Almost.*

***Chris:*** *I'm not fit company. TTYT (smiley face emoji)*

I didn't feel as happy as the emoji suggested, but that was the thing about messaging—no one knew the truth.

***Noah:*** *Here if you need me x*

***Chris:*** *Thank you x*

I wish I *was* going home to him. I wish my fucking knee didn't hurt so bad; or my back, which had taken the brunt of the force; or my face, which ached like a mother.

I didn't sleep well, so I did the only thing that felt right. As dawn broke, I called the school to say I'd be in late in, which Evie approved without hesitation. Then I headed up to the ranch to be with the horses, and maybe get a ride in. Thank fuck, Levi was there, and he must have seen something in me and just assumed I'd want to get out on horseback.

Maybe it was the shiner.

"Your face," he murmured.

"Should have seen the other guy."

"Do you need help to hide a body?" he joked.

"Nah, it's all good."

And that was all we spoke about until we were twenty minutes in, high on the land above the ranch, watching the world come to life. I'd finally emptied my head and pushed down trying to understand the hatred in other people when Levi cleared his throat.

"We're friends, right?" Levi blurted.

"Of course." I assumed he was going to ask me about my face. I liked Levi. And I was quite fond of his pink-haired millionaire fiancé, who was driving everyone crazy organizing his and Levi's upcoming wedding, which I seemed to recall was at the end of June. Not that Levi talked about the wedding, but god, he loved Quinn, and the love was everything to them both, as if it consumed them.

It was beautiful to see.

Levi's blue merle collie, Sky, ran along the fence, chasing god knows what, but other than the odd bark when Sky caught a scent, today had been a silent ride, comfortable, the landscape rolling by as we headed away from the ranch onto open Lennox land, inhaling the crisp, icy air and feeling very much alive.

Levi's quietness was very normal, but today, I saw him glancing at me more often, wrestling with thoughts, trying to find the right words. Finally, he broke the silence, his voice tinged with a hint of urgency. "I'm getting married," he blurted.

*Wait—this wasn't about my face?*

"Yes, you are." I laughed, trying to take the edge off the panic I could see in him. He was one of the most laid-back people I'd ever met, quiet, stoic. a cowboy in every way, but maybe even he was being infected with Quinn's wedding madness.

"No, you don't understand. I don't know how to write vows with all the meaning and the long words and poems. You're good with words, an English teacher and all. Could you help me out? As a friend, I mean?"

His request caught me off guard, but in a good way.

I smiled, warmed by the trust he was placing in me. "Of course I can," I replied, as we aimed left and up over the back fields. He didn't really want me to help him write his vows, he just needed me to go into teacher mode and tease out the information he already knew. "What kinds of things do you want to say?"

He sighed with so much pent-up emotion. "That's it, I don't know. I'll be standing there in front of people, and I'll just lose my shit, and that will be it. Quinn will hate me, he'll cry, I'll probably cry, the wedding will end, and I'll have to leave the state, or hell, move to Mexico."

I drew Beans to a stop, and Levi copied. "Well, that spiraled fast."

"Shit," Levi said again.

"What brought this on?"

He leaned on the pommel, patting Blake. "Quinn has this notebook that he sketches in, and I'm allowed to look." He stared at me; his eyes wide. "I promise, he says it's okay. It's not private or anything."

"Of course."

"He left this paper in with an entire essay, about me, about us, about the future, and I only read a little before he took it off me, but shit, he has all the pretty words, and I have nothing in my head, but horses and dogs." Sky took that moment to roll on her back in the snow, yelping and whining before belting off to follow another scent, and in general, having the best day of her doggie-life, which at least made Levi smile.

"Okay, so tell me what you want to say."

"That's the point, I don't know."

We clicked for the horses to move on, a leisurely pace that meant we could talk.

"Do you love Quinn?"

"Of course," he said, and threw me a frown. "Doesn't mean I can put it into words, then read it out it in front of people."

"So, what do you love about Quinn?"

We were quiet for a while, and I gave Levi space to talk.

"Everything."

"Okay… so what did you think when you first saw him?"

"His hair," he began, in a soft voice. "He was bright as sunshine, but pink, his hair I mean."

"Okay, as bright as sunshine. Got it. And now?

"He fits just right in my arms, when we hug, and when I'm holding him, my heart just seems to soar, like he's half of me. Like he's the best half of me. Like he makes my world better. He smiles at me for no reason, but he's not laughing at me, he's just happy to be in my space, and I'm happy back. He'd do anything for me, and I'd do anything back, and he doesn't care if I stink of horses; he just holds me, and loves me and…" He drifted off then, and we continued our ride.

He didn't really need me. He already knew what he wanted to say.

"Can you tell him everything that happened to you in a day, good or bad, in any kind of words, big or small?"

"Yeah."

"And does he ever think what you're saying is wrong? Or stupid?"

That earned me a sharp glance. "Of course not; he wouldn't do that. He loves me as I am." The frown stayed for a moment, and then, as he realized what he'd said, his expression softened. "Oh," he whispered.

"Yep, all you need to do is tell him how you feel in words that make it clear and that mean something to you."

And right on the heels of Levi's epiphany came one of my own.

After the day I'd had, after the fear and the tightness in my chest, wasn't that what I should do with Noah?

# Chapter Twenty-Six

## Noah

THE DINER WAS UNUSUALLY BUSY, A STEADY HUM OF conversation filling the air. It seemed as if the whole town had converged here, probably because of the diner's proximity to the sheriff's office.

The landline rang as I picked up two new orders, and with the receiver pressed between my ear and shoulder, I hustled into the kitchen.

"Lily's Diner, Noah speaking, can I help?"

Silence.

"Hello?" I asked, but then, the call ended.

That was the fourth call in as many days, and I knew it was probably kids, but it always seemed to happen when I was juggling food or plates. There was no number I could see, probably blocked, but it was annoying. Maybe I should think of changing the number.

As I moved from table to table, taking orders and serving food, Merle working the coffee machine and taking orders at the counter, I couldn't help but overhear snippets of conversation. Most of it revolved around Ainsley and his situation. It was the kind of gossip that thrives in small towns, where everyone knows everyone else's business, or at least thinks they do.

I should have been pleased about the business, the diner was buzzing, and the register was ringing more than usual. But the reason behind it left a bitter taste in my mouth. It felt wrong to benefit from Ainsley's misfortune, from the town's eagerness to dissect his pain.

I paused for a moment, leaning against the counter, watching the room. The chatter, the clinking of cutlery, the occasional laughter—it all seemed out of place.

"How can people just sit there, casually discussing a young boy's trauma as if it were just another piece of daily news?" Merle muttered as he filled an order for soup and sandwiches—today's special was roasted butternut squash and apple, served alongside grilled cheese with caramelized onion.

I remembered the look on Fox's face when he'd come in, the worry and concern for his friend. It was a stark contrast to the almost morbid curiosity filling the diner now. I felt a surge of protectiveness, not only for Fox, but for Ainsley, too. They were kids, caught up in situations they shouldn't have to deal with.

"Small towns," I murmured, but hadn't the same thing happened with me and Briggs? People turning a blind eye, then reveling in the fallout and the gossip?

Taking a deep breath, I forced myself to focus on the tasks at hand. I continued serving, refilling coffee cups, and offering polite smiles. But inside, I was struggling with a mix of emotions—frustration at the gossip, concern for Ainsley, and a growing sense of responsibility to protect these kids from the rumor mill.

The phone rang again, and this time, I at least had my hands free.

"Lily's Diner, Noah speaking. How can I help?"

Silence again, and then, as I was going to disconnect myself before the caller did, a familiar voice—the pastor.

"This is all your fault. Flags in the window are just the start of the road to eternal damnation!" His voice was slurred. Was the man drunk? I was about done with the call drops, and if this asshole thought he was going to be getting up in my face and disapproving of me, then fuck him.

Fuck, this pastor was obsessed, and I interrupted his speech.

"Sir, we believe in spreading love and acceptance here, just like your Jesus did. If you find a problem with that, maybe you're on the wrong side of the rainbow." Then I hung up on his blustering and felt Merle's hand on my shoulder.

"Okay, boss?"

I bit back the curse I wanted to let loose, aware that the sounds in the diner had stopped. I turned to see everyone in there facing me, and I waited for them to say something, or leave, and then, one guy started a slow clap, which was taken up by everyone.

At least I'd gotten that right.

The day dragged on, each hour punctuated by the sound of the door chime as more customers came in, drawn by the lure of fresh gossip, both Merle and I working like mad to keep the grill turning out the best food, and the coffee and desserts flowing.

And when the phone started ringing, Merle took the call. We couldn't turn away a potential order, but his eyes widened after he'd given his name. He said nothing, only returned the handset to the base.

"Well shit," he muttered.

"What?"

"Some guy wanted to know what the fuck I was doing here, and said he'd make sure I never got near you," he muttered.

"I guess the good pastor thinks I'm going to taint your immortal soul with my rainbow gay."

He chuckled at that. "I think we ignore the phone for the rest of the day."

"I can get behind that."

As the diner began to empty, I felt a sense of relief. Not only because the phone didn't ring again, but because it had been a profitable day, despite it coming at a cost I wasn't comfortable with. I hoped for quieter days ahead, days when the diner would be filled with the regular, mundane chatter of everyday life, not the buzz that was gossip.

Merle had just left when Fox came in from school, dumped his backpack on the counter, which I picked up out of habit to hide away, then sighed. Seems as if, maybe, his day was as shit as mine.

"Ainsley wasn't at school today," he mumbled, staring at the tabletop. "And I tried to make Clarke smile, but he's just really worried that Ainsley will move away…"

I reached across, placing my hand over his. “Everything will be okay.”

“Will it?” He sighed again, a deep, world-weary sound that seemed too heavy for someone his age. “I wish I could do something.”

“You’re being a friend to Clarke, so you’re doing more than you know,” I reassured him, squeezing his hand.

“I have homework, but I’m soooo hungry, Dad.”

I made him a drink and snack—albeit not quite as sugar filled as yesterday’s, and he settled down to homework in the back booth, but every so often, he would stop and stare into the distance.

I wish I could make things better for him.

At five, as I was flipping the sign to *Closed*, Chris arrived, and without hesitation, he limped into my arms for a hug, which I returned with all the reassurance I could give him. His eye looked swollen, and I cradled his face to examine it.

“What happened?”

“I got in between Pastor McKenna and Ainsley yesterday,” he said and leaned into me as if he couldn’t hold himself up. “It’s so good to see you,” he murmured.

“For real? Shit.” I kissed the bruise by his eye as if I could make it better. He made it sound as if it were nothing, but protecting Ainsley and getting hit wasn’t nothing. “Pastor Asshole called me this morning and gave me a speech about fornication and fuck knows what.”

“I heard someone posted bail for him.” Chris was frustrated. “But Ainsley’s safe, so now he’s straight on you, for real?”

“Yep, he sounded drunk.”

"I wouldn't be surprised."

"Then he told Merle not to get near me."

"Wait—he was threatening you?" Chris asked.

"Just words, nothing Merle and I can't handle." I locked the door behind him and drew down the last blind. "I missed you last night."

"I missed you, too."

"Was today another bad day? Fox mentioned Ainsley wasn't in school."

Chris ran a hand through his hair, a sign of his unease. "Yeah, it's been a tough day. Ainsley's situation… it's gotten around town. And you know how stories get exaggerated."

I knew all too well the speed at which rumors traveled in small towns, and I'd seen it in here today.

"Is Ainsley going to be okay?" Fox asked as soon as we headed to the back of the diner. "Is he coming back to school?"

Chris hesitated, probably wondering what facts he could share amidst the flurry of rumors.

"I don't know anything about that, Fox."

Fox scrubbed at his eyes. "I should never have told him to talk to you. Now I've messed it all up."

Chris placed a hand on Fox's shoulder and squeezed.

"You did exactly the right thing. Okay?"

"But you weren't in homeroom this morning. Did they fire you for being on Ainsley's side?"

I frowned at Chris, who met my gaze, then glanced back at Fox. "I was late in this morning, then I took the rest of the day for admin."

"Not fired?" Fox asked, a little desperately.

"No, not at all."

Fox hugged Chris, tight, brief, but it made my heart lighten a little. "Good. Because you're my favorite teacher, and not just because of..." He thumbed at me, and then Chris smiled. "Homework." He left us then, heading back to the booth, stealing more diet soda as he went past.

"Staying for dinner?" I asked Chris, who looked exhausted.

"Yeah, thanks."

"Why are you standing..." I waved at him there with crutches, shaky and pale.

He closed his eyes briefly. "Too exhausted to think about the chair, or walking."

"Sit, sit, I'll get you food. You want coffee?"

He slumped to the nearest table, and I set about taking care of him, starting with soup.

He loved the soup and had a hundred questions. "And what is in the soup, besides squash and..."

"Apples."

"I'm eating apple soup?" He didn't sound turned off by the fact, taking another mouthful. "What else, though?"

"Cinnamon and nutmeg for warmth, but not in-your-face hot, just subtle. Also, there's a splash of coconut milk in it, and of course you can see the toasted pumpkin seeds." At least talking about soup was a safe thing.

Then he took a big bite of the toasted cheese and rolled his eyes. "I love this almost as much as I love you."

Silence.

He placed the toasted cheese on the plate and stared at me, shocked at what he'd said.

I laced my fingers with his free hand. "I love you, too."

I leaned over the table and our lips met in a kiss that felt as if it could stop time. It was one of those perfect moments where everything else faded into the background.

We might have stayed like that, lost in each other, if Chris hadn't suddenly pulled back with a grin. "We should probably eat before the soup gets cold," he said, his eyes still sparkling with mischief.

I laughed, settling back into my seat. The aroma of the grilled cheese and the butternut squash soup filled the air, and I was about to take a bite when Fox's voice startled me.

"You know, Chris, you could stay the night," he said, glancing up from his homework. I turned to him, reminded of his presence, and feeling a pang of guilt for having gotten so caught up in the moment with Chris. "I don't mind, now you're boyfriends and all that."

His suggestion didn't sit right. I was pleased Fox felt comfortable enough with Chris to include him in our little family unit meant more to me than he probably realized. But a part of me wondered, what kind of father was I? To have been so absorbed in my own feelings that I'd forgotten my son was right there. I searched his face for any sign of discomfort or hesitation, but all I saw was a genuine acceptance.

I cleared my throat, trying to find the right words, but Fox shrugged, a small smile on his lips. "I like you for my dad." He was talking to Chris. Then he faced me. "Don't mess it up, Dad, because he makes you happy. "

His words struck a chord in me. He was right. Chris made me happy, happier than I had been in a long time.

And Fox's approval, and simple acceptance of my relationship with Chris meant the world to me. Still, it didn't feel right, not yet.

"Maybe not tonight," I murmured, and Chris squeezed my hand. "Another night?"

Fox nodded, then smirked. "Best I get some more sleepovers at Clarke's house, then." Chris snorted into his soup, and I stared up at Fox and really tried for innocence. Fox pointed a finger gun at me. "Nothing stealthy about you kissing your *boyfriend* in front of me, Dad," he said with a smile, his approval of me and Chris clear.

Fox headed upstairs for his hour of gaming.

"It's good that he's cool with us," Chris said. "Something about kids today, the good ones, I mean. They see nothing wrong with two guys kissing."

"My family wasn't very supportive when I came out," I admitted. "Maybe that's why I ended up with Briggs. I felt isolated in who I was, like I had nowhere else to turn to help understand what a genuine relationship should be like."

Chris listened; his eyes filled with empathy. "I was luckier," he said. "When I realized I was bi, my family were there for me." I envied him that, the familial support I'd craved. "Owning that part of me wasn't something I saw coming, you know?" Chris said, his gaze distant as he reminisced. "I'd always known I liked men, but I never acted on it. I just followed the path I was given, y'know? I was a jock, going to the big leagues, dated the homecoming queen and everything." He waggled his eyebrows. "Then, after the accident, like way after, when my head was less messed up, I let myself fall for someone new and I met Marcus." A small smile played on his lips—Marcus must be a fond memory. "He was my physical therapist after the accident. Something about him… well we had a thing, and I knew I was bisexual."

I couldn't help but feel a pang of jealousy, even though I knew it was irrational. "Marcus, huh?" I teased, trying to keep the atmosphere light.

"Long gone. He moved to the east coast, and we weren't this big thing where I pined for him, just missed him a little, but this was ten years ago now."

"I guess I should thank him for helping you figure things out."

Chris chuckled, picking up on my teasing tone. "Yeah, he played a big part in my long-ass journey up to finding and falling in love with you. So, I owe him a lot."

I smiled, my initial twinge of jealousy fading away. "Well, if he ever comes back to Whisper Ridge and into the diner, I'll have to offer him a free meal. For opening your eyes."

Chris laughed, the sound filling the quiet space between us. "I'm sure he'd appreciate that."

# Chapter Twenty-Seven

## Chris

I MIGHT NOT HAVE STAYED THE NIGHT, BECAUSE I respected Noah and Fox, but something had shifted between me and Noah today. Maybe it had something to do with Fox's quiet acceptance, or the way Noah had taken care of me with the soup, or hell, it could just be the wound-up parts of me easing, but a week later, with the *good* Pastor remanded and refused bail—gotta love a local judge—my next visit to my therapist was less angsty about the past, and more focused on pulling together the threads of a life I really wanted. I started by explaining about McKenna and how I'd felt when he'd stormed in and threatened me and his own son.

"I stood up to him, put myself between him and the kids, and I know, if it had gone on, maybe, he would have gotten past me…" I paused and threw her a rueful smile. "I *know* he would have gotten past me, but I delayed him reaching his son, and it felt good."

"Empowering?"

I nodded because that was a word I'd never thought would apply to me, but yeah, that was how I felt. "I understand there will always be things I can't do, but I know that no matter how capable I feel, or don't feel, I'm me." I scratched my knee. "Christ, did that make any sense at all?"

"Of course."

"And I'm okay. Better than okay."

Susan smiled then. "You're a survivor, Chris, and that's something to be proud of."

"I think maybe I don't need another appointment," I said with caution because I'd become used to PTs and counselors, and anyone else around me, warning me I still had a long way to go.

"I agree." She smiled. Had I heard right? "Stay present, be aware of what you're feeling, and if your thoughts spiral, and you feel you need to talk, then you know what to do and where I am."

"Thank you." I let the brakes off the chair—I was far too sore to stand or use crutches, although Daniel had given me his best medical opinion by telling me to take my damn meds and suck it up, until the muscles above my stump and around my other knee healed. He'd known that I needed the straight talk, but did I really need the tussle we'd had afterward? My siblings were all assholes. Well, apart from Michelle. Oh, and Mark. So yeah, mostly just Daniel and Scott then.

"Goodbye, Chris."

I wheeled out of there, headed to the car, and gave the biggest grin when Daniel gave me a stupid thumbs up.

He'd had to drive me over because… pain… and he'd teased and tormented me the entire way about buying a Superman cape for my new heroic status in town. Whatever.

"Head examined, okay?" he asked as he helped me into the car.

"Fuck you," I fake-snarled.

"That's my husband's job," he said.

I made a show of covering my ears. "I do not want to hear about you and Micah going at it."

"Are you sure? It's kind of hot being happy with my man." He smiled and narrowly avoided my swipe at his head.

The drive with Daniel was filled with the comfortable silence only shared by siblings who'd grown up together. It left me plenty of time to think about Noah and Fox, and wondering what kind of life we could all have together if we tried.

"Talking of that…" Daniel pulled me out of my daydreams of how we might convert their small apartment for me, or whether it was more practical for them to live at my place if things went on as they'd started.

"Talking of what?"

"Me and Micah being happy," Daniel reminded me.

"What about it?"

"You and Noah?" That was a question full of meaning and hidden agendas, and I was sure I'd be getting a lecture about safe sex if I let him. Big brothers suck, big brothers who are also doctors suck even worse.

"We're good. Better than good. I'm um…" I stumbled

over the words, struggling to explain what I felt. How did I explain that Noah and Fox filled a void in my life I hadn't even known existed? That they'd become an integral part of my world in a way I never expected?

"You fell in love," Daniel finished for me, his voice soft, but certain.

I nodded, even though he was focused on driving, his eyes on the road ahead of us. "Yeah, I did," I admitted, the words feeling so right.

"That's the best news," he said, his voice all kinds of warm and reassuring. Reaching over, he patted my knee in a gesture that was both comforting and congratulatory. "Welcome to the club."

I chuckled, a mix of relief and happiness bubbling up inside me. It felt good to have his support, to know that he understood and was happy for me.

"It's new, you know? And a bit scary," I confessed, watching the scenery pass by. "But it feels right."

Daniel glanced at me, a smile tugging at the corner of his lips. "Love usually is. Scary, I mean. But it's also the best thing you'll ever experience."

I thought about Chris and the quiet comfort and the sense of belonging I felt with him. "Yeah, it *is* the best thing. And I'm just… really happy."

As we drove on, the conversation drifted to other topics, but a sense of contentment settled over me. In sharing this part of my life with Daniel, and him not laughing me out of the car, it was like a final piece falling into place. I was where I was supposed to be, with people who mattered to me more than I could have ever imagined. For the first time in a long time, I was in love, and it was the best feeling in the goddamned world.

Daniel sailed right past my house, and I didn't argue when he parked outside the diner.

"Lunch?" he asked, checking his watch. "I have thirty."

"My treat. As a thank you for taking me to get my head fixed."

He shot me a smile as if it meant nothing, but it meant *everything*. Then, I stopped him with a hand on his arm, and he faced me. "Are you okay?" he asked, searching my face for a reason I'd stopped him from getting out of the car.

"Thank you for finding me that day in the bathroom."

The words fell heavy into the quiet car, and Daniel turned in his seat to face me, then reached out and grasped my hand. "Thank you for making me see the real Micah, so I could fall back in love with him."

We hugged awkwardly, and when we separated, I gave him a stern look. "And we never talk of this moment again."

He held up his little finger, which I curled mine against. "Pinkie swear."

---

AFTER DANIEL and I finished our burgers, he had to go to the clinic, so he headed off, and when Noah caught me yawning, he suggested I head upstairs to relax on their sofa and refused to take no for an answer. I just wished that last week's confrontation hadn't wrecked my back so much or made my other knee twist because I needed help on the tight staircase, but Noah was right there, supporting me as I navigated the steps and reminding me that my current aches, incurred while helping Ainsley, warranted some special treatment.

Also, that he enjoyed looking after me, and asked if I wanted a bowl of ice cream.

Of course, I did.

I let him fuss, settling me on the sofa, helping me remove my prosthetic and placing it to the side. Then, with a bowl of chocolate ice cream, I was left alone with my thoughts, the quiet hum of the apartment, and the faint noise from the diner below. The combination of food, talking with Susan, taking low-grade pain medication, and snuggling up with a cozy blanket, soon lulled me into a snooze.

Only to be woken by Fox talking to me. I blinked up at him, recognizing a Scrabble board in one hand and a plate of snacks in the other. "We're doing Scrabble; are you staying tonight?" he asked with a hopeful glint in his eyes.

Before I could answer, Noah walked in, confirming with a smile. "Yeah, he's staying." He, then, leaned over and kissed me, a gesture so full of affection it made my heart swell.

As we gathered around the small kitchen table for Scrabble, my first blind pick of tiles included five vowels and two Ps that fit nowhere, but with the Scrabble tiles scattered in front of me, it didn't matter that words weren't happening and I was going to lose, because everything felt right. It might well be a simple Saturday night, but there was something special happening here.

Fox clutched his tiles, his gaze darting between the

board and his letters. "My turn!" he declared, placing his tiles on the board with a flourish and riffing off my appallingly bad PEA. "Voila—Yeet and Peat!"

Noah raised an eyebrow, trying to stifle a laugh. "'Yeet'? Is that even an actual word?"

"I think there's some cheating going on here," I teased.

"I'm not cheating," Fox said. "When you 'yeet' something, it's like throwing something hard. It's totally a word, Dad. A young word for young people."

I snorted a laugh, then leaned back in my chair, grinning. "I think we're getting old, Noah. We can't keep up with this cool, hip lingo."

"It's a word! I promise it is, Dad!"

Noah pretended to be deep in thought, stroking his chin. "Hmm, 'yeet' huh? Well, I'll let it pass this time. But only because you're so convincing."

Fox beamed, pleased with himself. "You just wait. I've got more where that came from."

The game continued, filled with laughter and lighthearted teasing. Now and then, Fox would come up with some more trendy words, each one causing more amusement. At each one, Noah and I would exchange whispers; "Do you have any idea what that means?" way too often.

As the evening wore on, the scores didn't matter. What mattered was the sound of laughter filling the room, and the way Fox's eyes lit up when he won.

Sitting there with Noah and Fox, I realized this wasn't just a game of Scrabble; it was a snapshot of a life I wanted with Noah and his son.

"I'm tired." Fox did this huge fake yawn and stared at

his dad. "Night, Dad." He hugged Noah, and then, shocking the hell out of me, he hugged me too. "Night, Chris."

It was around nine, not even late for a Saturday, but by unspoken agreement Noah and I headed to bed, and without my crutches, I had to maneuver into the bedroom on one leg and a lot of balancing against things.

"Not that sexy, eh?" I deadpanned, only to be pushed back onto the mattress where I landed with an *oomph*. Noah shut and locked the door, then straddled me.

"Wanna know something?" he asked as he began to unbutton my shirt.

"Go on."

"You're so freaking sexy."

He leaned down and sucked on my left nipple, then my right, then back to kissing down the scar before heading south. He bypassed my cock, heading further down, and then, reaching for a tub of cream on the side table, he picked it up and showed it to me.

"Daniel said this works," he whispered. "Can you show me how I help with your knee?"

I blinked as he leaned down to rub my nose with his. "You want to know how to handle Mr. Stumpy?" I deadpanned.

"Yeah."

So, I showed him, and his massage turned into more, and we tested how quiet we could be as he gave me the most intense blowjob I'd ever experienced, and again, when we traded positions, I showed him exactly how much I loved sucking him right back.

"I love you," he said into lazy kisses.

"I love you," I whispered back, and then, sated and smiling, we crawled under the covers. He turned away from me, then shuffled back so he was the little spoon.

Wrapped in each other's arms, we slept.

And Saturday turned into Sunday, and I stayed over again.

# Chapter Twenty-Eight

## Noah

THE DINER BUZZED WITH THE EARLY CHATTER OF PATRONS; the air filled with the aroma of fresh-brewed coffee and sizzling bacon. I stood behind the counter, lost in thought. After two nights of Chris sleeping in my bed, I couldn't help but worry about how practical it was for him to move in to our place when he had a perfectly fine house that was most likely set up for his needs. Maybe without rickety stairs and the tiniest shower known to man.

Not that I'd seen his place yet, but he assured me his shower was large enough for two, and next time Fox went for a sleepover, I'd be making a point of visiting and staying over.

Staying over was amazing.

Sex with Chris was amazing.

Him letting me massage his stump, then massage the rest of him, then the blowjobs… yeah…

"Earth to Dad?"

I blinked at Fox, who grinned at me, and I snapped back into Dad mode. "Lunch," I said, and passed him the box, and he stared at me. "What?"

"Nothing." He was smirking now, and I shooed him out of the diner to the bus.

I slipped back into diner mode and tried not to think too much about Chris.

I was behind the counter, wiping down the espresso machine with a sense of contentment that had become a rarity in my life, prepping for the morning rush, tuned into the fact it was seven-thirty, and Chris would be here any time. He'd left at six, going back to his own place to get ready for school, saying he was more than capable of wheeling himself to his house and daring me to argue. I expected him back again, as he had this routine of stopping by for his usual order—a strong black coffee, no sugar—before heading off to his day at school. Almost to the second, when I looked up, I saw Chris crutching in, saying hello to a few of my breakfast regulars, and making his way over to me.

As he approached the counter, there was a soft smile on his face, one that never failed to set my heart racing. He greeted me with a warmth in his eyes, and without a word, he leaned over the counter, and I met him halfway, and he kissed me. It was a simple gesture, yet it held so much weight because it was our hello, a moment stolen from the rest of the day before it began.

"You made it home, then." I nodded at his smart schoolteacher pants and shirt with a purple tie.

"Did you doubt me?"

"Nope." I handed him his coffee in the to-go cup, and he took a quick sip, appreciating the taste, then kissed me goodbye. It was a sweet, lingering kiss, and even though I wanted it to continue, it was going to have to be enough to set me up for the day. He kissed me in full view of anyone who was in the diner. In those moments, I wasn't a secret to be kept; I wasn't something to be hidden away because I didn't fit some sports agent's narrative. Chris made me feel I was precious, as though I was worth being seen.

As he pulled away, there was this sense of everything being right. "Love you."

"Love you, back," I said.

"Bye." He exchanged fist bumps with Levi, whom I hadn't seen in a few days and who came in with purpose. Chris gave me a last smile, and with a casual wave, he was out of the door, off to face the day, while Levi made his way over and took a stool.

"Pancakes?" I asked—going from the fact Levi hadn't deviated from his favorite on the four or five occasions he'd been in here. "Extra-crispy bacon? Black coffee?"

"Yes, please," he said and wriggled on the stool to get comfortable. "Quinn tried to make me eat tofu this morning. Tofu, for fuck's sake." He shuddered, and we exchanged smiles. "All that hippy-dippy health shit will end up killing me. Give me pancakes, bacon, and real syrup every day."

I passed him his coffee before heading out the back. "You think Quinn might have a point?"

"It's like you want to talk yourself out of a sale!" He was flabbergasted by my suggestion.

I smirked. "Never."

I headed into the kitchen—the only outstanding order being his, and Merle was working the coffee machine—and I made the fluffiest of pancakes, crisped the bacon to perfection, and poured the maple syrup into a small jug.

"Here you go," I said, and placed everything in front of Levi—if I could bottle his happy expression and sell it, I'd be a millionaire.

"I'm heading over to Abby's with the pastries," Merle announced, "then the wholesalers, you want to add anything to the list?"

I shook my head. "It's all good."

Merle headed out, but a few moments after he left, the door opened again, the bell jangling, drawing my attention, Levi's, and that of a few regulars. I turned, expecting to see Merle heading back in with another question, or to say he'd forgotten something, but my gaze landed on a figure I thought I'd left behind.

Briggs.

My ex-husband was here, posturing just inside the doorway, tall, blond hair, and his piercing gaze that had once captivated me, was fixed right on me. Clad in figure-hugging jeans and his baseball jersey, emblazoned with his number, and no coat—despite the cold—he was impossible to miss. He'd made the grand entrance he was used to. It was obvious he was waiting for the diner to quieten as the great Briggs Lewiston arrived to grace us all with his presence.

It warmed me that not a single person was bothered or interested in his appearance, with everyone turning away.

"Hey, Cal," he drawled, loud enough for people to hear,

sauntering over to the counter with a confidence bordering on arrogance. His tone might have been casual, but I knew him well enough to see the hint of caution in his expression.

"Noah," I said, in a careful tone.

"You'll always be Cal to me, sweetheart."

*Don't make a scene. Act cool. Remind him about the restraining order.*

I struggled to find my voice at first, and he smirked, and any hesitation in him vanished, and his familiar confidence returned in spades as he tipped his chin and leaned on my counter.

"You can't be here," I said under my breath.

"But here I am," he said, loud enough for others to hear.

*Fuck this. He wants an audience, then he'll get one.* "What do you want?" I managed, my tone sharp enough to still the conversation in the diner, and for the person sitting nearest to us, Levi, to take note of what was going on.

Briggs's gaze didn't waver. "Thought I'd visit Fox."

"It's a school day," I reminded him, "and you're violating the order to stay away from both of us."

He fake-pouted—tried to look contrite. "But I've changed, Cal. I've realized what I lost, so I'm here for you. And for Fox, of course." A smirk undermined the sincerity in his voice, and the rehearsed humility that didn't quite mask the arrogance I knew too well. I'd always been the type of person to cling to the idea of second chances, in redemption, but with Chris's kiss still lingering on my lips, and the kind of man I'd fallen in love with for real, I couldn't bring myself to even try to understand Briggs.

Particularly, when all I felt was anger, resentment, and—*fuck*—a healthy dash of fear. The phantom bruises on my wrists and stomach ached with the remembered pain.

Briggs leered at me, all grin, and white teeth, but his smile didn't quite reach his eyes. "I'm also here to see *you*, Cal," he repeated, a hint of something insincere lurking beneath his words that only I would ever understand.

"Noah," I snapped again, and I felt strong.

"Aww, baby, why change your name?" Then he nodded. "Hiding. I see. But Cal is such a pretty name." He was still loud, and he wouldn't leave. I should just call Neil now, get him to act on the restraining order, but maybe I could deal with this myself. I'm stronger now.

*Loving Chris has made me stronger.*

I lowered my voice, casting a glance at Levi, who was pretending to ignore the conversation, but sitting far too close not to hear everything, studying the menu as if it had changed overnight, and as if he hadn't already eaten half his pancakes. He might be waiting to see what was going on, then maybe he'd tell the town. He was Chris's friend, but maybe I wasn't ready for him to go running to Chris, and he was too damn close.

"Go away, Briggs."

"Just give me one minute, and I'm gone," he said. "I have so much to apologize for."

"You're making a scene," I warned—aware that everyone could hear him.

"I don't mean to." He clutched his chest. "You broke my heart."

Fuck this shit. Against my better judgement, I decided to talk to Briggs alone. I pulled out my cell and pressed buttons. "I'm recording this for the restraining order, Briggs."

He waved at my cell.

Waved like he was on camera.

"In here!" I demanded, catching Levi's concerned gaze, and went into the small hall, and Briggs, complete with oily grin, followed me.

"I've missed you." He reached for me as soon as the door blocked us from the diner, and I stepped back.

He pouted again, all kinds of playful, but there was a hard edge to his expression that, maybe, only I would ever see. "You know, everything was a misunderstanding. You were angry, and I was drunk and—"

"You hit me, you punched me in the stomach, and you threw me against a wall. You broke my wrist—"

He moved so fast that I didn't have a chance to react, placing a hand on the wall next to me, caging me between the stairs and the door to the diner. "It was once, and you provoked me." He laughed, and there it was, that dangerous hate. "What did you expect when you told me you were taking my son from me, threatening to go to the cops about what you *thought* was happening. How did you think I was going to react when my husband was betraying me?" He spoke as if this was funny, as if all of what had happened was just some huge cosmic joke.

Fuck, he was delusional if he thought any of his downfall was my fault.

I glanced down at my cell. "Okay, your minute is up. I'm calling 911."

He snapped in a moment, gripped my hand—hard—and levered the phone from me, then glanced at the screen, stopping the recording as he held me back, deleting what I'd recorded, then frowning at the photo of me, Fox, and Chris playing Scrabble, which I was using as my background.

"My boy," he said, and I think he was trying for a fond parent tone. "Who's this guy with you? Is this that Merle guy? Is he fucking you? I told him to stay away. You're mine."

"You did what?"

"Merle! He answered your phone as if he was a lover."

"Merle works here." I tried to get the phone back, but he used his height to hold it high, the fire of temper in his dark eyes. "Give me back my phone," I said, not letting any of the fear I was feeling filter into my demand. He fed on my fear, and it was all too easy to be scared of someone as fast and nasty as Briggs.

"You need to change that photo, stat. I don't like it, and it should be me there, not some random guy who wouldn't look so pretty after someone takes a baseball bat to his head."

I froze, panicked, and fear gripped me, but I took a deep breath, steadying my resolve. "You can't just walk back into my life and expect me not to have moved on."

His smile faltered, a crack in his confident facade. "That's bullshit—"

"Fox is happy here with me, can't you accept that?"

"I'm Fox's real father. He's not even really *your* son. He's mine to take if I want—"

The door from the diner opened, Levi stepping through, acting as if he was surprised to see us standing there. I was pressed against the wall, Briggs brandishing my phone above my head.

Levi smiled as if butter wouldn't melt. "Sorry," he apologized, blinking, all innocent. "I'm looking for the bathrooms."

Briggs changed in an instant, the mask of civility falling so fast that a person could blink and miss it. "Think you're going the wrong way, bud." He smiled, handing me back my phone, and patting my shoulder. "Nice to see you, Cal, sorry… *Noah*." He confronted Levi, who confronted him right back, then stepped to one side to allow Briggs through. As soon as the door shut on my ex's ass, I slid to the bottom step, bending at the waist, all my bravery sliding away in an instant.

"Noah?" Levi was in a crouch in front of me. "Noah?"

I stared at him. The adrenaline that seeing Briggs had created was like acid inside me, burning its way through all of my peace.

Levi rested a hand on my knee. "Come on, Noah, are you with me?"

I blinked at him. "Uh huh."

The door opened again, and fear knifed through me, but it was Neil, in his sheriff's uniform, another man lurking behind him. Connor? What was scary-ninja Connor doing here? The sheriff took in the spectacle we had going on before placing a hand on Levi's shoulder. "Levi?"

"Some guy came in, called him Cal, took his phone. I didn't like it."

"You didn't need to call the sheriff," I murmured, or at least I think I did—everything was a blur—and I scrubbed my eyes. All the pain and fear, all the coping strategies I'd worked on, had slipped away in one stupid ass minute of me thinking I could handle even sixty seconds of Briggs.

"I've got it from here," Neil said. "Hey, Noah? You want me to call Chris?"

"Fuck. No!" I said. "He's at school, and I don't want Fox to… oh shit… Fox."

"Okay, how about we take this upstairs and have a chat?" Neil sounded so reasonable, so level-headed, but Connor was still there, arms crossed over his chest, all kinds of badass. Neil glanced back at Connor. "School, Fox Bennett, don't make it obvious," he said, and Connor nodded and left. "Connor will go to the school and keep an eye on Fox, okay?"

I think I said okay, or something like that. Connor was as big as Briggs, but he didn't have the same mean expression.

I'd wanted so badly to avoid *the chat*. I wanted my old life to be somewhere else, in a place I didn't have to visit ever again, but it would always end up following me here. It wasn't as if I was in witness protection; it was no secret where I was—Briggs had known about the inheritance when he tried to force me to sell—but the restraining order was supposed to keep him away, and the deal we made for him to leave us alone in exchange for me not fighting for any money was supposed to mean it was over… I tipped my chin.

Neil was talking. "Levi, can you … can I ask you to close the place or call Merle or something."

"Merle's at the wholesalers," I interjected.

Levi nodded. "I'm on it."

Then, I faced Neil, who was compassion and focus personified. "Let's go upstairs."

It was the climb toward everyone knowing everything, and I was new to town, and I may well be part of Chris's life, but who was everyone going to believe? Briggs, out there, winning people over with stories of his glory days as a pro-ball player, or me, with nothing to my name except a diner.

Just as I was reaching to the community, finding love, he had to come back and take it all from me.

But not Fox. I was Fox's legal guardian.

Fox wanted to stay with me.

He'd chosen me.

When Neil and I reached the living room, I sat on the sofa, and he took the facing seat.

"I have a restraining order against Briggs Lewiston," I began, and Neil nodded.

"I know."

I blinked at him. "You do?"

He gestured at his uniform and smiled. "Also, Connor ran your name when you arrived."

"I know—he came in and told me."

Neil rolled his eyes. "Yeah, well, he's an asshole treading on everyone's toes, messing in things he shouldn't, and giving me all kinds of grief. But he's good, and he has his eyes on Fox, okay?"

"He won't go marching in and pulling Fox out, right? I don't want Fox scared. I should go and—"

"It's okay." This was a blur—everything was white noise. "Connor won't do that. Now, do you want to expand on it for me? Give me an idea of what we're dealing with when it comes to your ex-husband."

"Fox saw him hurt me," I blurted. "But Fox doesn't know he's here..."

"Okay."

I stopped—how much did Neil need to know? Even as sheriff, he didn't have to understand everything about my private life. Right? I'd told Chris about Briggs, but only in loose terms. He'd shared so much of himself with me, but what had I given him back? Not anything of Briggs and what he'd done. I covered my eyes, all the regrets shoving at me and not letting me breathe.

"Briggs shouldn't be near me," was all I said, and Neil nodded. "He threatened..." I stopped—had he actually said he was going to hurt Chris, or was that just his usual crap? "I don't know. It wasn't a threat, but he said Chris wouldn't be so pretty with a baseball bat to his head."

The words fell into silence. Neil's jaw tensed, and he went icy cold.

"Okay then," he said. "We'll leave it at that for now. I'll have an informal chat with this Briggs guy if he's still in town. Run this encounter up his local PD for breaking the restraining order."

"Okay." *Just don't make him angry.*

"But, Noah, what Connor found when he did the background on the guy..."

"I know. Briggs is..." I had to search for the right words. "Arrogant, feels as if the world is against him, or rather he *owns* the world. He knows he shouldn't be near me, but he..." I stared right at Neil. "He acts like none of that will touch him." I massaged my wrist again, and I swear it hurt.

Neil nodded, probably making a mental note that Briggs was an asshole, and that was all I could read of him. His job as sheriff would have him on my side—the restraining order was covering *me*. He was helping *me.*

"You want me to mention it to the school for your son?"

I thought I had more time—I thought he'd leave us alone, that we were done with him. I'd been naïve. Stupid. Wrong.

"I'll talk to Fox first," I half whispered, and then raised my eyes to meet Neil's steady gaze.

*This was my fault. I shouldn't have let Briggs take me out of people's sight. And if that photo hadn't been on my phone... hell... if I wasn't with Chris, then Briggs wouldn't have gotten angry.*

Fuck that noise. I didn't want it in my head.

Neil nodded, then clapped a hand on my shoulder. "I look after this town, and, Noah, you're part of Whisper Ridge, okay? You know where I am."

"I know."

"What about Chris?"

"What about him?" I blinked at Neil, who sighed.

"He'll hear about this. Plus, I don't want to see my friend, someone who likes you a lot, get hurt. He's a good man to have in your corner, and he loves you, anyone can see that. I'm going to ask you, off the record, friend to friend, does Chris know about Briggs?"

Chris and Whisper Ridge were one and the same thing, and he and Neil were friends, and I was messing everything up by keeping secrets. "He knows enough." But not all of it. Not the pain, or the fear, and how could Chris truly love me when he didn't know the real me? I was in some happy land where I was divorced and moving on, but that wasn't enough. I was afraid of Briggs and my past, and he could still hurt me with words. I owed Chris the truth about my ex, about him hitting me, hurting me, threatening me, and to have an honest talk about what that meant for me and Chris.

I reworded it. "He doesn't know enough."

Neil left after a few more questions, and I moved into Fox's room, staring at the mountains, coming up with all this conviction that everything was going to be okay, and I'd not mess this up. Fox had replaced the poster of Briggs in his glory days with a montage of photos of us, his friends, the town, and in pride of place, a blown up shot of him and Molly hugging, and another of the four of them—him, Molly, Clarke, and Ainsley—from the double date.

"I won't let your papa hurt the life you're building, Fox," I promised the montage. "I won't."

# Chapter Twenty-Nine

Chris

My mind was preoccupied with grading papers and planning the next day's lessons as I left school. The teacher's parking lot was almost empty as I approached my car, lost in thought, and that was when Connor appeared beside me like an apparition.

"Jesus, Connor!" I exclaimed, my heart racing. "You scared the hell out of me." Quinn had always said his security guy was stealthy, and now, I believed that.

"Sorry, didn't mean to," he said, his tone serious. "I need to talk to you."

I unlocked my car and tossed in my files, but didn't get up out of my chair, sensing the urgency in his voice and getting this feeling of unease. "What's up? Is everything okay?"

"It's about Noah," he began, glancing around as if to make sure we were alone. "His ex showed up at the cafe today and caused a scene."

A cold knot formed in my stomach. "What happened? Is Noah okay?" I glanced over to where the line of buses usually parked—Fox would have left for the day. "Is he still there? Is Fox okay going back home?"

"Fox will be fine," Connor reassured me, then strangely for him, he seemed at a loss as to what to say and cracked his knuckles. "Neil is there, or at least he was, and he sent me to keep an eye on the school." He shrugged. "I'm heading back, but look, situations like this, they're shit, especially for kids. I'm telling you this for Fox's sake, so when you go home, you'll treat him right with this. Don't go barreling in all protective and asking questions. I'm talking from experience." He was rambling a little, but I got the sense he knew more than he was telling, and I had an uneasy feeling. How bad was it that Briggs had visited his ex and his son? I knew Briggs and Noah were divorced. I'd gotten the impression Briggs was out of their lives and that it had been an unhappy marriage, and of course, it had to be bad for Noah to have sole custody of Fox, but Connor was acting as if Briggs was a threat. Was he a threat?

I levered myself out of the chair and collapsed it, placing it into the converted trunk, then heading back to Connor as I tried to process what he was saying. "Thanks for letting me know, Connor. I appreciate it."

"Just don't tell Neil I gave you a heads up. He hates it when I meddle." Connor shrugged. "He won't like that I'm telling you, but I did a thorough analysis on your man, and his ex, and I didn't like what I read about Briggs Lewiston, so the goddamn sheriff will have to live with it, and I'll deal with the fallout." He frowned as if he had more to say about Briggs, or the sheriff's opinion of him; I didn't know which. "Just thought you should know, for Fox."

I nodded, grateful despite the unconventional way the message was delivered. "Thanks, Connor. I'll check in on them now."

"And if you time it right, you'll get there before Fox gets home—he's one of the last drop-offs, and I'm gonna go follow his bus."

With that, he slipped away as fast as he'd arrived, and I almost missed him rounding the corner. Then, with worry creeping into my thoughts, I headed back to Whisper Ridge and parked behind the diner, foregoing the chair despite the aches from today, I took my crutches just in case, and headed inside. The place was open—Noah behind the counter chatting to Fred who was still axing lyrical about herbs on eggs—and when Noah glanced over to see who'd arrived; he smiled in welcome.

Only I knew him now, and Noah's smile didn't reach his eyes.

I waited for him to tell me about Briggs as we kissed hello, until he'd made me a snack, poured me a coffee, and handled customers. I even waited for him to tell me when he was chatting to me about the Spring Rains Festival and his recipes, and the posters he was putting in the window.

Nothing.

He was all sunshine and smiles to customers, made them food, and made them laugh, but everything he did hid a frightening brittleness I thought might crack him in two. Fox came home about thirty minutes after I'd gotten there, strolling in without a care in the world, stealing cookies, side-hugging his dad, asking if he could have chicken parm for dinner. He didn't notice his dad was close to a meltdown.

Was it just me?

Was it because I'd expected the worst?

This weird normal that Noah was striving for was killing me because he was busy with anything he could find to do, and at seven on the nose, it was me who ushered out a lingering Freddie and shut the door before turning the sign to *closed*. Behind me, I heard a noise, a soft sigh, or a sob. I pulled the blinds and headed back to the counter, but there was no sign of Noah, and I followed the sounds I could hear to the hall and the bottom of the stairs, wincing when I saw Noah on the bottom step. How the fuck was I going to get down there and then get up again?

I didn't give a shit.

I sat next to him and reached for his hand, which he took and held tight. His breathing was harsh, as if every emotion he was trying to keep in check was stealing air from his lungs, and he squeezed my hand so tight it hurt.

Still, I didn't try to remove it.

"Noah?"

He pulled up his knees, taking my hand and kissing it, unpeeling my fingers, and kissing each one in soft but deliberate movements.

"My ex, Briggs, was here today," he murmured.

"Okay."

"There's things you should know." He glanced at me, and I nodded in encouragement, and he swallowed hard. "I have a restraining order against him, and a contract he signed that said he'd stay away in exchange for any money I might have got from him for Fox."

Shit, this sounded bad.

"It all started just after we got married," he began, then stopped. "Before we were married, he was the perfect gentleman—attentive, thoughtful—and I never saw through him. First, it was just words, y'know? Like, Fox was only five when we met, and after the wedding, I became this stay-at-home dad because… well, Briggs was on the road a lot, and I'd taken a sabbatical from the restaurant, working on a cookbook, and teaching sometimes, when I could, at the restaurant I'd worked at. That's where Briggs and I met, when he threw this huge party to celebrate his thirtieth birthday, and I'd been part of the team…" He blinked. "I'm confusing myself. Shit, I'm getting off track."

"That happens," I murmured, "when things are painful."

He sighed. "Fox was into everything, so bright, so intelligent, always pushing the limits; a good kid." He looked at me, his eyes bright with emotion. "Messy, all over the place. We had so much fun, and I taught him all kinds of cooking, and we always cleared up before Briggs got home because that house was like a mausoleum, a temple of neat. He got thrown out of a game, Briggs I mean, and he came home early, found the two of us in the kitchen, flour everywhere, and he kind of lost it with us. Fox didn't understand. I took him upstairs. We cleaned up, and he was happy with his toys, and I went down, and that was the first time Briggs told me I was doing things wrong. He was so calm, explaining how I could be better, what he expected from me," Noah recounted, his voice laced with a pain that was hard to hear. "I changed, lost parts of myself, became more like a shadow."

Listening to him, I felt a growing anger towards this man who had hurt Noah so badly.

"And it got worse?" I asked, dreading the answer.

"Fox was at an academy, attended lots of extracurricular stuff, weeks away, and so I started covering shifts at the restaurant—special events, that kind of thing—but I always made sure I was back for Briggs because, otherwise, he'd get upset, and by this time, I'd become a man who didn't upset Briggs Lewiston." He leaned into me, knocking my shoulder. "Then, the shit hit the fan. It turned out that Briggs had slowly lost his money, allegedly thrown games, lost bets, emptied Fox's college fund, forged my signature on paperwork, took out a second mortgage on the house that he'd signed over fifty percent of to me on our wedding day. Bankrupted us. Got angry. Took it out on me and threatened to take it out on Fox if I didn't back down from harassing him over his actions." He snorted a laugh. "Harassing *him*!"

"You must have hated it there."

"Part of me did, the other part tried to make it work; classic reaction to abuse. Then, he hit me."

I inhaled sharply. "Noah…"

"I don't even recall why, but he hit me here." He pressed a hand to his stomach, then to his chest. "And I threatened to leave, and he said he'd never let me take Fox. He reasoned Fox wasn't my child by blood, and if it went to court, whatever he'd done, I would have to walk away from Fox. I couldn't do it. You get that, right?" He sounded desperate.

"Of course, Jesus, you would never leave a child to get hurt."

Silence, and he stared down at our joined hands. "I stayed, and it carried on. He was arrested for laying bets on his own team, and for verbal abuse in the locker room, but miraculously, everything was paid off to go away, probably by his team because, hell, he was still pitching the wins, right?"

"Yeah." Sports overlooked all kinds of shit while the wins kept coming.

"He came home one afternoon, didn't know Fox was home ill, and he lost his shit and hit me so hard he cracked a rib, and then, he threw me against a wall and broke my wrist, and worse than that…" He scrubbed his eyes, and I couldn't believe there was anything worse than what he was describing. He gasped for breath, his hand on his chest. "Fox saw it all."

"I did," Fox said from the top of the stairs, and we both inhaled, horrified that Fox was even there.

"Fox—"

"It's okay Dad," he interrupted. "I was thirteen, and I saw him hurt Noah, because Noah was protecting me, never leaving because it would mean we'd be apart." He came down the steps, then sat a few steps up. "I love you for that, Dad. I love you protected me. I hate he hit you, but I love you got me away. I love that you love me. I just… thank you."

Noah cleared his throat, tears sliding down his cheeks, and I pulled him close to me.

"He's the best dad, Chris," Fox said, warning me in his way, with so much defiance, as he stared down at me. "And if you hurt him like Papa did…"

The warning was clear. "I would never hurt Noah. I love him, and I love you, and…" *I want us to be a family.*

Fox and I held each other's gaze, and he paused before he replied. "Yeah," he said. "I know."

Silence fell between the three of us, but Noah still hadn't talked about today, and I hated I knew he had things to tell us.

"Why are you telling him this now?" Fox asked, sounding confused.

"Because your papa was here today," Noah admitted.

Fox's reaction was immediate, a mix of protectiveness and fury. "When? Was I upstairs? Is he here now?" Fox asked, poised for action, scanning the diner.

"No, you were at school. He's gone. The sheriff took care of it," Noah assured him.

Fox clambered over us to the hall and went into a crouch in front of his dad, his gaze skimming his dad from head to toe. "Did he hurt you?"

Noah smiled and reached out his other hand to his son. "No. Levi was here, and he scared him off, called Neil, and then, Connor arrived as if he and Neil were an avenging superhero duo, and your papa left." Everything spilled out in an instant, and Fox sat down then, to curl into his dad's arms.

"He's not coming back; I won't let him," I said with strength.

"He won't be back," a loud voice came from the door,

Connor staring down at us, all three of us jumping a freaking mile.

"Stop doing that!" I snapped, then, "How did you get in?" I was sure I'd locked the main door.

"Ninja," Fox whispered.

Connor crossed his arms over his broad chest, dressed all in black and looking bad ass. "Briggs Lewiston won't be breaking the restraining order again," he said, in a tone that sent shivers down my spine.

"Did you kill him?" Fox asked, wide-eyed.

Connor stared at him dead-on, then quirked a smile. "No kid, no killing. But I got a cop buddy of mine to flag him down on the way back to Columbus, to inform him that there would be financial implications and other dire consequences if he messed with you and my town."

"Oohh, *your* town." Fox sounded impressed, staring up at the real-life action hero.

I wasn't sure whether that was a good thing or a bad thing and waited for Noah to take point.

"Thank you," Noah said. I guessed he was okay with Fox being all starry-eyed over hero-Connor for now.

Connor nodded. "No worries. You take care now."

Then, he sauntered out, and I didn't hear the bell at the door. The fuck?

I exchanged a glance with Noah, who mouthed *ninja* and cracked a smile, and I couldn't help the words that spilled out of me.

"We'll talk more, all of us, yeah? Upstairs on the sofa." I wriggled and winced.

Fox nodded and jumped up as if he had a tail made of

springs. "I guess you're both too old to be sitting on the floor."

"Just you wait!" I warned. "As soon as I get up, you're in trouble."

Fox made a show of examining his nails. "I'll have left home by then," he deadpanned, and Noah snorted a laugh, all the tears and the sadness gone for a moment.

"We're gonna be so good together, the three of us," Noah said and held his hand out in front of him. "What do you think, Fox? You, me, and Chris?"

Fox laid his on top. "Yep."

Then, it was just me who needed to say my part, and they both stared at me expectantly. "So good," I said as I slapped my hand on theirs.

And we would be.

I knew it right into my bones, and I certainly felt it in my heart.

# Epilogue

Chris

The Spring Rains Festival was in full swing, and the whole town seemed to have turned out for it. The diner's stall was a celebration of color, adorned with Pride flags that fluttered in the gentle breeze. Each flag was a burst of brightness against the backdrop of the festival, their rainbow hues weren't easy to miss. Pastor McKenna might not have been part of this community anymore, but that didn't mean everyone left in town was inclusive, but so far, no one else had an issue with the flags in the diner's window. The stall for the fastest pitch was right next door, the team taking turns to man it, and money was flowing in.

In particular, a significant sum from Quinn, who'd handed me a check a few days back, making me promise to tell no one. I'd asked if I could share the money with Jerry's soccer team—he just handed me another one and smiled as though he was the happiest man on Earth.

I really liked Quinn.

Wheeling among the stalls, I observed the vibrant life of the festival. Kids ran around with painted faces, the aroma of various foods filled the air, and the sound of laughter and music created a backdrop of fun, despite the bout of spring snowflakes spinning in the air. It was cold, but most of the snow was gone now, and in its place the brooks and rivers ran deep and fresh, and the hope of summer felt real. Today was one of those perfect days when the community came together to celebrate, and I loved every minute.

I'd checked out the other stalls, said my hellos, and I wheeled from the Lennox ranch stall where a grumpy Levi was in charge of the *guess the weight of horse* competition, and headed back to the diner's stall. I couldn't help but feel a sense of pride seeing Noah there, managing everything with his usual efficiency. His rainbow cakes and filled croissants were proving to be popular, with people lining up to sample the food he'd prepared with my help.

Well, not much of my help.

But I tried.

Fox was hanging around too, supposedly to assist Noah, but I noticed that he was spending more time after his turn on the baseball stall roaming the festival with Molly, along with Clarke, who was in a bit of a funk. It was clear that Clarke was missing Ainsley, who'd moved to live with his aunt, changing schools in the process.

I was happy he'd had somewhere to go, other kids who were disowned by parents weren't as lucky, but I was sad for his and Clarke's young love, and also, that Fox missed him as well.

"Ainsley!"

I glanced up and saw a familiar face-- Ainsley, walking towards Fox, Molly, and Clarke. Clarke's face lit up with a mixture of surprise and joy, and Fox grinned from ear to ear, mirroring Clarke's excitement, their faces breaking into wide grins.

Wanting to say *hi,* I headed over to them just in time to catch the tail end of their conversation.

"… so, my aunt is actually thinking about moving here, to Whisper Ridge," Ainsley was saying, his eyes bright with the prospect, hugging Clarke close.

"Seriously? That would be awesome!" Clarke exclaimed with unmistakable relief and happiness.

Fox chimed in. "Wow, that's cool. We've missed you around here."

I couldn't help but join in their conversation. "Hey, Ainsley, it's good to see you back, even if it's just for the festival."

Ainsley glanced over at me, a shy smile on his face. "Thanks, Mr. Sheridan. I've missed being here. And if things go as planned, I might be back for good, and I can come back to your class." He lowered his voice and leaned away from Clarke so only I could hear. "The teachers I have now are bad. Like *epically* bad."

"Come back soon, then," I said and preened a little that he thought I was a good teacher—not that he'd specifically said that, but it was implied. Right?

"That would be great for the town. And for you guys, obviously," I added, nodding towards Fox and Clarke.

The group fell into an easy conversation, chatting about the festival, school, and everything in between, and I left them to it, catching Noah's eye and the kiss he blew me, making a show of pocketing it and smiling.

It'd been a full month now that we'd been living in my place.

Initially, I'd moved into the diner's apartment, but it wasn't working, and so my house became our home, which Fox loved, given he had his own space in the attic, complete with a den of his own. When Connor had approached us, asking if he could live over the diner, fed up of the hotel room after a year of living there, Noah couldn't jump on it fast enough.

Built-in diner security from a ninja? Check.

Quinn arrived at the diner's stall, his distinctive pink hair matching perfectly with the Pride theme, and a few steps behind him, almost blending into the crowd, yet watchful, was Connor, keeping a stern eye on everything. From a distance, Connor caught my eye and gave a subtle nod of acknowledgment before returning his gaze to the crowd. It was clear he was on duty, ever the vigilant protector of the town.

"Hey, Chris, Noah, these look fantastic," Quinn said, gesturing to the few remaining baked goods as I wheeled into place next to the stall.

Noah glanced up and smiled. "Thanks, Quinn. They've been a hit. You guys want to try something? It's on the house."

"Did you ask him yet?" Levi abandoned the ranch stall and joined his fiancé, his arm slipping around his shoulders, hugging him close.

Quinn was studying the pastries and sent Levi a fond smile. "Not yet. Shhhh. So, I wouldn't know where to start, Noah. What do you recommend?" I watched as Noah described each of the remaining items with great enthusiasm. It was clear he put a lot of love and thought into his baking, and he had an answer for every one of Levi and Quinn's questions.

"I love everything."

Noah, handing over the baked goods Quinn had chosen, replied, "Glad you think so. It's always a bit nerve-wracking, wondering if things will go over well."

I laughed. "I don't think you have anything to worry about. Everything you make is amazing."

Levi agreed. "Definitely. You've got a gift, Noah."

After a brief discussion, Quinn selected a couple more items more. "These will be perfect for later," he said, smiling. "Also, we have something to ask you."

"Sure," Noah said, distracted by rearranging the remaining croissants.

"We hoped you'd agree to make our wedding cake."

I saw Noah do a double take, glance around him as if they'd been talking to someone else. "Huh?"

Quinn pointed at Noah. "You. Our cake. Are you interested?"

Noah blinked, then grinned. "Yes."

"Official though, paid and—"

"I owe Levi a freebie for helping me that day with my ex," Noah interjected.

"Absolutely not," Quinn said.

I touched Noah on the hip. "Quinn's a millionaire," I deadpanned.

Noah tilted his chin—God, I loved stubborn-Noah. "It would be our gift to you."

As Levi and Quinn prepared to leave, Connor drifted closer, though he still kept a respectful distance. "Everything good here?" he asked, his tone casual, but his eyes scanning the area.

"All good, Connor. Thanks," I responded.

Levi clapped a hand on Connor's shoulder. "Don't work too hard, man."

Connor grunted, a ghost of a smile on his lips. "Someone's got to keep an eye on things."

With a last wave, Levi and Quinn wandered off, pastries in hand, blending into the crowd. Connor lingered for a moment longer, ensuring everything was indeed okay before he, too, melted away into the festival.

Watching them go, Noah turned to me. "A cake," he said. "A wedding cake."

"The best one ever," I said.

Noah wrinkled his nose. "No pressure, then."

As the day progressed, the festival continued in full swing. I spent time at the stall with Noah, helping where I could, and watching Fox and his friends enjoy the festival. There was a sense of community and togetherness that made Whisper Ridge feel like more than just a place to live. It was my home, and Noah fit into it so perfectly.

When the day wound down, and the crowds started to thin, I was aching and tired, but happy, and as we packed up the diner's stall, I looked over at Noah and saw the fatigue mixed with satisfaction on his face. "Great job today," I said, placing a hand on his shoulder.

He smiled, a little tired, but happy. "Thanks. Couldn't have done it without you."

When there was nothing else to do, we headed home in the rain, a welcome change from the ice and snow, although just as wet. Fox, Clarke, and now Ainsley, were in tow, as the boys were having their first sleepover with us.

As we walked in, the boys started making plans for the night, and they practically bounded up the stairs in a whirl of energy and chatter.

Noah and I exchanged amused glances, following them at a more leisurely pace—I know I was exhausted, and Noah hadn't stopped since five this morning. "I'm glad Ainsley's here," I commented, as the boys' laughter echoed down the stairs.

Noah chuckled. "Snacks for them, then I'm dying on the sofa."

In the kitchen, Noah and I busied ourselves preparing snacks for the boys—a mix of healthy options and a few treats, knowing all too well the appetite of growing teenagers. We worked in comfortable silence, occasionally sharing a smile or a quick kiss, still riding the high from the successful day at the festival.

Once the snacks were ready, Noah called the boys down, and they retrieved them. "Don't stay up too late," Noah warned them with a mock-stern expression.

"We won't, promise," Fox replied, the very picture of innocence before he went back upstairs, and then, it was the two of us, and a sofa that called to us.

It felt good to have the house filled with such energy and laughter. We settled in the living room; he helped me take off my prosthetic, chattering about the wedding cake, and then, a comfortable silence enveloped us as we curled up on the sofa in each other's arms listening to the rain.

It was moments like these, simple and unassuming, I cherished the most. The laughter from upstairs, the warmth of home, and Noah's company were a reminder of the importance of family—whether born or found.

As the evening wore on, the sounds from upstairs grew quieter, signaling that the boys had succumbed to sleep or were playing games.

It was a perfect end to a wonderful day, and as I sat there with Noah, I felt like everything was complete.

"I'd like three flavors in our wedding cake," I murmured, "Lemon for sure, chocolate with that chili, I think, and then one I don't even know about that you surprise me with."

Noah stiffened in my arms, then wriggled free and straddled my lap.

"'Our wedding cake'?" he asked.

I realized what I'd said without even trying. "Yeah, ours. What flavor would the layers be?"

He blinked at me, but didn't look shocked, instead he smiled. "The lemon sponge cake? I'd infuse it with freshly grated lemon zest and a hint of vanilla, and between the layers, a tangy lemon curd would add a burst of citrus."

"And?" I carded my hands into his hair, losing my fingers in the silkiness there.

"Dark chocolate for the middle layer, not chili though for a wedding. So, maybe a hint of espresso, cream obviously, and then, a thin layer of chocolate crunch, perhaps a praline or a light feuilletine."

I didn't know what feuilletine was, but I bet it would be wonderful. He kissed the tip of my nose.

"What about the surprise layer?"

Noah chuckled. "That's where I could get creative and add a personal touch. It depends when we're getting married. Maybe a spiced pumpkin cake for a wedding this fall, or a strawberry and basil combination for next summer?"

"I'm thinking this fall,"

"Really?" He tilted his head.

"Yeah, changing leaves, cool evenings, bonfires." I cradled his face, tugged him close enough that we were almost kissing, and then, "Will you marry me in the fall, Noah Bennett?"

I could feel his smile against my lips, then he kissed me gently.

"Spiced pumpkin cake it is, then," he whispered.

"Wait. Is that a yes? Are you saying you'll marry me?"

We separated for a moment, and I found myself lost in his mesmerizing blue eyes.

"Yes."

And the spring rain quickened against the window.

What's next in the Wyoming series?

Read Connor and Neil's hate to love story—**Into The Fall** —the final book in the Wyoming series

**rjscott.co.uk/books/into-the-fall**

**A former SEAL and a small-town sheriff clash and collide into love amidst a backdrop of mystery and danger on the Lennox Ranch.**

Connor, a former SEAL with a past shrouded in mystery, has found an unlikely home in small-town Wyoming. His fierce loyalty to his best friend and his appreciation for the tranquil existence Whisper Ridge offers have anchored him and made a new life seem possible. His fights with the town's sheriff, Neil, crackle with an unresolved tension that Connor is determined to explore, aiming to get the irritating but irresistible lawman into his bed.

Neil harbors a deep-seated resentment towards Connor, whose brazen attitude and tendency to overstep boundaries crosses the line of the law. Neil's professional integrity battles with his personal desires; If only Connor wasn't everything he wanted in a man, with his green eyes and his stupidly handsome face, then Neil could ignore him, arrest him, lock him in a cell. Instead, all Neil wants is to kiss said face and deal with the regrets later.

When a devastating landslide at the Lennox Ranch destroys a barn, Neil and Connor discover a weapon and a body, thrusting them into an uneasy alliance. With dangers from the Lennox family's past creeping into the present, they work together to unravel the mystery and protect their friends. Then sex and distrust blossoms into something neither man can deny—love.

**rjscott.co.uk/books/into-the-fall**

## Never miss another release

Follow me on my completely FREE Patreon for news
patreon.com/RJScott

Or keep up to date with news and releases, free stories and sales, sign up here:

Newsletter - rjscott.co.uk/rjnews

## FREE READS

You can also find free stories on my website

## Shadow Team

1. How Much for the Whole Night
2. *How Much for a Broken Heart*
3. *How Much for a Life of Lies*

### How Much For The Whole Night?

**A seductive stranger gives Josh everything he wants, but one night of lust could get them both killed.**

Driven by a combination of alcohol-induced recklessness and an overwhelming desire for something real, Josh ventures into a dark and seedy bar and lusts after a sexy, enigmatic hooker. When Josh negotiates a price for one night of pleasure he can't know that when his time with Ethan is over, he'll be left shattered and forever changed by the encounter. Fleeing with his son is the only means of ensuring their survival amidst the chaos of what comes next, and there's only one man he can trust to keep them safe.

A hooker who isn't a hooker at all.

Ethan is on the brink of completing a covert operation that will enable him to infiltrate a human trafficking ring. Yet, when his conscience clashes with his mission, Ethan disobeys orders, jeopardizing everything he's worked for. Forced to escape, he takes Josh and his son, but he has nowhere to go, and now, their only hope lies in seeking refuge in an isolated safe house far from prying eyes.

Protecting Josh, Ben, and a tuxedo cat called Oreo, is Ethan's priority. Only he has no choice but to resume his undercover role, and he must leave Josh and Ben behind.

When a gun is pointed at his head, his final thought is that he's lost everything that matters; can he make it home to his new family? Or will he have to die to protect the people he loves?

# Single Dads

The Single Dads Series

Single | Today | Promise | Always

Listen | Pride | Miracle | *Rainbow (Dec 2024)*

Single (Single Dads 1)

Reeling from the painful rejection of a man he thought he loved, Asher is left holding the baby.

Ash wants a family and is determined to continue with a surrogacy he'd begun with his ex. Bringing baby Mia home, he vows that he will be the best father he can be. Nothing in this world matters more to him than caring for his daughter, not even accidentally falling in lust with the doctor next door. Challenged by his growing attraction to Sean, and confronted by painful memories of his family, Ash has to learn that love is all that matters.

When ER doctor Sean moves in with his friends next door to sexy single father Ash, he falls so quickly it takes his breath away. The sex they have is hot, but Ash is adamant his heart is too full with love for his daughter to let anyone else in. Why is Sean the only one who sees how scared Ash is, and how can he prove to his new lover that he desperately wants the three of them to become a family?

http://rjscott.co.uk/read-single

---

## Single Dads Series

The Single Dads Series can be read as standalone, but some characters will appear in other stories :)

**Single** | **Today** | **Promise** | **Always**

**Listen** | **Pride** | **Miracle**

## Texas & Legacy

Texas (Cowboy, Rancher, Millionaire, Family)

The Heart of Texas | Texas Winter | Texas Heat | Texas Family | Texas Christmas | Texas Fall | Texas Wedding | Texas Gift | Home For Christmas

Legacy (spin-off from Texas series)

Kyle | Gabriel | Daniel

## The Heart Of Texas (Texas 1)

*Bachelor Riley is looking forward to two things: running his father's successful company and staying single forever. But when suddenly he's required to marry in order to receive his inheritance, Riley convinces rival Jack into marrying him for one year...*

Riley Hayes, the playboy of the Hayes family, is a young man who seems to have it all: money, a career he loves, and his pick of beautiful women. His father, CEO of HayesOil, passes control of the corporation to his two sons; but a stipulation is attached to Riley's portion. Concerned about Riley's lack of maturity, his father requires that Riley 'marry and stay married for one year to someone he loves'.

Angered by the requirement, Riley seeks a means of bypassing his father's stipulation. Blackmailing Jack Campbell into marrying him "for love" suits Riley's purpose. There is no mention in his father's documents that the marriage had to be with a woman and Jack Campbell is the son of Riley Senior's arch-rival. Win-win.

Riley marries Jack and abruptly his entire world is turned inside out. Riley hadn't counted on the fact that Jack Campbell, quiet and unassuming rancher, is a force of nature in his own right.

This is a story of murder, deceit, the struggle for power, lust and love, the sprawling life of a rancher and the whirlwind existence of a playboy. But under and through it all, as Riley learns over the months, this is a tale about family and everything that that word means.

**The Heart of Texas**

## Lancaster Falls (Romantic Suspense)

1. What Lies Beneath
2. Without a Trace
3. All That Remains

What Lies Beneath (Lancaster Falls 1)

In the hottest summer on record, Iron Lake reservoir is emptying, revealing secrets that were intended to stay hidden beneath the water. The tragic story of a missing man is a media sensation, and abruptly the writer and the cop falling in love is just a postscript to horrors neither could have imagined.

Best Selling Horror writer Chris Lassiter struggles for

inspiration and he's close to never writing again. His life has become an endless loop of nothing but empty pages, personal appearances, and a marketing machine that is systematically destroying his muse. In a desperate attempt to force Chris to complete unfinished manuscripts his agent buys a remote cabin. All Chris has to do is hide away and write, but he's lost his muse, and not even he can make stories appear from thin air.

Sawyer Wiseman left town for Chicago, chasing the excitement and potential of being a big city cop, rising the ranks, and making his mark. A case gone horribly wrong draws him back to Lancaster Falls. Working for the tiny police department in the town he'd been running from, digging into cold cases and police corruption, he spends his day's healing, and his nights hoping the nightmares of his last case leave him alone.

**What Lies Beneath**

## Heroes

1. A Reason To Stay
2. Last Marine Standing
3. Deacon's Law

A Reason to Stay (Heroes, 1)

**It takes a Navy SEAL's training to keep them alive, but when the mystery on the mountain is solved, will Viktor and Aiden's love story survive the fallout?**

Viktor left small-town Vermont to become a Navy SEAL and had no intention of tying himself down or falling in love. A succession of men and women share his bed, passion and danger are his addictions, and he's the first of his team to run headlong into trouble. When his nephew witnesses a murder, Viktor returns home to protect his family and lands in the middle of an active case led by none other than the man he left behind. He can handle getting punched out by Aiden, but teaming up with the sheriff to find a killer is not on the cards. For Viktor, love is dangerous, makes a man vulnerable, and one mistake could get Aiden killed.

Aiden never expected to find lasting love with a decorated active SEAL, but he didn't expect Viktor would leave his bed never to return. Even two years later, disappointment simmers below the surface, and he never wants to see Viktor again. But, when seemingly unrelated deaths draw Viktor back home, Aiden has to find a way for them to work together despite their past. With Viktor's training and Aiden's local knowledge, they partner to work the case, but Aiden isn't just fighting the bad guys and mother nature; he's falling in love with a man who will surely leave him again.

What links the string of deaths in the Green Mountains? Can hate and distrust turn back to love? And if they make it down from the mountain alive, can Aiden persuade Viktor he has a reason to stop running from love?

## Montana

Crooked Tree Ranch | The Rancher's Son | A Cowboy's Home | Snow In Montana | Second Chance Ranch | Montana Sky

### Crooked Tree Ranch (Montana 1)

**The cowboy, the man from the city, and the ranch where hate turns to love, and family is everything.**

Amidst the chaos of his crumbling life, Jay seizes the opportunity to apply for a marketing role at a dude ranch in Montana. Leaving New York behind, he embarks on a fresh start at Crooked Tree Ranch. However, the infuriating cowboy who constantly challenges him begins to stir up more than just frustration. Falling for the gruff cowboy shocks Jay, but when kisses turn to more, could love be possible?

Nate, a former rodeo star and the ranch's foreman, has been shouldering the responsibility for five years after his mentor fell ill. Encouraged by his brothers and determined to keep the ranch thriving, Nate realizes the necessity of bringing in an expert to propel the business forward. Yet, when the new arrival arrives with a troubled family, Nate is caught off guard by the magnitude of the challenges they bring. As he and Jay work together to transform the ranch, Nate finds himself unexpectedly drawn to the charming city guy.

Against the backdrop of the Montana mountains and in saving Crooked Tree Ranch, Nate and Jay fall in love, one kiss at a time.

---

Crooked Tree Ranch | The Rancher's Son | A Cowboy's Home | Snow In Montana | Second Chance Ranch | Montana Sky

## Hockey from RJ Scott & VL Locey

*When hockey wunderkind Tennant Rowe meets his new coach, he knows he's in trouble. Jared Madsen is nine years older than Tennant, impossibly attractive, and — worst of all — his brother's off-limits best friend. Is their chemistry worth the risk?*

Changing Lines (Railers 1)

Can Tennant show Jared that age is just a number, and that love is all that matters?

The Rowe Brothers are famous hockey hotshots, but as the youngest of the trio, Tennant has always had to play against his brothers' reputations. To get out of their shadows, and against their advice, he accepts a trade to the Harrisburg Railers, where he runs into Jared Madsen. Mads is an old family friend and his brother's one-time teammate. Mads is Tennant's new coach. And Mads is the sexiest thing he's ever laid eyes on.

Jared Madsen's hockey career was cut short by a fault in his heart, but coaching keeps him close to the game. When Ten is traded to the team, his carefully organized world is thrown into chaos. Nine years his junior and his best friend's brother, he knows Ten is strictly off-limits, but as soon as he sees Ten's moves, on and off the ice, he knows that his heart could get him into trouble again.

**Changing Lines**

---

## All hockey romance from RJ Scott & VL Locey

### Harrisburg Railers (Hockey Romance)

Changing Lines | First Season | Deep Edge | Poke Check | Last Defense | Goal Line | Neutral Zone | Hat Trick | Save The Date | Baby Makes Three | Rivals | Perfect Gifts | Family First

*Railers Volume 1 | Railers Volume 2 | Railers Volume 3 | Railers Volume 4*

### Owatonna U Hockey (Hockey Romance)

Ryker | Scott | Benoit | Christmas Lights | Valentine's Hearts | Desert Dreams

Arizona Raptors (Hockey Romance)

Coast To Coast | Across the Pond | Shadow and Light | Sugar and Ice | School and Rock

Boston Rebels

Lost In Boston (Free Novella) | Top Shelf | Back Check | Snowed | Royal Lines / Blade | Rental

LA Storm

Script / *Second / Shield*

Chesterford Coyotes

Off The Ice | On Thin Ice | *Dance on Ice*

## The Lake Prophet Mysteries (Romantic Suspense)

1. Solstice
2. Equinox
3. Zenith

**Solstice (A Lake Prophet Mystery)**

*The Lake Prophet Mysteries, book 1*

**From the dramatic peaks of the Olympic mountain range to the small town of Prophet, murder is only a footstep away.**

Gabriel is a former undercover cop haunted by the things he's seen and done. He returns to his small hometown of Prophet, taking on the role of sheriff, hoping to mend his fractured relationship with his estranged brother and rebuild his life. But when a chilling murder occurs at Sentinel Rocks, a sacred Makah site on Lake Prophet, Gabriel's dreams of peace and reconciliation are shattered.

Gabriel navigates a web of intrigue, where suspects abound; from local tribal elders to fervent Solstice worshippers and even those hunting the elusive Big Foot. When the brutal murder leaves Duke, a loyal Labrador retriever, as the sole witness, Gabriel stumbles upon an unexpected ally—a local animal behaviorist named Tiber.

Tiber, a newcomer to Prophet, seeks refuge in this remote haven, attempting to escape his own inner demons. Armed with his extraordinary ability to communicate with animals, he offers his expertise through video consultations, helping pet owners with their beloved companions. While he attributes his skill to his academic background, his intuition and flashes of insight owe as much to his Navajo heritage as to science.

With the relentless rain washing away sins and good intentions alike, Gabriel and Tiber must begin to confront their own vulnerabilities and unravel the truth.

**What Lies Beneath**

## Christmas stories

**The Wishing Tree** - Small Town Romance, silken kink

**Stop the Wedding** - Best friends to lovers, stop the wedding

**Cupcakes and Christmas** - Reality TV, opposites attract

**Love Happens Anyway** - Fake boyfriend for Christmas

**The Christmas Throwaway** - A young man thrown out of his home before Christmas for being gay

**Christmas Prince** - A prince, a castle, and the magic of Christmas

**Dallas Christmas** - Hockey Romance, closeted, second chance

**Jesse's Christmas** - Grinch ends up in the best ever Christmas town

**New York Christmas** - Second chance romance in New York

**The Road to Frosty Hollow** - Road trip, best friends brother

**Angel in a Book Shop** - Magical, book store, love across the centuries, waiting for love

**Seth & Casey** - teacher/firefighter, trapped in snowstorm - less Christmas and more snow!

## All books from RJ Scott

For a full list of ebooks and links please scan the code above or visit rjscott.co.uk/rjbooks

# Meet RJ Scott

RJ discovered romance in books at a very young age and realized that if there wasn't romance on the page, she could create it in her head. With over one hundred and fifty books published, she is a full time author of gay romance.

She lives and works out of her home in the beautiful English countryside, spends her spare time reading, watching films, and enjoying time with her family.

The last time she had a week's break from writing she didn't like it one little bit and has yet to meet a box of chocolates she couldn't defeat.


www.rjscott.co.uk | rj@rjscott.co.uk

**NEWSLETTER - rjscott.co.uk/rjnews**

facebook.com/author.rjscott
x.com/Rjscott_author
instagram.com/rjscott_author
amazon.com/author/rj-scott
bookbub.com/authors/rj-scott
goodreads.com/rjscott
pinterest.com/rjscottauthor

Printed in Great Britain
by Amazon

43137308R10188